the
dancers,
dancing

the
dancers,
dancing

éilís ní dhuibhne

BLACKSTAFF
PRESS
BELFAST

First published in 1999 by Blackstaff Press
Reprinted 2007

This edition first published in 2010 by
Blackstaff Press
4c Heron Wharf, Sydenham Business Park
Belfast BT3 9LE
with the assistance of
The Arts Council of Northern Ireland

Typeset by CJWT Solutions, St Helens, Merseyside

Printed in Ireland by ColourBooks Limited

A CIP catalogue record for this book is available
from the British Library

ISBN 978-0-85640-860-1

www.blackstaffpress.com

For Bo, Ragnar and Olaf

This darksome burn, horseback brown,
His rollrock highroad roaring down,
In coop and in comb the fleece of his foam
Flutes and low to the lake falls home.

A windpuff-bonnet of fawn-froth
Turns and twindles over the broth
Of a pool so pitchblack, fell-frowning,
It rounds and rounds despair to drowning.

Degged with dew, dappled with dew
Are the groins of the braes that the brook treads through,
Wiry heathpacks, flitches of fern,
And the beadbony ash that sits over the burn.

What would the world be, once bereft
Of wet and wildness? Let them be left,
O let them be left, wildness and wet;
Long live the weeds and the wilderness yet.

GERARD MANLEY HOPKINS, 'Inversnaid'

The map

Imagine you are in an airplane, flying at twenty thousand feet. The landscape spreads beneath like a chequered tablecloth thrown across a languid body. From this vantage point, no curve is apparent. It is flat earth – pan flat, plan flat, platter flat to the edges, its green and gold patches stained at intervals by lumps of mountain, brownish purple clots of varicose vein in the smooth skin of land. Patterns of fields, rough squares and rectangles, are hatched in with grey stone. The white spots, sometimes slipping disconcertingly out of focus, are sheep.

You see what the early map-makers imagined – Giraldus Cambrensis or Abraham Ortelius, Francis Jobson, Richard Bartlett – those whose outrageous ambition it was to visualise and draw on a two-dimensional surface of wood or parchment or vellum or paper or whatever was to hand baronies, counties, countries, continents. Their minds' eyes flew as high as this, and higher: hundreds of thousands of feet above the earth while their bodies remained glued to land. And then the eyes descended, bringing with them the diminished, distorted images from their imagined flight, back to earth, back to the drawing board. This is it, their maps said. This is the earth, the place you live in. This is what it looks like really! See you! Look!

Sea and land, hill and hollow, lake and river. Blue spots and brown spots, green patch, dark line. And more, more. Other details, tiny but plain, not like the symbols you find on modern maps but resembling the illustrations of the earlier, more licentious cartographers who, after strenuous efforts to be scientifically objective, often gave in at the end to a childish and thoroughly understandable desire to decorate. When the lines of latitude and longitude were in place, the tables and compasses painted in the corner, they set to work with brush and paint: little men plough and hunt; wolves and bears and – yes! – unicorns and griffins gambol in the forests. Dolphins and whales frolic in the gorgeous ocean. And these are the best, the truest, maps: at once guide and picture, instrument and toy, as they valiantly attempt the all-but-impossible, as they try to show the woods and the trees, the whole world and all the people in it.

The burn. A narrow bold blue-black line meandering in the nervous way of mapped rivers from one edge – the brown triangle hills – to the monoblue sea. From your superior angle you see it all, every inch of it, from its source on the side of a low hill, along its eager early course to where it flattens, broad and whorish, drunken and listless and loses itself in the sea.

You see it, and the little people on its banks. Little dolls, little stick shapes, at gates and in yards. A straggle of tiny children winding along a navy-blue lane. A field full of footballers.

You can't see their faces from where you are. You can't hear their names. You can't see those who are secreted in the boxes. Inside is what you can't see, maker of maps. Behind or below, before or after. And yet you can see plenty. The burn on its endless journey, endlessly beginning and endlessly ending, endlessly moving and endlessly unchanging. And the figures on their little journeys, back and forth and up and down and in and out, until they move out of the picture altogether, over the edge, into the infinity of after the story.

You see the woods and the trees and the sea and the river, and it is a pretty picture. What Ptolemy saw. Mercator. Bartlett. What we see before the plane hurtles down. What the holiday agents and the people advertising summer camps present on the covers of their brochures. What you can't see is what it is better not to see: the sap and the clay and the weeds and the mess. The chthonic puddle and muddle of brain and heart and kitchen and sewer and vein and sinew and ink and stamp and sugar and stew and cloth and stitch and swill and beer and lemonade and tea and soap and nerve and memory and energy and pine and weep and laugh and sneer and say nothing and say something and in between, in between, in between, that is the truth and that is the story.

Every picture tells a story.

A truism. Half true like all truisms. Half false.

The rest of the story is in the mud. Clear as muddy old mud.

Washing

Four girls sit on rocks in the middle of the stream: a dark plump girl; a girl whose hair burgeons from her head in a mane of light; another with long white legs and short black shorts, clipped jet hair; a willowy branch of a girl, blonde. The sun shines through green leaves, glancing off the chestnut water and all the hair. Both hair and water pick up the sun and play with it, respond with similar glimmers and flashes, darks and dimples of light.

The girls hunker on the clumps of lichened stone and lean into the water. They bend over the water, and over them bend great elm trees, some oaks. The stream is running through a garden, passing under a barbed-wire fence at one side, flowing out under an arch in a stone wall at the other. It is an old country garden, shady, overgrown, rich with greenery and secrets, rich with growth, both planned and unplanned: roses along the wall, delicate creamy pink rambling roses; woodbine twined around the trees; a jungle of nasturtiums tumbling over one bank of the stream. On the other bank grow leggy cabbages, fat onions, and a row of blackcurrant bushes.

Foam floats down the stream on the chestnut water, the thick clotted foam of mountain streams. It is mingling with white sudsy foam. The girls are washing their clothes in the river. They dip in socks and knickers, blouses and T-shirts, rub them with pink toilet soap, and rinse them out in the brown boggy water.

The gurgling of the river mixes with their giggles and the murmur of their voices. One of them sings a song, the kind of song ten-year-old girls sing as a party piece. The voice rises from the stream. 'Will I be pretty? Will I be rich? Here's what she said to me.' They all join in, cheerfully: 'Che sera sera! Whatever will be will be. The future's not ours to see. Che sera sera. What will be will be!'

The girls are from Derry and Dublin. The future, even of the song, is not theirs to see. But by now their future is their past, an open book, a closed chapter, water under the bridge.

All Irish they speak too

'Tubber is so beautiful!' Elizabeth, Orla's mother, said to Orla and to everybody else within earshot. Elizabeth is not from Tubber but she had adopted it as her own, with enthusiasm. 'It is only fantastic. It is really the most beautiful place in the world, I'm not telling you a word of a lie! And it's all Irish they speak there too.'

The pearl in Tubber's crown. Not only west, not only beautiful, but all Irish as well – not half Irish, not a quarter Irish. All. The Crillys go there on holiday every year and speak all English.

Tubber is one of the maps Orla has held in her head since babyhood. There is another. That is the map of Dublin. Two sides of the Crilly coin: the good and the bad, the tourist west and the dull east, the rare Irish and the common English, the heathery rocky lovely and the bricky breezeblock ugly, the desirable rural idyll and the unchosen urban reality. Holiday and work. Past and present.

The unchronicled jouissance
of summer bus journeys when
you're young

The bus is parked in the centre of a ring of houses behind the
school. The ring is in Dublin and is called Oldchurch Crescent,
and on it the back gate of the school is situated. This gate is kept
locked. It has to be, because the residents of Oldchurch Crescent
object to the very existence of schoolchildren, and refuse to
allow the dry and deadly silence that habitually pervades their
precious crescent to be sullied by the playful patter of juvenile
feet or the sweet music of youthful voices. And at this time and
this place their view is considered perfectly acceptable; it accords
with a widespread, if not universal, belief that children are
merely substandard grown-ups, to be ignored or whipped into
adulthood, but never tolerated on their own terms. And so all
the children and their parents and, needless to add, their teachers
(two of whom reside there anyway) bow to the wishes of the
delicate denizens of Oldchurch Crescent. Even the one child
who lives or tries to live – attempts to survive – there herself,
namely Nuala Marie Blanaid Hanafin, has to walk all the way
around to the front gate half a mile away every morning to go
to school, although the majestic back gate stands just a few steps
from her own hall door.

The crescent is quiet and still, as always, when Orla and her
mother arrive there. The sun shines down on it, but in a

diffident, pale yellow, respectable way, more like a moon than a sun. The prim houses turn their silent doors, their curtained windows, to the road and to Orla, their façades as forbidding as the cracked sad faces of ancient shabby ladies born in another century. And, indeed, for the most part it is such people who inhabit the houses. So Nuala Marie Blanaid informed Orla once. Almost everyone on Oldchurch Crescent is about eighty years of age.

Even the wallflowers in the horribly symmetrical gardens look as if they were planted for Queen Victoria's coronation, and perhaps they were. This is Rathmines, one of Dublin's oldest and once – but not any more, not quite – most respectable suburbs.

The bus is plonked right in the middle of the crescent, a desecration, like a giant plastic frog in the middle of an exquisite marble fountain. Why? Maybe there was more room for it there than around at the front of the school. Or maybe Sean O'Brien, the teacher who is organising the trip to the Gaeltacht, just did not know the unwritten rule of Oldchurch Crescent. He comes from Drumcondra, a place that happens to look like Rathmines but might as well be in another world.

All the children and their mothers went to the front gate first, and then had had to walk all the way around to the back, dragging bulging suitcases along the footpath.

It is July 1972.

Mothers are standing around the bus now. They are making signs to their children ensconsed inside, waving their hands and twisting their lips into what they hope are lip-legible words. Have you got your anorak? Have you packed your toothbrush?

All superfluous and, if not, too late. But the mothers cannot pull themselves back from the bus; they are drawn to it as if it were a giant magnet and they fragile helpless safety pins. For most of them it is the first real parting from their children. They all know the experience of going to the Gaeltacht will be beneficial. It will make the children independent, it will knock the corners off them. It will also improve their Irish so they will have a good basis for Secondary, one up on the children whose parents have not sent them to the Gaeltacht. And besides all that it is great value, a cheap holiday in the fresh cold air of the West of Ireland, that will see the children through the best part of the long summer holidays and give them, the mothers, a chance to draw their breath. Only August then to put in and then they'll all be back at school and usefully occupied once again. It is a godsend, the Irish college.

But the mothers are also scared stiff that this is the last time they will ever lay eyes on their children in this world. The bus might crash and tumble down a bank into an abyss or into a lake or a river or a quarry. You often heard things like that on the news. A bus carrying eighty schoolchildren crashed this afternoon. There were no survivors. Usually these crashes happen in far-off lands, in Spain or France or England. But still . . . And even if the bus made it safely there and back, the children might get knocked down, individually, in the Gaeltacht, or they might have an accident with farm machinery, or fall into something: a slurry pit, a quarry, the Atlantic Ocean.

The mothers are thus excited and terrified to exactly the same degree. And this mixture of emotion textures their faces. It keeps them lingering, uselessly, at the windows of the bus, gesturing frantically at the children, who wish they would go away, who wish they would stop embarrassing them and leave them in peace to start eating the sweets and drinking the lemonade they have purchased for the journey.

The bus stands in Oldchurch Crescent for ages and ages and ages and ages, the way buses and so many things do, when you are thirteen. Waiting. The driver is busy for an hour packing the suitcases into the boot of the bus. He is a snail, he is a sloth, he is a tortoise in a blue peaked cap. It is unbelievable that it could take so long to put away fifty cases.

The man who is organising the trip, Sean O'Brien, is no Ronnie Delaney either. There he stands, inept and slow, by the door of the bus, checking names off a list. Aisling Brosnan, is Aisling Brosnan here? Aisling? Brosnan?

A tall thin man he is, with floppy thick blond hair and thick square black-framed glasses that make each eye look like a television screen. Edgy and jagged, every five minutes his anxious face breaks into a transforming smile, a smile that cheers Orla's sinking impatient resentful heart when she sees it, a smile that is the sun breaking through a November cloudcap like a streaking spoonful of fiery honey mixed with hope and laughter. Yes. And this happens often, the honey flames, all it takes to inspire it is a mother shoving a child up the step into the bus, and him able to tick one more name off his interminable list.

Orla gets on and squishes along the aisle until she finds an empty seat. She sits at the window and places her plastic bag at her feet, inhaling the curious oxygen-deficient touring-coach smell and hoping it will not make her sick, as it usually does. She is in luck: the very next person to get on is Aisling, whom Orla hopes is her best friend. Aisling has little option but to sit beside her. And then Sandra Darcy arrives, Sandra Darcy who used to be Orla's best friend before Orla decided that she wasn't, and she has to sit behind them on her own and wait for someone else to join her. They all keep their fingers crossed that it won't be someone awful like Monica Murphy or Noeleen Talbot, but they know it probably will be: everyone else will have their own best friend to sit beside.

Sandra and Orla and Aisling are the only threesome. A threesome because no mutual commitment could be made between any pair of them, even though they all like one another well enough.

Their good luck holds. The seat beside Sandra remains empty. So Sandra has space to spare for her duffel bag and her anorak, and she allows Orla and Aisling to put theirs on her seat as well, which saves them having to take things down from the rack every five minutes, like everyone else on the bus.

Orla is thirteen and two months and Aisling is twelve and a half and Sandra is almost fourteen: two Pisces and a Gemini. It annoys Orla that Aisling is a Pisces like Sandra, the artistic sign, while she is a Gemini, a sign with no special qualities except for a tendency to duplicity. But Sandra has many disadvantages to outweigh that one good quality, so it does not matter too much.

Aisling has no disadvantages, in Orla's eyes. She has very curling auburn hair, frothing around her tiny face like a lion's mane, tumbling so far down her back that she can sit on its edges. She is slim enough almost to satisfy the very stringent standards of the time as to female size, and her clothes are always correct for the year and place and her age. Just now, they consist of medium-blue Levi's, a white-and-lemon striped T-shirt, an anorak in a clear lovely innocent yellow, new, bought especially for the holiday. That is Aisling. She has the best of everything, and is perfect in every way. This she does not realise herself, but Orla noticed it long ago. It is for these reasons that Orla has to have Aisling as a friend.

Orla is fattish. To be precise, since judgements in this area can be so subjective, she is five foot four in height and weighs ten stone twelve pounds, i.e. almost eleven stone, in her vest, pants and bare feet, in the morning before breakfast. She has a round pretty face to compensate, if anything could, and straight brown hair that can shine like a river, even though it hangs dull as a plank when it is in need of a wash. She would have been so pretty if only, if only ... ! The fat, and the clothes, and the background ... So many ifs.

Her fat bottom bulges inside her green corduroy trousers. And peeping out from their green hems are shoes Elizabeth bought in Clover's for ten shillings, which have a dainty little heel and a white pearl buckle in front, very attractive, but which are a very peculiar colour for shoes, namely tangerine. The surface even has the dimpled, slightly repulsive texture of orange peel. Of course Aisling said 'Very patriotic!' when she saw them. Orla had anticipated this and didn't mind it, much.

She should have known better. But she'd loved the shoes when she'd seen them first. The pearl rosette had shimmered like the inside of an oyster shell, and the tangerine material – not leather, yet not plastic – glowed in the dark cave of Clover's shop window, glowed like two summer oranges on a bottle-green tree. Clover's was a wonderful name, one of Orla's favourites, redolent of hills and holidays, fresh lake breezes. In fact the shop is a chaotic place, dim, and crammed with shoe boxes and shoes out of boxes, new shoes with clean soles and the reassuring tangy smell of leather, old shoes bent and creased like old age pensioners on the bus, smelling of dirty feet. Elizabeth and Orla love it all, its messiness and its plenitude, and especially its cheapness. Every time they pass that shop they are seduced inside. And often they buy.

Elizabeth had been delighted with the tangerine shoes' price, although Orla could see that even at the beginning she had doubts about their style. (Why didn't she voice them then, rather than later? Why don't people?) Not until she got them home did Orla begin to understand why. Not until they were sitting under her bed, their dimpled orange toes peeping out, did the delusion fall from her eyes. Tangerine shoes. Nobody wears tangerine shoes.

Elizabeth has also given Orla a pair of sandals, plain sandals made from the same flabby, dark tan leather as schoolbags. They have a T-bar strap and three slits over the toes to let the air in and the pong out. 'Ideal for Irish college!' Elizabeth had said to the woman in the shop, name unknown, Mrs Clover perhaps. 'Oh yes, they will be, maam,' she had said and nodded her little picklehead. As if she'd ever left Camden Street in her whole life! As if she even knew what Irish college was!

The sandals look like boys' sandals. Shoes that are worn by boys are worse than shoes that are tangerine. Orla has no intention of ever wearing those sandals, ever in her whole life.

'What did youse bring?' Sandra says *youse*. It damns her for all eternity as far as Orla is concerned. Orla has a special linguistic mission in life, and it is not the mission of every good citizen, which is, according to the teachers in her school, to speak Irish. It is rather to stamp out every trace of local English dialect from her surroundings, rather as Church and State in Ireland have recently been aiming to eliminate sex from the Irish way of life. Words like *youse* cannot be tolerated. Orla has her work cut out correcting the terrible English of her mother and her brother. She'd love to work on Sandra but can't. All she can do is despise her. Youse.

'Two Fanta and two bags of Tayto and a packet of chocolate goldgrain and a bar of Whole Nut and two apples.'

'I brought a Coke and a shillingy box of fruit pastilles and five bags of crisps.'

'Do you think they'll let us out in the North for Mars Bars and Marathons?'

'Oh yes they're bound to.' Thus Orla, speaking with confidence. 'My mother said we'd stop in Omagh, we'd probably stop in Omagh for lunch and we could do some shopping there.'

Elizabeth has even given Orla sterling to buy something for her: three packets of Persil.

'How am I supposed to carry three packets of Persil all the way to Donegal and back?'

'They'll give you a bag, sure, won't they? None of your backchat. I can tell ye I never got a month's holiday when I was your age or any holiday at all.'

Old times. How Orla hated them.

'Maybe I can get them on the way back?'

'It's all the same to me. Just get them. They're fifty pence cheaper on the large size.'

Elizabeth has given Orla something else as well: a present for her Auntie Annie, who lives in Tubber. It is a brown bag containing a pair of elastic stockings. Aunt Annie has varicose veins and will be glad of their support. When Orla remembers her suitcase, hidden deep in the bowels of the bus, a magic chest packed with ironed blouses and crisp cotton dresses, she can see under all the neatly balled socks and folded pants that soft, disgusting brown paper bag. It makes her stomach turn. She tries to push the picture away but it pops back at intervals, all through the long journey, like a dark shadow on the brightness of the day.

The bus is due to depart at ten but it is after eleven when it finally leaves. It takes a very long time indeed to check everyone's name on the list. Sean O'Brien keeps glancing at it, askance, as if he doesn't quite know what it is. Then he scratches his head and laughs a thin, hopeless laugh. He reads out all the names four times. The first time, two boys don't answer even though everyone sees them on the bus, biffing one another and pulling long faces which are supposed to mimic Sean O'Brien's. The second time, five people don't answer. The third time, everyone says yes, because they are getting very bored. But then he checks one last time and half the children on the bus refuse to reply.

'I think they're all here!' says Bean Uí Luing – Mrs Lang – another teacher for the Gaeltacht. Her voice is furry and cheerful, like sponge cake, with jam and cream and sugar – a cream sandwich. 'I think we can leave, Sean!'

'You better get started or yez won't be there before dark!'

Orla closes her eyes. It's Elizabeth.

'Are you sure, Mrs Crilly?'

'Sure of course I'm sure. We know them all don't we?'

He scratches his head again. But you can tell, even Orla can tell, that he trusts her more than he trusts Bean Uí Luing. Anyone could tell that she is scatty, even after two minutes. Her blonde hair falls onto her cheeks in untidy wisps. She is wearing a pink suit and a silk scarf and a little pillbox hat. Her shoes are slingback, also pink. Mother of the bride, Aisling whispers. Where did she get that hat?

At last, at last, at last, when hope is thinning to an elastic band of desperation, the engine roars. At its cheering shudder, Orla and Aisling open their Coke, Fanta and crisps. By the time they are in Finglas, the goodies are gone. Orla has one of her stomachaches. Sandra still has crisps and two bars of chocolate.

'I do like to make them last,' she lisps. Sandra has a very minor speech impediment: apart from her dialect and accent, there is something – something you can't get your ear around – wrong with the way she talks. That's one of her terrible flaws. There are others: she lives in a flat, not a corporation flat but any flat is bad enough. Respectable people live in houses. 'Never go in there!' Elizabeth warns. Orla has ignored the warnings, and found the flat comforting and warm, cosy in a way her home never can be. She hasn't let on. 'She has nits in her hair, I've seen her scratching,' Elizabeth says. Sandra's eyes are odd colours, one blue and one brown. Her hair is long and thick, gold and brown and yellow mixed together. 'I've never seen hair the like of that on any child before,' Elizabeth says. 'What does she put in it?'

They stop in Monaghan for chips.

Monaghan is all right as market towns in the middle of Ireland go. Better than most. But there is one problem: it is not the North.

'Can't we wait till we cross the border?' Orla implores Sean O'Brien.

'No, a stór. It's past lunchtime already.'

And whose fault is that may I ask?

Everyone on the bus tries to make him wait for the North, where eminently desirable bars of chocolate and tubes of sweets, Opal Fruits and Mars Bars and Bountys, can be bought. (Everyone in the world must know this by now, what the North meant to the children of the Republic: it meant Mars Bars.) The children have been planning their shopping for weeks. Orla has saved money specially for the stop in the North, and so have most of those on the bus. But nothing they can do can convince him that any of that matters. One sweet is the same as another, perhaps, is his point of view, indicating how little he understands his charges. The little buggers don't matter, perhaps, is his point of view, indicating how little he likes them. Or stopping in the North is too risky, perhaps, is his point of view, indicating that he's a true-blue Dubliner.

They park on a hill and crocodile down the main street in Monaghan, where they eat eggs, beans and chips. The food is good – fat soft sweet chips, sopped in vinegar, crispy eggs. But as soon as the children return to the bus they start to sulk. First they sulk to force Sean to tell the driver to stop, and then they sulk to punish him for not stopping. They sulk from one border to the other, all the way across the North of Ireland.

They only stop sulking once, when the bus has to stop. This happens at Aughnacloy, just over the Monaghan border. A soldier wearing fatigues and carrying a heavy gun boards the bus. He gives the children a sweeping cold glance: thrilling. They all gaze eagerly at his face, a round pink boyish face, fresh from the rain that now pings down outside. They stare happily at his helmet, his gun, his green-and-brown Action Man clothes. It is the first time they have ever seen a real soldier, on duty: it is as if an alien from outer space, or Fred Flintstone or Donald Duck, stepped onto the bus. 'Come down the aisle,' Orla prays. 'Please!' She sees him, prowling along, his pink face concentrated and intent, prodding duffel bags with the point of his gun.

'Would you describe the contents of this bag for me, young lady?'

'Three Coke tins and a pair of socks.'

'And what is this object?'

'A stuffed rabbit.'

She hears his happy laugh.

But he doesn't come. He doesn't move down the bus at all. Instead he looks at them once again, in a bored way, and grunts something to the driver, who grunts back. Then he just leaves.

They resume their sulking.

And they don't stop again for an hour.

Even when they are momentarily distracted by the fascinating sight of more soldiers, crouching outside shops called Sheila's Bakery and Dairy or patrolling petrol stations, they continue. They know if they slacken for a second, Sean or, more likely, Bean Uí Luing, will take advantage. She'll see the opportunity and seize it, cheat them into relaxing. She knows how tired they are.

So they concentrate fiercely on Opal Fruits and Mars Bars. They exchange pithy descriptions of sweets they once ate and adored. Chewy tangy lemon and lime. Thick rich chocolate peanuts. Flavours denied to the children of the Republic, but available daily, like so many other advantages, to the children of the North.

Wall's ice cream.

Which always reminds Orla of walnuts, her favourite nuts when combined with chocolate and cream, as in Walnut Whips.

The Wall's pennants wave tantalisingly in the rain as they whiz past the little roadside shops. Her mind considers walnut ice creams: chocolatty, creamy, crunchy, walnutty.

'You could've understood him not stopping in a town,' Aisling says. 'We might've got lost.' As in Monaghan, where it had taken half an hour to locate Maurice Byrne and Damien Caulfield. Why they are going to the Gaeltacht nobody knows. It nearly takes the good out of it, people like them going. 'You could've understood not stopping in a town. But a shop. A shop on the side of the road. Nobody could run away from there.' A shop called Sheila's Sweetery or Anna's Bakery or Winnie's Dairy. Nowhere to run from them except the country.

But he won't give in. Not after Monaghan.

'At least I don't have to get the Persil,' Orla breathes quietly to herself. But she does not bother mentioning this to Sandra or Aisling. Sandra would laugh and Aisling would give her one of those long incomprehending looks, darkened by pity, that make Orla want to curl up and drown. It's her secret, the Persil, like the elastic stockings for Auntie Annie, like Auntie Annie herself – one of Orla's many, many secrets.

By the time the bus passes the custom post at Lifford, crosses from Tyrone into Donegal, Sean O'Brien looks as if he's been run over by a steamroller. Bean Uí Luing is knitting, a strawberry-coloured jumper, with fierce concentration. She does not talk to Sean or even look at him, but focuses on her stitching.

And then the children stop sulking. The air in the bus lightens and loosens, like an animal calmed after a shock. The tones of voices change. Someone laughs and it is a natural laugh of joy, not a sarcastic snarl.

Bean Uí Luing lets her knitting rest on her knubbly pink lap. She raises her pink bird face and beams at Sean O'Brien, who scratches his black hair and ponders the wonder of childhood.

He looks outside.

The navy-blue roads with their neat white stripes along the edges have given way to a narrow country lane. The tidy hawthorn hedgerows, clipped like crew cuts, have yielded to ragged brambles and bushy fuchsia, dipping and waving and scratching the bus. The sun is setting rosily in a featheration of blue and white, grey and peach, in the western sky (it is gone eight-thirty: thanks to all the messing, the journey has lasted more than nine hours).

The landscape in the delicate ether of twilight is beginning to look like all the places Irish people go to on their holidays. It has a windy, sandy, opalescent, carefree look, a happy-go-lucky few cows in a field it might rain any minute but who cares look, a bittersweet cry one minute laugh the next emotional hopeful poignant wistful delicate damp look. A newborn baby old as the mountains prayerful look.

The landscape has stopped being the east and the midlands and the North of Ireland and started being the West.

18

The children do not know why they had to stop sulking. They do not know why they are beginning to sing.

'She'll be coming round the mountain when she comes
She'll be coming round the mountain when she comes . . .'

Sean O'Brien scratches his head philosophically, takes three Aspros and a slug of Coke – he's kept a bottle of Coke hidden beneath his seat for nine whole hours, which is what it means to be an adult.

Bean Uí Luing puts her knitting in her tapestry bag and starts to sing too. She sings an Irish song, 'Beidh aonach amárach i gContae an Chláir'. All the children know it but only one or two join her. The others listen to Damien Caulfield's robust rendering of 'The Captain's Wife Was Mabel', until Sean O'Brien rushes from his seat with a convincing show of fine macho frenzy and clips him on the ear.

'I'll fucking sue you,' Damien Caulfield snarls. He knows it is against the rules, hitting a child on a bus on the way to an Irish college, where they are supposed to be on fucking holidays.

Bean Uí Luing starts 'Ten Green Bottles Hanging on the Wall' by way of compromise. They sing it all the way from somewhere south of Letterkenny to the Gaeltacht.

Irish college

Not the kind you find in Paris or Louvain, homes from home for priesteens bravely defying the Penal Laws during the eighteenth century and being schooled for ordination in ancient Catholic cities far from the chilly Mass rocks and dark secret byres that await their heroic return, bearers of the sacred mysteries, the magic words, the holy chalice which encloses in its deep gleaming heart the identity of the nation. Our body, our blood. Our hope our redemption. Our paradise. Our link with Rome and Jerusalem, Spain and Paris. Everything that is exotic, different, warm, unreal and other. Other but not English.

It is an Irish college of the other kind, born in the heady days of the Celtic Revival, allowed to fade somewhat during the long dull struggle for self-assertion, the deprived harsh childhood of the new Ireland, and revived again now that the country has reached adolescence and is breaking away from its Roman fathers. An Irish college modelled loosely on American summer camps or the folk high schools of Scandinavia. But instead of counsellors you have schoolteachers, instead of staying in tents or cabins you lodge in the farmhouses and bungalows of the native population. Instead of learning weaving, canoeing or carpentry you learn one thing: Irish. At least that is what you are supposed to do, and that is the reason why the government, generous and benign now that the Common Market is there to protect it, and recognising that the children have grown up and have suddenly realised that having fun may not be wrong, that it may, in fact, be necessary, may even be their birthright, subsidises the students who attend the college. Fifty-fifty. They pay fifteen pounds and the Department of Education pays fifteen.

I'm speaking English
so youse'll all understand

The bus pulls up outside a square cream block of a building with eight high narrow windows on one side and eight on the other, and a porch boasting two entrances, one marked *Buachaillí* and the other *Cailíní*. The children scramble down from the bus clutching their anoraks and plastic bags. The bus driver and Sean are already at the boot, lifting suitcases of all shapes and sizes and ages and social classes onto the road. 'Take your own luggage and go into the school, take your own luggage and go into the school, take your own luggage and go into the school,' Sean chants in a low, terse voice, over and over again, as he reaches into the dark underside of the bus with his long tweed arm and hauls out cases. His face is opaque as his hair now, thickly concentrated. There is threat in his voice but he does not look any child in the eye. The time for eye contact has come and gone, forever, as far as he is concerned. With surprising ease, the three girls retrieve their belongings, and, with difficulty since they are so heavy, drag them into the schoolhouse.

It is different from an ordinary school in the city, in that it has no rooms: the entire school consists of one large chamber. This is what they see when they walk in: a large hall, wood-floored, its green walls covered with the maps of the world, posters of black children with large pleading eyes, and posters of nursery rhyme figures drawn in thick black ink and coloured in vividly, red and blue and yellow, with which they are familiar. Perching on windowsills here and there are statues of the Virgin and the Sacred Heart – but they seem to be carelessly placed, as if someone had taken them and plonked them down anywhere at all, not giving them the careful consideration, the little blue lamps and vases of flowers, the lacy doilies, with which the teacher in Orla's school in Dublin, or her mother, honoured such statues. One of the statues, the Sacred Heart, is back to front, looking out of the window instead of into the room. What does he see? From the vantage point of the children, the windows reveal nothing except patches of cloudy sky. Even though there are so many of them, they are so high in the wall as to grant no view whatsoever of what lies outside. These windows, the windows of every national school in Ireland, have been designed expressly to prevent children looking out of them.

At the back of the hall, clustering around a cosy nest of chairs, table, record-player, is a group of adults: the teachers. The children know this because Bean Uí Luing has already joined them, and is laughing heartily at some joke. She is the only woman. There are four men, Sean outside, and her. She's going to have a good time, and you can see that this good time has already started.

The oldest man in the group begins to shout at them, in a voice designed for leading battalions of idealistic young warriors to some terrible doom. He is a small penguin of a man, black and white in colour: a black suit with a white shirt stretched over his tummy; a black fringe of hair giddily circling his tender white scalp; black-rimmed spectacles forming a protective pallisade around his piercing black eyes. 'Sit down!' he roars. 'I'll be with yez in a minute!' His voice booms through the room like a truck backfiring, and everyone sits down – there are benches along the walls, wooden benches with rough, splintery surfaces.

After what seems a very long time all the children are in the hall and seated on these benches. Then the small dark man comes into the centre of the room and stares intimidatingly around until there is absolute silence and a thrill of danger flitting through the children.

'Welcome!' he says. 'To Tubber College. I'm speaking English today so youse'll understand what I'm saying. But this is the last word of English youse are going to hear from me or from anyone else for the rest of your stay here. Understand?'

The question is rhetorical, of course.

'Now. Youse'll all be tired after the journey from Dublin. So I'll tell you where you're to stay. As soon as I call out your name go to the teacher I've assigned you to, bring your luggage, and wait there until you find out what to do next.'

'God!' Aisling sighs. 'This is like the Jews.'

He glares at her until all sound flees from the hall once again and the thin heartstopping silence, the proof of his absolute authority, has filled the vacuum. When he is satisfied that everyone has got the message, the calling of names begins. Children are assigned to different teachers, who will drive them in their cars, sometimes in relays which means more waiting for some, to the house where they are to stay. It goes smoothly enough.

Until he gets to Sandra. Sandra has been given the wrong house. She was to be with Aisling and Orla.

'I put it on the form!' She is deeply distraught, although she does not cry. She does not cry because she can't believe that this mistake is happening.

'Tell him,' says Aisling. 'I will!' She raises her hand. 'Look, Sandra is supposed to be with us,' she says to the round black man.

He glances at her over his glasses.

'What's that?'

'Sandra Darcy. She's our friend. She put on the form that she was to be with us.'

He scratches his head.

'OK. Sandra? You wait there until everyone else is gone. Then I'll see to you.'

Sandra smiles and sits back on her bench. Aisling and Orla punch her in the shoulder and go off to their teacher, who immediately makes them get into his car. They explain about Sandra and he nods and says, 'Don't worry' as he ushers them out of the hall. Sandra gazes after them, feeling frightened again.

The woman of the house
and the daughter of the house
meet the young visitors

Orla and Aisling are driven to Sava and her mother, the Dohertys of Caroo, one mile and a quarter from the conglomeration of chapel, post office and schoolhouse that constitutes the nearest thing to a village the Gaeltacht parish of Tubber possesses.

The teacher, whose name is Máistir Dunne, introduces them to Banatee (their Woman of the House), and Sava (her daughter). Everyone nods and says hello. Then Sava and Banatee scuttle off to the kitchen to make tea, leaving Máistir Dunne at a temporary loss. Taking out his pipe and tapping it for inspiration, he gazes at Aisling and Orla and they gaze back. He whistles a bar of 'The Croppy Boy', sighs deeply, and shows them to their bedroom.

It is an old-fashioned dark room at the front of the house, chilly and forbidding. What is more surprising is that it contains only one bed.

'Are we both going to sleep in that?' Aisling asks.

He looks at it hoping perhaps that the mattress will supply him with an answer, or the pillow. 'Well . . . would you mind?'

'Oh no!' they say in unison. They never mind anything. 'Oh no!' 'Oh yes!' 'Whatever you say!' Since babyhood they have been schooled to perfect acquiescence. 'Oh no! No bottle for

26

me today! Don't go to any trouble! I'll just lie here in my cot and scream my head off. It's good for me!'

'It's a ... em ... double bed,' he says thoughtfully and unnecessarily.

They all stare at the em double bed for a minute, experiencing a variety of emotions, including amusement, repugnance, anger, disbelief and sorrow. Then, without another word, Máistir Dunne walks out of the room, bowing his head under the doorway. Sackfuls of tension and embarrassment go with him.

Aisling and Orla do what girls do in such situations. They screw up their faces and giggle.

'Gonny!' Aisling plonks herself on the bed and tries to bounce. But it does not respond: it's a mattress without a bounce, made of tangled balls of crinkly yellow straw packed too thick to yield to any pressure. They both spend a few minutes attempting to change its nature, then capitulate and fall to examining their surroundings.

The quilt on their double bed is a candlewick counterpane, coffee-coloured. In between counterpane and sheet is a heap of blankets of all ages and materials: ancient thin hard wool, fluffy new synthetic. The sheets are purple nylon, with bits of straw from the mattress sticking up through them. The other furniture in the room is minimal and old-fashioned, which does not mean that it's picturesque. Country furniture, but not the kind people in cities imagine as typical. A huge, dark walnut wardrobe, its door impregnated with a foxy mirror. A painted dressing table – painted brown. The floor is covered with brown linoleum, with a trellis pattern in red. It is new, probably bought especially for the Irish scholars, to comfort and impress them.

Orla is used to rooms that look like this, rooms that create an overriding impression of brownness, even if technically some other colours are present, rooms that are sadly lit from one bleary cataracted bulb. For Aisling it is different. Her room at home is soft, pale green and pink, girlish and comfortable. She thinks this place is an absolute howl. At least that's what she says.

'It's a howl, isn't it? Did you ever see such a wardrobe?'

'No.' Orla laughs, opening the black cavern for the first and the last time. Its door will never stay shut again. In fact she has seen such a wardrobe many times. She has one just like it at home, in the room she shares there with her mother and father. They all share the wardrobe too, hanging several garments, one on top of the other, on every wire hanger. Aisling has never seen Orla's bedroom and never will if Orla has anything to do with it.

Sava calls them down to supper. They meet two other girls who will share the house with them – big tall thin girls who look about sixteen and are called Pauline and Jacqueline.

Aisling is polite. She says hello and when did you arrive? Pauline answers these questions monosyllabically. Jacqueline stares unashamedly at Aisling and Orla, saying absolutely nothing. Sava totters into the room in platform shoes to pour tea. She also is silent. When she has filled the cups and tottered away again, Jacqueline looks at Pauline and starts to giggle. After a while they are both in an uncontrollable, hysterical fit of laughter. Pauline glances at Aisling from time to time and says, 'Oh I'm sorry!' Then they giggle even more furiously. 'Excuse us!' she says. Jacqueline doubles over.

Orla is alarmed at first. She smiles weakly, even tries to join the girls in a laugh. But it doesn't work.

When they have been giggling for about five minutes without pause, Orla gets cross. She grimaces at Aisling and begins to eat her tea, sausages and fried tomatoes. Aisling raises her eyebrows. They talk to one another in Irish.

This sets Pauline and Jacqueline off even more.

'Oh excuse us!' Pauline says, tears streaming down her face, after about ten minutes. She gets up from the table, a lanky girl dressed in a short denim skirt. 'Come on you.' She digs Jacqueline in the ribs. Jacqueline looks blank, then follows her from the room.

'Honestly!' says Aisling.

'They're very slim, aren't they?' Orla dips a sausage into a small pool of brown sauce, Chef sauce, she has made at the side of her plate. 'Is there any room here for Sandra, do you think?'

'Oh gosh!' Aisling exclaims. 'I don't know.'

The casual betrayal of Sandra

Sandra waits in the hall until every other child has left. A dim, dusty, ancient glow, supplied by one bulb, settles in a puddle on the floorboards: outside, the light is fading at last. The windows are black. It is almost ten o'clock

The round man folds up his wad of papers neatly and places them in a slim black briefcase. He takes a packet of cigars from his pocket and lights one up.

'Ahem,' Sandra says.

He looks over and sees her, a small figure in a pink anorak, her yellow and brown and white hair falling over her drooping shoulders, her large eyes red-rimmed.

'Oh be the hokey!' He draws on his cigar. 'You're the girl with the problem.'

'I'm supposed to be in Aisling's and Orla's house. I put it on the form.'

'What's this your name is again? Sorry, love.'

'Sandra Darcy.'

The voices echo in the hall, which begins to seem vast to Sandra. The round man sits down on the bench beside Sandra and opens his briefcase again. 'That's a nice name,' he says, looking at her hair. He sighs. 'Yes yes. Sandra.' He takes out the list and checks it. 'You're down for Carrs' house.'

'I want to be with the others.'

'And what's their names?'

They find the names and the house.

'Ah yes.' He puts away his notes again and draws on his cigar. Sandra waits for him to solve the difficulty. She likes the smell of the cigar, and likes looking at the wisps of blue smoke drifting across the room. They transform it from being schooly to something completely different.

He looks at her again, takes off his glasses and wipes them on his sleeve. Without them his face is red and pudgy, a baby face. His eyes are smaller than you think when you see him in the glasses, and sunken.

'I'll bring you down to Carrs' tonight. They're waiting for you there. And tomorrow we'll sort this out. Is it a deal?'

Sandra feels her stomach drop. This is not the end she had foreseen when she smelt the comforting cigar smoke, savoured the air of competent masculinity that filled the room, softening its edges with its velvet-cushioned safety.

'But . . . ?'

'You're a great girl, I can see that, Sandra.' His eyes fall on her hair again. 'It's late, love. You can go to bed and have a good sleep and tomorrow we'll do something about it.'

Sandra has to agree.

Enid Blyton sings the blues

It's the first time Orla has ever been away from her parents: Irish college. She made herself believe it would be like a summer camp, like something she had read about in *The Bobbsey Twins*. When she saw the word 'college' – the word 'Irish' she had to disregard, obviously – she saw the Bobbsey twins by a campfire, roasting marshmallows; she saw the Chalet School, Jo and Mavis and all of them in the snow-capped mountains, going for hikes and being funny, wise, tasteful, English – what Orla would love to be. She'd like to be Jo at the Chalet, or the twins at St Clare's, or, most of all, Darrell Rivers at Malory Towers, with whom Orla has always identified absolutely. Darrell was beautiful, in a low-key way – you knew this although it was never stated in the book, where the ostentatious beauties, like Alison at St Clare's, the girls who had blonde hair and polished their nails (they didn't even use nail varnish, which is what you get in Ireland, but *polish*), were always stupid, and bad. They got expelled usually. Darrell wasn't like that. She thought nail polish was unspeakably vulgar; she was the kind of girl who would rather be martyred at the stake than give up her right not to wear make-up. A shirt and tie is what she liked to wear: when she left Malory Towers she was going to be a surgeon in Edinburgh, like her father. But above all she was noble, fair and kind, an excellent judge of character and situation. Darrell was always right, about everything.

And Malory Towers! The castle on the Cornish coast, the midnight feasts, the dotty teachers and the stern, just headmistress (very like Darrell, although this did not occur to Orla). Above all, the swimming pool, a huge pool cut out of the rugged Cornish rocks. Darrell perhaps was an ace swimmer, diving fearlessly into the bracing blue water. (Only horrible people did not dive, Orla knew. Girls who didn't dive were like soldiers too cowardly to rush from the trench into the rain of enemy fire. They were the scum of the earth. Orla herself was afraid to dive but believed she would be brave enough soon, given the right circumstances.) Orla had dreamt of the pool once, in the best and most memorable dream she had ever had. She had dreamt of the dark rocks jutting around the edges, and the huge blue expanse of pool, and the laughing girls in red swimsuits diving from the diving board. In the dream she had swum from one end of the warm salt water to the other, and white terns had dived in the background from a clear blue sky. Rocks, ripples, red swimsuits. Lovely perfect English accents singing through the clean air. English as she should be spoke. Girls as they should be taught. Life as it should be lived.

But Orla knows the score

Of course Irish college could not be like that. Of course not. Orla knows. She should: she's been to Tubber before, three or four times at least. It's where her father comes from, so she knows exactly what it's like, who lives there, their names. Half of them know her as well: they are related to her in one way or another. Her aunt, Auntie Annie, lives down by the beach. (When Orla thinks of this her stomach turns over in fear and shame. She does not want to have an aunt here, at Irish college. Darrell did not have an aunt in Malory Towers, only a perfect absent father, as far away as he could be, in Edinburgh, at the other end of the country.)

Orla, if not permitted by fate to be Darrell Rivers, which unfortunately is the case, would settle for being like Aisling, her friend; would be glad to be like any of the other children, free of connections apart from her schoolmates and the teachers. She would settle for being anybody but herself, Orla of the double allegiances, Orla of the city and the country, Orla who belongs in both places and belongs in neither.

Why she was sent here is not something she questions: Elizabeth decided it was to be. Elizabeth encouraged Orla's classmates to go with her, practically organising the trip from the Dublin side. Why did Elizabeth think it would be good for

Orla to go to Tubber rather than any of the other dozens of Irish colleges in Ireland? Maybe to promote Tubber, to show it off to the people of Dublin? She is always doing that anyway, verbally. Tubber is all she has to show off in the little terrace of houses where she lives, the narrow streets where the sun barely shines. Tubber Tubber Tubber, they hear about it from morning to night, how great it is, how perfect, how beautiful. (Elizabeth does not really believe the credit for this perfection is mainly hers, but sometimes you would think she did, listening to her.)

Or she could have wanted Orla to feel protected, away from home but not away as it were, away but among her own. In imagining Orla would like that, she showed how little she knew her. Or maybe she wanted to show off to the people of Tubber: this is Orla and her friends. They can afford to pay to go to Irish college. They can be Irish students with the best of them.

Yes. Orla thought it sounded like a good idea, until she got here and realised she was two people: Orla the daughter of Elizabeth, the niece of Auntie Annie, the cousin of the people of Tubber, and Orla the schoolgirl from Dublin, the friend of Aisling, the Irish scholar. She has either to be two people at the same time, which is a hard thing to be, especially when you are thirteen and a half. Or she has to choose to be just one of them. That also is very hard – not the choice, which is simple, but the consequences.

The choice itself is all too quickly made: she will have to try to be Orla the schoolgirl from Dublin. All her old Tubber habits, her specialised Tubber knowledge, will have to be suppressed, her innumerable relations ignored. The mantle of innocence and anonymity worn by the other children Orla will drape over herself, and hide whatever is underneath. Plenty. Plenty is underneath. But she is so used to hiding things that the decision to do it is automatic. What other course of action is open to her? It has been clear to her for years that all her friends would hate her if they knew what she was really like, and especially if they knew what her family was like. The inferiority of Orla's family to the families of Orla's friends is immense. It is an ocean that no bridge or ship or airplane or seagull or albatross or anything could ever cross. Friends on one side, family on the other. If the friends got wind of it . . . she'd be done for. It's friends or family, and she is thirteen and a half. She needs friends.

Still, it is odd pretending not to know things that she has known since the year dot. It is odd changing the way she looks at Tubber and the people in it, seeing them and talking about them with the eyes of Orla the schoolgirl, not the eyes of Orla the niece of Annie Crilly, the daughter of Tom who went to Dublin. It is odd how different the two sets of eyes have to be, and even odder how different the languages of the two Orlas are.

The college has its own special jargon, which is in Irish. So all the people and the places have a different set of names from those Orla has known – or they have known themselves. Before, everyone and every place in Tubber had an English name, but now they are all Irish. Tubber itself is An Tobar. The Dohertys are Muintir Uí Dhochartaigh. Charlie Paddy Andys are Muintir Uí Ghallchóir. They all sound much more important, it seems to Orla, more correct and elegant, than they do in their own funny Donegal English. The Mollies are Muintir Uí Chnáimhsí. Quilties is Na Coillte. In the English of this area, as of many areas in Ireland, all names sound, to Orla, faintly ridiculous. People have clownish names. Murphy and Meaney and Sweeney and Mulligan. Bally this and Ballyslapdashinmuckerishthat. Irish restores to them dignity and elegance. So she thinks, happily abandoning her own name in English, Orla Crilly, and calling herself Órla Nic Giolla Chrollaigh. That nobody, not even she herself, can pronounce it correctly does not bother her, not now. Anyway she mumbles it, when she says it, so nobody ever hears it properly. But she thinks it looks lovely, with its conglomerations of consonants, its long string of words. She thinks it looks difficult, and important.

Along with her own name, she puts all the old familiar names aside, and adopts the new, outsiders' labels. These are as safe and neat as blackboards or school uniforms, and thus eminently acceptable to her. But she knows there is something wrong with them. Their tone is false, they ring laughably in her ears, like the tinny sounds of children playing on xylophones when you are used to old accordions or fiddles, used to deep ancient drums.

The people and the places cannot themselves change much, whatever about their names. The men still wear old grey suits and wellington boots as they walk around the fields looking at fences and cows and the sky. The women still wear navy-blue wraparound overalls, their deep pockets perfect for storing stray eggs. Or clothes pegs. The children look wild and dirty on weekdays, stiff and clean on Sundays, as before. And the houses have that funny country look to them, be they thatched cottages, which Orla loathes, or slated council cottages, be they the forbidding grey blocks of the old farmhouses or her favourite kind of house, the new stucco bungalows with generous windows, glowing green- or red-tiled roofs.

The Dohertys' house looks like Auntie Annie's place, but it is bigger and better-kept. It is one of the square grey farmhouses, door in the middle, windows like eyes set at either side, chimney perched on top of the black slates. It is set in a shady yard, and its front windows command a view of a corrugated iron barn, painted dark red, a field in which the milch cows, ducks and geese graze, a small green pond. Beyond that stretches the whole of Tubber, and beyond that the sea.

Unusually for an Irish farmhouse, behind the house there is a garden, surrounded by a stone wall, with a stream running through it. The stream runs into a large field alongside the house before taking a turn and continuing on down through the valley. The girls are quick to discover the stream, as they discover everything in the house and around it. Banatee tells them to keep away from it. It's deeper and more dangerous

37

than it looks, she says. She calls the stream the burn. 'That there's the big burn and it's a dangerous burn. Johnny Charlie Patsy was drowned in that burn five years ago, so he was, he was down in it fishin for eels. Terrible fond of the fishin, Johnny Charlie, so he was, a lovely wee boy only ten year old and he was drowned at the burn down at yon bend in Mattie the Island's cornfield. Keep away!'

The girls nod, but make a note of the burn. They need all the water they can get, to wash their clothes and their hair and their bodies. The supply in the house is not plentiful, one bathroom for everybody. People in Gaeltachts pay little attention to water supplies, lulled by the eternal downpours into the belief that there's more than enough to go round.

Irish Irish and only Irish
and if you don't like Irish
it's back to town you go

You are supposed to speak Irish all the time.

'That is the rule of the college,' shouts Headmaster Joe, for that is the name of the round dark man, on Monday morning when the whole college is assembled for the first time. He is a bold comma of a man, fond of high drama. He is wearing his black suit, white shirt and red and black tie, striped, today as every day. All the teachers wear jackets of some kind, mainly tweed, but Headmaster Joe is never seen without his suit. 'If you break the Irish rule you will be sent home on the next bus. And don't think we won't hear you when you are away from the schoolhouse. We'll hear you. We'll hear you on the road and we'll hear you in the fields, not that you are allowed in the fields anyway. We'll hear you when you're at your banatee's table and we'll hear you when you are in bed at night. We'll even hear you when you are asleep.' His round black eyes twinkle. 'So don't think you can dream in English and get away with it. In this college, boys and girls, you are not allowed to dream in English. Do you read me? That is the rule.'

Inoperable. Headmaster Joe knows it and so does everyone else; the listening teachers already know it, nodding or shaking their heads in disapproval at such nonsense; the students, stiff and frightened by his stentorian tones, know it after one day in the place. Everyone is here to speak Irish, is supposed to speak Irish, but most of the time nobody actually will.

Many of them can't. Pauline and Jacqueline, for instance, know no Irish at all, even though they claim to learn it at their school in Derry. The Banatee and Sava speak the dialect of Tubber, a northern dialect which differs slightly from all other kinds of Irish still spoken and which is almost extinct. Aisling, who speaks Irish all the time at home, claims to find it incomprehensible. The Banatee does not appear to understand much of what Aisling or Orla say either, when they speak their fluent Dublin Irish.

Orla understands most of what she hears, from the Banatee and Sava, from Pauline and Jacqueline, from Aisling. From everyone. That's the problem: she's trying to be free as a baby, blissfully ignorant, but she's not. She's knowing, what Elizabeth calls 'oul- fashioned'. Girls are often oul-fashioned, their eyes are cunning and knowing, peering from their polite and silent faces, while boys are innocent, lovable and cherished. Orla has been taught this since she was about two years old.

Knowing too much is a burden Orla has been given to carry, because she is a girl. Girls read and learn and in consequence know too much. Nobody in Ireland likes a child who knows anything. Now on top of everything else she knows languages: tongues – or at least myriad dialects. Comprehension of myriad tongues is one of the gifts of the Holy Ghost, bequeathed by the same at Confirmation. Some understand many tongues and some speak many tongues. You would think, Orla thought, when she heard the gaunt, thief-eyed Bishop McQuaid citing these words, that the same people must do both. But no. Here she is, quick to understand but slow to speak. Her own limited, shoddy, modern, inaccurate Dublin Irish is what comes out of her mouth when she talks. Anything else would be pretentious. She remembers what happened to Mary Darcy when she came back from Connemara with an accent fit to catch a whale. Children laughed in her face, mimicked her every intonation until even she, bossy, priggish, know-allish, self-assured and old-womanish as she was, had to cave in and revert to the language of her peers. Orla would not make the same mistake, magnified enormously since Donegal Irish is so much more outlandish than Connemara Irish and so much more unusual. Orla has never come across anyone in Dublin, apart from her father, who speaks it at all. She's not going to be the one to start. *Caidé mar atá tú* instead of *Conas atá tú*. *Falsa* instead of *leisciúil*. *Fosta* instead of *freisin*. *Geafta* instead of *geata*. They manage to mess up almost every single word, even before they start changing the tune of the sentences.

A traditional Irish schoolhouse

After Headmaster Joe's battle cry, the scholars are assigned to their classes. Orla, Aisling and Sandra find themselves in the highest class, with Máistir Dunne. Pauline and Jacqueline are in the lowest, with Bean Uí Luing of the bus.

Six classes there are, all and every one of them in the school-house. Traditional Irish schoolhouse, as the brochure puts it: windows so high in the walls that the pupils cannot see outside. Will not the folk and animal life of Tubber be putting in on them. Boys' Side and Girls' Side, folding wooden doors in the middle.

Now, although not separated are the boys and the girls, the room divided is into six sections, separated from one another with flowery curtains a-hanging from skipping ropes. Able is every class to overhear all the others, and their eyes to see as well if peer they do under the curtains, which do some, of course, all the time.

'What's your house like?' asks Sandra.

'OK.' Cute as a fox is Aisling; it's little she lets on.

'Mine is awful. There's eight of us in one room, eight of us, and the food is disgusting. I'm changing today.'

'That's great,' says Orla. 'Did they say you could?'

'I haven't asked them yet,' says Sandra and a puss on her.

'Well you'll have to ask.'

'But who will I put a question on?'

'Put a question on him.' Points Aisling to their teacher, leaning against the blackboard, a pipe being smoked by him. Is the room a-filling with pale grey, rose-scented smoke. Pulls in Orla a breath, she fine and contented. Sweet to her the scent of tobacco.

'Him?'

'He's our teacher.'

Rises Sandra and asks him.

Pulls he his pipe out of his mouth and taps against the easel. Falls black tobacco, some of it still burning, on the floor, and tramples he out it with his brown shoe. A look of confusion on him.

'Hm,' says he. 'Hm. We'll talk to the headmaster after class, all right?'

Returns Sandra sadly to the bench.

Reads aloud Máistir Dunne's class from the great classics of Ireland: *Jimín* and *Rotha Mór an tSaoil, Peig, An tOileánach*. Organises he debate: Life of the Town versus Life of the Country. Teaches he poem: 'Fornocht do chonac thú' (Stark naked I saw you).

Hear they Bean Uí Luing under bottom the curtain.

Sentences a-teaches she.

I am in sixth class at school.

I am four years teen of age.

Better to me tea than coffee.

Hurler good is my brother.

Footballer good is my brother.

There is a cat white to me.

There is a dog black to me.

It is lovely with me my dog black.

Repeat the pupils the sentences after her, and then learn they them by clean mind. And they learning by clean mind it is able

with you to hear their brains working, like to a machine a-
humming, even only over the curtain. Pleasant, comforting
sound it is.

At noon taken are the curtains from their ropes, by pets of the
teachers; unpartitioned big room again is the schoolhouse. Bean
Uí Luing takes over. Stands she on chair, figure little dressed in
cardigan green, and starts to teach the whole college how to
sing. 'Feidhlimí's Boat' the first song.

> Boateen of Feidhlimí that went to Tory
> Boateen of Feidhlimí and Feidhlimí in it
> Boateen of Feidhlimí that went to Tory
> Boateen of Feidhlimí and Feidhlimí in it.
>
> Boateen tiny, boateen lively, boateen noble
> Boateen of Feidhlimí
> Boateen intrepid, boateen lovely
> Boateen of Feidhlimí and Feidhlimí in it.
>
> Boateen of Feidhlimí broken in Tory
> Boateen of Feidhlimí and Feidhlimí in it.
> Boateen of Feidhlimí broken in Tory
> Boateen of Feidhlimí and Feidhlimí in it.

Have knowledge some of the pupils the song already, and sing
they it with gusto. No knowledge of it have others, and sing
they hesitantly. Able some people to sing, and other people not
able. Over all the voices voice of Jacqueline rises, voice of fairy,
voice of angel – soprano.

Notice it Orla and Aisling, and look at each other, surprise on
them and joy – something that puts even more surprise on them,
jealous-hearted little bitches as they are.

Makes Sandra a wan smile, singing with weak heart, waiting
for the end of choir.

Looks she over the room for Máistir Dunne, but not there is
he. Not any teacher there now but only Bean Uí Luing.

'What will I do?' asks she, her voice cracking.

'What do you mean?' asks Orla, although knowledge has she well what Sandra means.

'He said he'd talk to the headmaster but I don't see him anywhere.'

'Maybe he is talking to the headmaster.'

'Will I ask her about it?' Looks she at Bean Uí Luing.

'Yeah!' says Orla, turning and walking away.

We meet the native speakers

The cornerstone theory of the Irish college system is that, as well as learning Irish in the classroom, the city children will interact with the indigenous inhabitants of the Gaeltacht, the native speakers. The first and most tangible benefit of this contact should be an improvement of their appalling Gaelic accents. But there is another, more nebulous aim: it is believed that by getting to know native Irish speakers, inhabitants of a rural, western, relict zone, the children will learn something other than Irish, something cultural, the nature of which nobody quite understands. All that is known about this quality is that it is healthier than the culture the students are accustomed to in the city – as the air is fresher, the fields greener, and the water clearer, so is the culture itself more spontaneous, fresh and unadulterated.

You can't put your finger on what the difference is. But it exists all the same. Even the children sense it.

The smells of the Gaeltacht enhance the atmosphere of goodness: the turf smoke, the salt breeze, the tang of cow dung relax Orla, and the other students. Their noses recognise that they are undergoing a purifying experience.

It is more difficult for their brains to grasp this. Their contact with indigenous Gaeltacht life is confusing, to say the least, and usually less than refreshing.

For Orla and Aisling, the accessible natives are Banatee, Sava, Faratee and Micheál.

Faratee is not easy to access. They catch elusive glimpses of him as he walks across the farmyard or drives his tractor up and down the lane. His name is Charlie but he looks like Tom in *The Riordans*: big and fat, dressed in a greyish suit. Most of the day he seems to spend moving lumberingly from one place to the other, up and down, back and forth. When he meets one of the girls he touches his cap and parts his lips fractionally, presumably uttering some word which they do not, however, hear.

Micheál is similarly silent and evasive. Although unlike the rest of his family he sleeps in the house, the girls see little enough of him. If they bump into him on the landing or stairs, he averts his eyes, blushes, and ignores them entirely. He looks like an ordinary teenage boy; shabbily dressed in very old clothes, since that is the way all young farming men seem obliged to dress, but otherwise normal enough. He is tall and, Orla guesses – wrongly – about eighteen years of age. His hair is dark red.

Orla, encountering him as she leaves the bathroom, looks away. But he smiles at her and says hello.

She replies, somewhat to her surprise.

'You know Micheál . . . ?' she risks with Aisling.

'Oh gonny!' Aisling says. 'What a weed!'

Orla doesn't mention him again.

The remaining natives then, are Banatee and Sava.

Banatee does not talk much.

She is a darting bird-like women. Her white hair is bobbed like a child's and she wears basket-coloured glasses on her high shining cheeks. Her everyday dress is a navy-blue overall sprigged with red flowers, and on Sundays she wears a black tailored suit, worn with a straw boater and shoes with thick Cuban heels, strapped across the instep, the kind tap dancers wear. All her clothes look as if they are thirty years old, and they are. Orla regards her with a curiosity that is mixed with affection: there is something neat and attractive about Banatee, even though her entire appearance makes her so anachronistic as to be inaccessible to Orla or any of the girls. To them she might be another species, or at least a race all of whose symbolism is foreign and impenetrable. Occasionally she pours tea for the girls, or can be seen through the open door of the kitchen. But after the first day, she has had little to say to any of them. She is as shy as they are, and the sum of the mutual shyness of city girls and country woman is an effective barrier against even minimal communication – even if the language were not getting in the way.

Most of the time Banatee does not see the girls, nor they her.

Leaving Sava. Sava the Silent.

It is Sava who serves the meals, in the parlour at the front of the house, carrying the plates of dinner in on a tray or bringing in extra plates of bread at teatime. She too is shy and silent, even though she is only a few years older than the girls. Small and thin like her mother, she has her mother's neat, fine features but in a younger form, so much younger and softer that the girls cannot see any resemblance at all. Besides, she has colour. She is, in fact, extremely colourful – her hair is black, black as a river at night, not black as a raven's wing. That is Sava's colour, as to hair, and her skin is pearly, a translucent white. Red mouth, needless to add. She is Snow White, she is Étain, she is Deirdre of the Sorrows. She is a great beauty, as her mother is, but although the girls understand, faintly, that there is something attractive about both of them they cannot see beyond the clothes and style to recognise their beauty. Sava also dresses wrongly. Not wrongly as her mother does, but wrongly in the opposite direction. She dresses like a tart. Her skirts are minier than mini, her T-shirts skintight. Instead of navy-blue and black, she likes shocking pink, lime green, any colour so long as it is loud and horrible. She doesn't wear make-up on her perfect skin, because it is too delicate to stand it, but her eyelashes are coated in thick, stiff mascara, and they stand around her large blue eyes like black railings around a pond.

You would think, in such a get-up, that she would have a strong brash personality to match. But it is not so. On her plastic platforms, she glides in and out of the parlour as silently as a cat. Occasionally she smiles and says 'Caidé mar atá tú?' Lately – they have been here only four days – she smiles at Pauline, who has quickly emerged as the most important girl in the house; Pauline, because she acknowledges the recognition and acknowledges that Sava, by virtue of her position as permanent resident, has some status, smiles back. Today, when Sava carried the bacon and cabbage into the parlour, she even said, 'How's Sava?' in her jokey, grown-up way. And Sava managed a rejoinder. Even under the gazes of Aisling, Orla and Jacqueline, all mildly disturbed by their consciousness of being left outside this communication, however insignificant it was, Sava managed to respond. Pauline has no gift at all for languages. But she has a gift for tones and moods. She can adjust her wavelength to anybody's, if it suits her. She can sense a tone, or set one to match what is around her.

As soon as Sava leaves the room, Pauline gets up and mimicks her tottering walk. The others giggle, pleased to be pulled back into Pauline's circle, and tackle their meal. The saltiest bacon, the steeliest cabbage, Orla has ever tasted.

Jacqueline screws up her small nose. 'God it's the pits,' she says. 'Really, isn't it? I wish I was at home with me mammy, so I do.'

'It's not right. In Carrs' they get the Irish flag every day for their dinner. Eggs peas and chips. It's a fact. And the banatee Gerry has makes hamburgers.'

'I'm not goin to eat this ——, pardon the language, girls!' Jacqueline pushes away her plate. Aisling raises her eyebrows and Orla feels sick: Jacqueline has used a very bad word indeed.

49

'I'm not going to eat it either. So I'm not.' Pauline holds her nose. 'It's fit for pigs!'

She stands on the chair and honks. Then she sings:

> 'They say that in the Gaeltacht
> The food is very fine
> You ask for Coca-Cola and
> They give you turpentine
> I don't want no more of Gaeltacht life!
> Gee ma, I wanna go!
> Where do you wanna go?
> Gee ma I wanna go
> Home!'

The burn scene one

Sunday afternoon. Orla, Aisling, and Pauline and Jacqueline are away down the garden, washing their clothes in thon burn I ask ye! Banatee is away to the hawspital in Letterkenny. Connie Tinney was brought up there last Tuesday after the wheel of his new tractor fell on top of him. Four ribs cracked and a broken leg but wasn't he the lucky man not to be killed? Man dear! Faratee drove Banatee to town, and who knows where that wee skitter Sava is. Or Micheál. Thon Micheál is no good.

Well the morning was very wet. But after the dinner the sun came out, it did aye. And it was then that Pauline came up with the bright idea that the whole lot of them, herself and the other one from Derry and the two weans from Dublin, would head out into the garden. And not alone that but into the burn. It's naw that anyone had said to them that they shouldn't go there, you understand, but they wouldn't have bothered if the woman of the house was at home. Because when she's at home she can see right out into that garden from the window of the kitchen. From where she'd be standin for the most of the day washin up after that lot of scholars. But she wasn't there. She was away off to the hospital in Letterkenny to see poor Connie and the way was clear for them to do whatever the hell they liked. They're not supervised on a Sunday afternoon for some reason and that was the root of the whole problem. Aye indeed it was.

The Dohertys' garden used to be a wild lovely place when I was a wee lad. Aye. Do you mind the old woman there, she would have been Charlie's granny? Well she was an unusual sort of an old woman. She was that. She had a sort of special interest in gardens and I'm tellin you that in those days that wasn't very common around here at all, it was not. Except way down over the hill some of the bigger farmers would keep gardens. That would have been the other side, ye know. Them that dug with the other foot. They dug gardens. But over here very few had the time or the money or even the land to bother about them. Or the interest.

She was the exception, old Auntie Sheila. That's what we all called her, everyone, even them that were no relation at all to her. Aye. She was Auntie to everyone. She was always out in that garden plantin lettuces and cabbages and carrots and parsley and scallions. And then the flowers she had. I don't rightly recall the names of them all but she would have had nasturtiums and sweet peas and roses needless to say, all kinds of roses, and she had them snapdragons and sweet williams and a whole lot of other flowers that I don't know the names of. I'm telling you thon garden was a wild nice place. It was beautiful. Pure beautiful.

It has the essential ingredients – stone, lichened wall, stream crossing diagonally through it, big old elm trees at one end. But it has not been developed as Orla would wish it to have been. Banatee has planted a row of red salvia beside the wall, and put a number of rose trees, flowering profusely in red and yellow, in the shelter of the kitchen window. They are the kind of roses that do not have a smell. Nasturtiums have taken over one bank of the stream, so that it looks almost entirely orange. Orla does not like their garish colour. She looks around and imagines how the garden would look if there were instead a profusion of tall, drooping flowers in dusty pinks and purples, creams and palest yellows. Flowers she has seen on the lids of chocolate boxes, or heard about in one of her favourite songs, 'An English Country Ga-a-arden'. Flowers she does not know the names for: delphiniums, columbines, hollyhocks, lupins. She sighs, turning away from the nasturtiums (she does not know that name either, knows hardly any names for flowers apart from the most common), and scrubs her underpants with toilet soap, watching happily as the suds float off to the arch in the wall through which the stream passes out of the garden.

'This was a great idea.' Pauline stands on a rock, wringing a pink T-shirt. 'I'm gonna always wash me clothes in the burn so I am!'

'It's better than that bathroom anyway,' Jacqueline drawls, sighing. 'I think the water is a wee bit hotter.'

Orla and Aisling giggle and look at one another. The Derry girls sound so knowing always, sophisticated and witty, with their tuneful accents and quick turns of phrase, with their sharp, northern vocabulary.

'The burn is beautiful,' says Orla. She and Aisling adapt to the Derry vocabulary, rather than the other way round. She does not know why this happens, unless it is that to her own ears the accent of Dublin, which Pauline to her astonishment calls a 'brogue', seems flat and lifeless, and its words consequently lacking in value. 'It's a pity there isn't a bridge across it or something.'

'Yeah, a little wooden curved bridge like in the Japanese gardens or something, that'd be lovely.'

Wouldn't it?

Sandra is dying for a swim

The scholars' day is divided into three parts: mornings are devoted to lessons, afternoons to outdoor activities, and evenings to dancing.

Lunch over, Aisling and Orla walk back to the schoolhouse where they will play rounders. Other children form a crocodile and sway off down the road, led by two teachers, to the beach. Boys play football.

Sandra wants to go swimming. 'I'm dyin for a swim, it's a gorgeous day!' she says.

'I can't.' Orla stares at her firmly. Aisling blushes.

'Oh!' Sandra understands.

'What did you get for dinner?' Aisling asks.

'Peas, eggs and chips.'

'We got corned beef and cabbage.' Aisling sounds more rueful than she feels. The corned beef had tasted quite nice, if not the cabbage.

'I told him I was supposed to be with youse,' Sandra says with emphasis.

'You're probably better off where you are,' Orla smiles.

'That's not fair. She's supposed to be with us!' Aisling moves closer to Sandra and turns her shoulder indignantly on Orla. 'What did he say?'

'He said he'll talk to me about it tomorrow.'

'Tomorrow!' Aisling sighs and shakes her head. 'Tomorrow and tomorrow and tomorrow! My way of life is fallen into the sere the yellow leaf!'

'They've started to walk to the beach.' Orla tries to re-enter the circle, while watching the line begin to move. She gazes at the sea, a gleaming turquoise lake below them. She remembers the feel of its water lapping against her, smooth as gelatine, and its intriguing rock pools. Orla loves swimming as much as Sandra does, and gets to swim much less often, since her mother will not let her use the public swimming baths in Dublin – Tara Street or the Iveagh Baths. They're common, them baths. Orla's mother will not even let her go to Blackrock, to the red-and-white open-air swimming pool where all the children of the south suburbs dive and swim all summer long, splashing from the high diving board into the cold black water. Sandra goes there every second day in summer and to Tara Street every Saturday throughout the winter.

'Why won't yez come? It's hot. I'm boiling!' Sandra's eye follows the line of children as it moves away from them.

'I told you, didn't I? I can't. You go. Go yourself.'

'Will you come, Ash?'

Aisling looks from one face to the other, Sandra's pleading and Orla's implacable. She is tired of Orla and her whims but too polite to abandon her. On the other hand she doesn't want to hurt Sandra. Such dilemmas, the impossible dilemmas of the nice girl she frequently has to face.

Such dilemmas are usually decided by a stronger-willed third party.

'She hasn't got her togs with her,' Orla says firmly, clinching it.

'Ah Janey Mack!' sighs Sandra.

'Go on, Sandra, you'll like it anyway.' Aisling encourages her, relief her main sensation.

The crocodile is rounding the bend on the road. Only its tail end is visible.

'I'll do rounders too.' Sandra flings her towel on the stone wall.

The fairy reel

The curtains are down, the large room glows in the evening sun. The children file into the schoolhouse and sit on the benches, now placed along the walls, under the cracked blue maps and posters of smiling families of outmoded appearance and unusual faded colours. Headmaster Joe takes up position beside the record-player and announces the dances.

All the formalities that have been dispensed with in the dance halls of Ireland are firmly enacted, even enforced, here – either because Headmaster Joe, who is aged about fifty-five, insists on clinging to the traditions of his youth, or because the male scholars are supposed to be educated to be courteous, gentlemanly, gallant, according to the high standards of the Gaels of yore. Girls on one side, boys on the other, no mixing between dances allowed. Every boy is required to dance every dance, no matter how disinclined he is to do so – since most of them are aged twelve, they are all very disinclined to do so, so it is important that they be given no choice in this matter. On the first night at the *céilí* the invitation formula was drummed into the scholars so thoroughly that even the dimmest and most linguistically clumsy of them can say it perfectly. 'An ndéanfaidh tú an damhsa seo liom, más é do thoil é?' And the response is, 'Déanfaidh agus fáilte.' Boys are obliged to ask every time, and girls are required to accept. Refusing is not permitted, on pain of expulsion from the *céilí* and, they believe, ultimately from the college.

As a system it works with great efficiency. The schoolhouse resounds to the thump of dancing feet and the creaky, silvery strains of three-time and four-time tunes from seven, when the *céilí* starts, until half past nine, when Headmaster Joe shouts, 'Oíche mhaith anois, a pháistí agus codladh sámh!' Or *culaith shnámha*. Nobody, not the shyest boy or the ugliest girl, sits out a single dance. They all pound away frantically. Headmaster Joe shouts out the instructions from his perch on the chair: Boy take his partner's hand. *Isteach! Amach!* I said *Amach!* Girl take other girl's hand. Swing around once. *Go mall go mall go mall!*

Slowly, awkward as elephants, they walk their way through the patterns, which to the uninitiated seem unbelievably complicated. It's like having to do a Euclid theorem with your legs. Prove that the sum of three angles of a triangle is equal to two right angles. *Droichead na nAsal*. 'Fallaí Luimnigh'. 'Ionsaí na hInse'. The Walls of Limerick and The Siege of Ennis are what they manage on the first night, the two simplest *céilí* dances in the world. They walk their way through them, then walk their way through them again. Then Headmaster Joe decides that the time has come to let them hear some music: the creaky record-player fills the schoolhouse with crackling, golden rhythms. The feet begin to thump, the bodies sway to the tune: 'Miss Martin's Reel'. The legs move a bit faster and to anyone viewing them from above – only one person is, Headmaster Joe – the patterns begin to take a loose shape. They are like the patterns on the crochet tablecloths sold in the souvenir shops in Tubber, or – he wipes his forehead – the swirls cut into the stones at Newgrange. In and out, round and round and round, in and out. And on to the next couple: the couples move along the floor two by two, eventually meeting all the other couples. By the time the set is over, everyone has danced with everyone else on the floor. It's a metaphor for the life of the parish.

The dances remind Orla of other things: the games she plays on the street at home: Red Rover and Pussy Four Corners and Kick the Can. Black shoe, black shoe, show me your other black shoe!

They dance almost without pause, awkwardness giving way to something like competence, nothing approaching grace, for two and a half hours, until their faces are red and their limbs exhausted. All they have to do now is walk a mile or two home to their banatees and stuff themselves with bread and jam and tea before flopping into bed.

Orla gets a boyfriend on the first night. Not a boyfriend exactly, not a golden penny exactly, but a boy who dances with her four or five times. He repeats this at every *céilí* for the rest of the holiday. It is a convenience for him more than anything else. It saves him the trouble of having to find a fresh partner every time. She knows this but she is pleased all the same, happy enough to appropriate him, or be appropriated. It is convenient for her, too, to know he is there, to have a boyfriend.

He and Orla do not exchange a single word, apart from the formulaic greeting and response, during all the time they dance together. And there is nothing sexual or sentimental in their relationship. Orla does not give him a second's thought when she is not with him, or even when she is with him. She does not consider whether he is attractive or not, whether she likes him or not. It just doesn't matter. She knows what his hand feels like – cool and dry – and how he dances: slowly. He is a slightly overweight boy, just about her own height, with a blond crew cut, large ears, and a pink-and-white face, smooth as an apple. He has an open, babyish countenance and she likes the colour of his jumper: wine. Alasdair is his name, and he is from Belfast. This means she would be unable to talk to him anyway, under the eye of the teachers, at the *céilí*: the boys from Belfast know even less Irish than the ones from Derry, in other words none at all. Their silence is therefore absolute when adults are around. They can only talk when they are sure of complete privacy.

Aisling establishes a similar partnership of convenience with a boy from Dublin called Seamas, who can speak Dublin boys' Irish – which is different from Dublin girls' Irish, as their English, too, tends to be. Sandra, in spite of her yellow and brown and gold hair, does not commit herself to anyone, and never knows who she is going to dance with. She doesn't like fellas anyway, that's what she says, tossing her mongrel hair, pouting.

'Neither do we!' laughs Aisling. 'God!'

Orla knows she's odd liking Alasdair, even in the way she does like him. If she were normal, like Aisling and Sandra, she'd think he was a weed. 'What a weed!' is what they say, referring to Seamas, or to any boy. 'Yuck! That weed!' Not talking to boys is not a question of language difficulties, for them, but of principle. Yuck! Who'd want to talk to them!

Not so the Derry girls. 'They're older,' Aisling says, blushing. Older, taller, thinner, prettier, with whiter bobby socks and shorter miniskirts. They pretend not to know Aisling and Orla once they walk in the door of the *céilí*. When the music starts their eyes light up, their bodies sway slightly, their long brown arms and legs flex and strengthen subtly, poised for action. Orla watches them from her bench, where she and Aisling and Sandra sit in their home-made cotton dresses and ankle socks, watching Jacqueline and Pauline metamorphose, girls becoming mermaids before their eyes. Before many eyes: all eyes are upon them; they are the tallest girls and the best-looking (nobody would say 'sexiest' but they know, happily or sadly or resentfully, that that is what they are).

Jacqueline and Pauline swagger to a corner and stand there, talking to one another, ignoring everybody. They have no make-up, and they are dressed in denim and striped T-shirts (they tend to dress more or less identically, Pauline calling the shots); only their footwear is adult: strappy sandals, such as

Roman slaves in films wear. But they exude glamour. Magical perfume, magical glow, it seeps from them and surrounds them like a holy penumbra. Their corner of the room glows with charm, sexuality, fashion. In the chalky cheesy schoolroom, they create an oasis of girlish femininity. Headmaster Joe glances over at them and quickly turns away again, with an irascible twist of the mouth: he has to line up the records, run this *céilí* as efficiently as he runs everything else. It's the end of the first week and exhaustion is catching up on him. Máistir Dunne gazes at the corner and pulls on his pipe, smiling. Killer Jack, another teacher, grins, while Bean Uí Luing smiles benignly at the boys and girls of her class, who are playing a clapping game down beside the blackboard.

As soon as a dance is called all the older boys rush to Jacqueline and Pauline. The fastest two walk off with them, holding their long thin hands, not sure what they are supposed to do now they have won the prize. Later Máistir Dunne and Killer Jack dance with them, and find Jacqueline the better partner: she is compliant, gives herself to the dance. Pauline remains stiff – if she is with someone she does not like, which is the case when teachers are involved – and makes them feel guilty and awkward. She is happier flying around with any of the older boys. Towards the end of the evening, the oldest boy scholar, Gerry, asks her to dance, and it soon becomes clear that she likes him.

Gerry is going to be the star boy, the overall star, of the college. Even after a week he has taken up his position. He is the kind of boy who knows everything, is clever and affable at the same time, the kind of boy who can chat amiably to the teachers and upon whom they feel they can rely, and who at the same time manages not to antagonise most of the boys. Inevitably he antagonises some, the rougher and more subversive, who despise every inch of his neat handsome body, who spit, metaphorically, on his carefully modulated tone of voice and his gentlemanly demeanour. Orla is surprised that

Pauline likes this boy, the ultimate teacher's pet, destined for success (he knows it, everyone expects it). She is so subversive herself, not caring a fig for authority, while Gerry, it seems, loves it. Does not kowtow, but actually appears genuinely to love authority, in the form of teachers or government or rules or traditions. But he is handsome, like Pauline, and aristocratic in a different way. Superior. Also he is from Derry. He is the best-looking, oldest, most presentable boy from Derry at this college, and she is the female equivalent. (Jacqueline doesn't count. Already she is dismissed by Orla, by everyone, as a person who does not make the grade, no matter how limpid her eyes.) It is inevitable that they find one another.

Gerry and Pauline do not talk much, but everyone can see that their eyes talk. Other girls who fancy him notice it soon enough, and abandon hope. He dances with Pauline only half the time, but that is because of his cautious and ambitious nature. He will do nothing to arouse the disapproval of the authorities, and nothing to compromise his own reputation as a star boy. Half the time is what he thinks he can get away with, enough to stake his claim to Pauline while keeping the ill will of others at bay. Gerry has an instinct for striking this kind of balance. He achieves it, but Headmaster Joe, sitting beside the record-player, sees through him. Still, he is not worried. As director of the Irish college his responsibilities are many. It is the hardest job he has ever done, much harder than being headmaster of a school, which he also is. This is full-time. Girls and boys, lessons and dancing, food and lodging. He has to deal with the local landladies, encourage them to feed the children with food they can eat, check that their standards of hygiene are reasonable, scrutinise them, correct them, at the same time mollify and encourage them. He has to keep the children occupied, happy if possible. But his most urgent task is to prevent any sexual disaster. Pregnancy. In a college like this where the average age is twelve or thirteen it is not a grave danger, but it still exists. Gerry seems safe. Too bent on self-advancement to step out of line. Too subservient to his sacerdotal teachers to put his reputation for purity at risk. But Pauline is fourteen, big for her age, and mad as a hatter. She is the sort of girl who needs watching. Anarchy personified. She is the sort of girl who could lead anyone astray.

Gerry feels the little eye upon him, and so half the time he abandons Pauline and prances around with the likes of Orla or Aisling, leaving Pauline clear for Killer Jack and the younger male teachers.

The dancers raid the shop

When the *céilí* is over, all the students who have pocket money go to the shop. Orla, Aisling and Sandra, pink and hot, race with the throng through the cool night air to the general store and post office. On its floor are sacks of flour, meal, layers' mash, and other dry floury substances with a strange, sharp smell. The shelves are packed with ordinary products: raspberry jam, Galtee cheese, packets of Omo.

By the time the girls reach the shop, it is full of students. They cram together, trying to get to the counter. Behind the counter are the woman who owns the shop and is also a banatee, and three of her daughters. With harassed faces they hand out packets of crisps, bottles of minerals, and ice creams.

Killer Jack comes to the door of the shop. A frisson of surprise runs through the children. They fall silent. He takes a look at the crowd and laughs sharply. 'So long! See you tomorrow!' he says, in Irish, to the woman of the shop.

'No no, come around the back, *a thaisce*.' The woman of the shop gets flustered, even more flustered than she already was. She, like the students, is red in the face. Her face looks as if it could be nice but at the moment it is crisscrossed by hurry and anxiety.

Killer Jack goes around the back. Minutes later the children observe him appearing behind the counter. The woman of the shop abandons her young customers and serves him: he is buying sixty Silk Cut and two boxes of matches. There is trouble with the matches. They can't be located. The woman of the shop's three daughters too now abandon all the other customers and hunt for them. Killer Jack lights a cigarette with a match he already has and stands watching them. He blows a ring of smoke up towards the ceiling of the shop. The children watch the grey smoke circling. A few of them laugh. Orla feels annoyed, but does not know why.

Finally the matches are found (behind some jars of raspberry jam). Killer Jack takes the little boxes and tosses them into the air before sticking them in the pocket of his tweed jacket. The woman of the house turns and scowls at the children.

'Who's next?' she asks crossly, sighing.

Not fair, think the children. But they are used to being pushed aside, all the time, if any adult demands prior attention. Impatiently they wait their turn, clutching their pound notes, their handfuls of silver coins.

The post

The curtains are taken off the ropes, the borders between the classes temporarily removed once again. This time it's for An Post.

Headmaster Joe pulls a grey sack to the top of the schoolhouse and stands beside the record-player. Like Santa Claus he dives into the bag and fishes out envelopes, cards, and brown-paper parcels.

Maureen Dowling, Sheila Dempsey, Maurice Coleman, Pauline Gallagher, Aisling Brosnan, Peter Brown . . . He reads the names in a bored monotone, hardly pausing between them, his ambition being to get through the post as fast as he can. The children wait, silent, holding their breath, fingers clenched. It's a lottery. It's a competition. It's a thrill. It's exciting. It's heartwarming.

It's disappointment. It's disbelief. It's misery. It's tears.

It's life. A foretaste of what's in store, the ups and the downs, the thrills and the spills, the luck, the chanciness. The joy and the pain.

Mary Trimble, John Walsh, Michael Duggan, Brian Merriman . . . I mean Monagle. Ha ha ha!

Orla writes to her mother every second day. She tells Elizabeth everything in great detail: the timetable for the day, the food they eat, the clothes the other girls wear. She makes humorous comments on Jacqueline's attitude to the food, on the hairstyle of Banatee, on the way Sava dresses. She names every teacher and relays information about their habits, their appearances, their spouses, their origins, their families. Everything. Her shortest letters are ten pages long, her longest twenty-five. They all end with the same injunction: 'Do not work too hard!' Elizabeth has not replied to any of them, not yet. Aisling has received a letter every second day; her Friday letter included a five-pound note. Pauline gets a postcard from Italy, where her parents are on holiday – alone at last – every day. She doesn't read the postcards, at least not in the hall, but stuffs them into her canvas bag. Even Jacqueline, with her chips and Brits and sagging old cardigan of a mother, got a letter and money on Friday. Everyone in the college has had at least one letter now, with the single exception of Orla.

The first day she didn't mind. The second was all right. By the third most people had received something. Now she has been in Tubber for four days and still not a word from home. She can hardly refrain from crying. She doesn't mention her lack of letters to anyone – there is more shame attached to it, at this stage, than disappointment. Aisling has noticed.

'No letter?' she says, not unkindly, although she is aware of Orla's damaged pride. 'Oh well!' she says. 'Maybe tomorrow!'

The kindness makes Orla want even more desperately to cry. She bites her lip and forces her eyes to dry up. She pushes the rocking fear in her stomach down, as if it were a frisky dog. Down!

Orla wants a letter because she wants to be like everyone else. She also wants a letter to reassure her. That everything is all right at home is not something she takes for granted. On the contrary. In the absence of evidence to the contrary, she assumes the opposite. Orla is afraid that Elizabeth will die.

This is the era of the sick, as far as Orla is concerned. Never again in life will she come across so many illnesses, or experience so many herself. What causes it? Houses are chilly, food is monotonous and starchy, teachers are violent, school is terrifying, babies are stuffed to the gills with cow's milk from packets and cans from the moment of their birth. (Women in Dublin don't want to acknowledge the existence of breasts: they haven't got them, and if they have, those protuberences certainly don't contain anything as messy, as repulsive, as animal, as *wet*, as milk. I ask you! Milk comes from bottles and Cow and Gate cans, thank you very much indeed! Bosoms are dry pointy pincushions, tucked away in brassières. And there they stay.) All this is for the good. Like the mounds of floury potatoes with a fried egg, mounds of potatoes with streaky rashers, mounds of potatoes with a frizzled chop, that are the daily fare. Being slapped in school is good for you. Being blue with cold is healthy: that old central heating, which hardly anyone has, will kill the nation.

But everyone is sick, regularly, four or five times a winter. Colds, bronchitis, asthma. Measles, whooping cough, mumps. Chickenpox, appendicitis. Orla has been in hospital three times getting things out: her tonsils, her appendix, her adenoids. Half her teeth have been removed, up to six at a time, in ghastly, bloody operations, performed while she was comatose, gassed to sleep by a strong, evil-smelling ether, in the dentist's chair she hates more than anything in a world of strange, unpredictable tortures. Visits to the doctor and from the doctor punctuate daily existence – although nobody in Orla's family has anything permanently the matter with them.

Mothers are sick with other, motherly, ailments, many so revolting that there is no name for them, or not a name that you or they would care to utter aloud. 'Headache' is the word they use. Mothers have headaches even more often than children have the flu. Nearly every day in many cases.

Elizabeth suffers from the headaches. She lies in bed in her brown room, with the brown curtains drawn, and a nylon stocking tied around her head. 'Oh, my head!' she says. 'Would ye get me an Aspro, there's a good child. Oh! Oh!'

The words come slowly. She has to squeeze them out. And her voice is transformed from its normal buoyant stridency to a faint hoarse croak. Orla catches her breath, caught between terror and anger, pain and disbelief. What she hates most is the nylon stocking around her mother's forehead. It is *not* decorative. Probably it is a clean stocking, but the look of it recalls the smell of grown-up women's feet, which is not, in Orla's estimation, an attractive scent. Elizabeth well looks lovely, in Orla's estimation, but Elizabeth ill is another story. Jekyll and Hyde. She can transform herself from being a queen to being a witch, a washy green-eyed monster wrapped in skin-coloured nylon stockings.

When the stocking appears on her mother's head, Orla runs up and down stairs, fetching cups of tea, dry toast, aspirin. She is torn by her wish to escape from Elizabeth – to run out into the back garden where she can lose herself in a game of tennis, batting a ball against the wall of the house, or sit on the roof of the shed in the sunshine reading a library book – and her wish to stay with her, hovering around the sickroom, which really is sick, stinking of sweat and various unguents that Elizabeth applies to her head, or her back, or her shoulder, or her legs. Wintergreen cream, a heavy dark minty odour. Balsam for colds. Vick for the chest. Elizabeth gets everything. Today a headache, tomorrow her kidneys may be at her. Gallstones, cystitis, trouble with the bowel movements. She will be yellow and liverish, or green and wan. Almost every part of her anatomy lets her down from time to time, and whenever it does Elizabeth is at death's door. Every night Orla prays that Elizabeth will live a little longer, that the sickroom odours will not be transmogrified to one homogenous odour, the perfume of death.

Now that Orla is away, she forgets about Elizabeth a lot of the time. But after An Post the fear grabs her. Elizabeth can't write because she has a headache. She has a headache because Orla has gone away, deserted her for the summer. She has a headache because of all the work she has to do, from dawn to dusk, day in day out, to support Orla and her brother, Roddy – who is at home but who is not much help around the house.

Elizabeth is more than any ordinary mother. She is a dynamo, a powerhouse, the centre of Orla's universe. Orla knows she could not live without her. That without her all order and sense would vanish from her life. Elizabeth arranges everything; everything revolves around her. The house is hers to order and command as she moves through it, on her good days, with the purpose and authority of a Napoleon. The kitchen is her command headquarters. A warm wonderful kitchen, dominated by a huge old range, even though the house is in the centre of Dublin. The range is like Elizabeth, a glowing powerhouse when on, which it is for much of the time, an ugly horrrifying deadly object when it goes out. Then it smells sour, with the dank ancient smell of burnt-out coke, and it requires hours of effort to get it started again, hours of riddling and shaking and scratching with long black evil-sounding pokers. But mostly it is hot and thriving and Elizabeth hovers close to it, drawing water from it in buckets, baking wheels of brown bread and white bread, scones and apple tarts, concocting soups, stirring mutton stews. Frying things. Elizabeth is a fast, efficient cook and everything she cooks tastes good. Her mother was a cook in some rich man's house, and she taught Elizabeth how to boil a pudding, trim an apple pie. Mostly Elizabeth sticks to basics, but she is adventurous occasionally too. At weekends she experiments with novelties taken down from Brenda's Kitchen in the *Sunday Press*, or ripped out of women's magazines when she visits the hairdressers. (Elizabeth would not dream of wasting money on something as frivolous as a woman's magazine, or any magazine or book for that matter. Money is for food, clothes, housing and, if absolutely necessary, education, which is a way to get more money. Good sense means getting all these things as cheaply as possible. That is her work in life, the goal that imbues her days with meaning. Illness is her release from work, her hobby merely.)

But Elizabeth is gifted. When well, she has extraordinary, boundless energy, a complete contrast to her dramatic and terrifying illnesses. She moves around the house, around the neighbourhood, under full steam, issuing orders, requests, comments, pouring forth an endless stream of talk in a loud, humorous tone. She has the perfect housewife's knack of being able to restore a messy room, a messy home, to complete order with great rapidity. Corners are never cut. When she washes dishes, the sink is left gleaming, with not a tea leaf lingering on its blue steel surface, no dishrag crumpled in a wet knot, like some frightened rained-out animal nestling in its corner, no pot or fork or frying pan procrastinating. She is a perfectionist. Orla is never happy in other people's houses, because they almost always fall short of her standards. She is not happy in her own house if Elizabeth is not up making everything shipshape.

Elizabeth's range of command is not confined to the domestic. It is she who organises every aspect of school life, who supplies the uniform and the books, the pennies for copies and pencils, the subscriptions for trips. It is she who checks homework and attends meetings and helps at sales of work. Orla can go to school, sit there and listen, go home and do her homework. But she would be helpless without Elizabeth.

It was Elizabeth who organised the transition from Primary to Secondary, who made sure, by hook and crook, that it took place, in spite of all the odds. Orla's father Tom, who is a silent and kindly man, could never have managed it. He doesn't manage anything in the Crilly household. All he does is go to work and hand over his little shiny brown pay packet to Elizabeth on Friday evenings. Tom would not even know how to spend his own money, the money he works for six days a week, from seven in the morning to six in the evening – later if he's on summer overtime, which he usually is, in the summer. Tom can work, like a slave, or a horse, or a child. But

71

you couldn't expect him to manage anything. That's what mothers do. And no mother more efficiently and absolutely than Elizabeth, a matriarch to strike wonder, if not more, into the heart of the most ardent feminist. Equality is not a concept known to women like Elizabeth, and she certainly would not wish to fight for it if she knew what it meant. Superiority is what she has always had, at least since the day she selected Tom as a suitable partner.

Elizabeth rules the house and the lives of its inmates with despotic efficiency and authority. If Elizabeth should die – and the threat, seldom uttered but dangled silently in the Crilly air, a sword of Damocles hanging over all the Crilly heads, is that she might, at any minute – they might as well all die too. Commit some sort of family suttee. Without Elizabeth to run them, they'll be as good as dead.

That is why Orla has to write so often. She has to keep in touch, keep Elizabeth informed that she is here, alive, that she cares, that she needs her. She has to receive messages back from Elizabeth to assure her that she is not ill, that her kidneys and her back and her head and all the rest of her substantial but absurdly delicate body is all right.

Elizabeth is not good at writing letters though; this much Orla remembers. It is a cold comfort, a straw, the thought that she has never seen Elizabeth, or anyone, sit down and write a letter. Christmas cards yes, but that is all. Elizabeth has never written letters to anyone before and it is too late to start now. Sometimes she receives things in the post: bills, mostly, or letters from the health clinic. These she reads quickly and anxiously, then sticks them on the file, a straightened wire coat hanger which hangs under the stairs, dangling in the dark among ancient coats and jackets, musty hats: the Crilly family archive. Perhaps that is where Orla's letters go?

The girls discuss the
North of Ireland question

It is the end of the first week. Saturday. Sandra is still stuck in Carrs'. Every day she asks some teacher, a different teacher every day, if she can change to be with her friends. They say, 'We'll see what we can do tomorrow.' They murmur, 'It's not so easy.'

Sandra is getting used to Carrs' and has made friends with a few of the girls there: Monica Murphy, Noeleen Talbot. But she doesn't like it. Dohertys' is where she should be. She filled in the names on the form. That's what she tells the teachers but they look impatient when she says that. Gradually she understands that she should not refer to the form, the pale blue form which had looked so considered and important, which she and her mother had filled in so carefully and with such anxiety. Gradually she understands that the pale blue form has no power to do anything, not now, and perhaps never had. All she can do is say 'It's not fair.' And Aisling agrees with her: 'It's not fair.' Orla feels that too, but she is still pleased, secretly, that Sandra is not staying with her, that she has Aisling all to herself.

In Dohertys' the girls are eating their supper, which they have at ten o'clock every night. On the table, there are two plates piled with white soda bread and raisin bread, as well as dishes of butter, gooseberry jam and rhubarb jam. A large pot of tea.

The girls have danced for two and a half hours and then walked home through the twilit valley. Their heads retain the smell of woodbine and bramble, acid tangs of redcurrants. Dance music perseverates their minds. 'Miss Murphy's Reel'. 'Planxty Martin'. The parlour is not quite dark. The light has not been switched on. The room feels cool and clean after the hurly-burly of the *céilí*, and its uglinesses are cloaked by shadows. Hungry as horses, tired out by the relentless activities of the day, the girls devour thick slices of bread and jam, slug down dark, strong tea. They all feel very happy. With the exception of Jacqueline.

'The jam is really scrumptious, Jacqueline.'

Jacqueline has gone on hunger strike, a hunger strike that is not likely to be very effective since she has not told the Banatee what she wants: chips. Yesterday she vowed she would eat nothing until chips were served.

'That's all she eats at home,' Pauline said. 'Every night. Chips.'

Cheps is what she says. Cheps. The burn. Bobby socks. Wee. Och. Turrible. Och that's turrible.

'Just chips? On their own?'

'Chips on their own, chips with batter burgers, chips with fish.'

'The jam is the best thing in this house, Jacqueline, you should try it.'

'No, thanks all the same.'

'She had a terrible letter,' Pauline explains. Turrible.

'I just want some decent food.'

'Cheps,' says Aisling, and her face reddens.

'It's no joke.' Pauline glares, defending her friend.

'Her folks were moving into a new house three days ago and the Brits stopped them.'

'The Brits stopped them?'

'The army. Tell them what happened, Jackie.'

'Och, I can't be bothered.' Jacqueline is tall, thin, blonde, red-lipped, frail, translucent, beautiful, limpid, lazy. 'I don't know where to start...' Not very intelligent, probably. To Orla and Aisling she is an unknown quantity. They have not managed to size her up at all.

'They got this house, a new house.'

'They bought a new house and the Brits wouldn't let them into it?'

'They didn't buy it. A Housing Executive house, you know; they used to live in a flat.'

Aisling and Orla exchange startled glances. They do not mix with people who live in council houses, as a rule, and would never have believed that such people could look like Jacqueline, dress like her, come to an Irish college. In Dublin they would immediately recognise somebody from a corporation house, if not by their appearance or habits, then as soon as they opened their mouth. The northern accent conceals class. Astonished, they continue to listen, but nothing Pauline can tell them will shock them as much as this bit of information. So that explains it, is what Orla is thinking. The chips. People in council houses might live on chips. People who own their own houses eat potatoes, carrots, stew, and other healthy, unpleasant things. Jacqueline does not look as if she has lice in her hair, Orla thinks, but maybe she has. Thank goodness she is not in our room.

'They used to live in a flat ... In a, well, a rundown block, really, wouldn't you call it? And they got this brand new house from the Housing Executive.'

'A corner house.'

'They always have enormous gardens, don't they?' Aisling nods encouragingly. She is always polite. Orla is buttering her fifth slice of bread, spreading it with the thick sticky seedy gooseberry preserve.

'Fucking Brits.' Jacqueline's saucer eyes darken.

Aisling and Orla gasp. Fucking!

'Why did it happen?' Aisling feigns innocence, unusually for her – usually she doesn't have to. Even she knows why, can guess why, but this knowledge embarrasses her.

'Why do you think?' Jacqueline snarls scornfully.

'Because you are Catholic.'

'Well . . .' Pauline begins.

'Aye, you bet.' Jacqueline butts in. 'Catholics don't get new houses in Derry, that's the rule until now.'

'But now they can – there's a new law or something. Only the UDA stopped them moving in last time. And this time the Brits did it,' Pauline interjects. 'There's a new law, it's all more equal now.'

'More equal? UDA, Brits, what's the difference? They wouldn't let us move into our new house!'

'But how did they stop you? The, eh, Brits?'

Orla smiles at Aisling because she has used this word. 'Brits'. All these words, the Derry words, seem funny to them. Whenever she uses one, Orla can hardly refrain from laughing. The Derry situation, with its Catholics and Protestants and its rugged aggressiveness, its lack of shame about its problems, seems both funny and shameful. They are dying to talk about it and to find out about it, but at the same time they shy away from it.

'How do you think? With machine guns and Panzer tanks. They blocked the road with them. That's what it said in her letter.'

'Gosh.' Panzer is impressive, whatever it is.

'You see, last time the UDA wouldn't let them move in. So this time they got a crowd together. Thousands of people.'

'Moral support.' Aisling always knows the *mot juste*. Her father is a journalist, the whole family is exceptionally articulate.

'Aye. They got dustbin lids and sticks and hurleys and they all marched along behind the lorries.'

'Lorries?'

'Of course there were lorries. With their furniture and stuff, dope.'

Orla pictures it. Children banging dustbin lids. Men striking the pavement with hurley sticks. And the women? She can't imagine them, can't see what they might be doing. Shouting and carrying on in a vulgar, fishwife way, she supposes. Jacqueline's mother, from what she has gathered so far, is old, fat, sagging. The kind of woman who wears an old jumper and slippers all the time, even out in the street. The word 'march' is not one she can connect with her image of this woman, or with anyone related to Jacqueline, who can barely drag herself, complaining all the time, up and down to the school.

'It sounds awful.'

'It was.' Pauline reaches for the teapot. She is exhausted by the topic by now and doesn't want to continue talking about it. Jacqueline's father is in Long Kesh. She should tell the Dublin girls that, give them something to think about. Cage Four, nothing to eat but watery porridge and brown water masquerading as soup. She can't go on. The sound of her own voice begins to bore her. And Jacqueline, of course, will tell nothing. Not because she is shy about these things – she is proud of them – but because she is too languid and too indifferent to these small, ordinary, Irish-speaking nonentities from Dublin to exert herself to talk. The subject, however, has its own momentum, like Jacqueline's refusal to eat. Even when it is time to stop and change, it will go on, and on, beating in her ears like the banging of the dustbin lids. The raucous banging, the cacophony of sounds, the shouting, the chaos on the sun-drenched, untidy streets. All for a few pathetic houses, so small and ugly you wouldn't want to think about them, much less live in them.

'The North of Ireland has its problems,' Aisling closes the subject piously.

'Aye,' sighs Pauline.

'What would you know about it anyway?' Jacqueline snarls. 'Your father . . .'

'Shut up.' Pauline wakes up.

Orla and Aisling wait with bated breath.

'Her da is a Prod.' Jacqueline simpers at the girls.

'Oh well, so what?' Aisling tosses her head. 'Our next-door neighbours are Protestant, the Andersons. They're extremely nice people.'

Pauline looks tired.

'So why aren't you a Protestant then?'

'Her mother's Catholic, that's why.' Jacqueline gets up and leaves the table. 'If yer ma's a Catholic you hafta be one as well. It's the law.'

Aisling looks as if she is going to contradict this but thinks better of it.

'Oh yeah, I see.' Orla nods. 'Does it matter if it's your father who's a Catholic.'

'Och no,' says Jacqueline. 'I don't think so anyways.'

Too bad, really, thinks Orla, who would have liked to meet a proper Protestant. But she looks at Pauline with increased respect.

A thought occurs to her. 'Why do you want to learn Irish? If your father is a Protestant?'

'Why do you want to learn Irish?' Pauline is scornful.

'Well . . . I am Irish,' Orla declares.

'So am I well. So is he. Ye don't have to be Catholic to be Irish do you?'

Orla wishes she hadn't asked the question. She blunders on. 'Well I mean . . . you're Northern Irish. It's different isn't it?'

'I'm sick of this conversation,' says Pauline. 'Time for beddy-byes! Yawn yawn yawn yawn. Who'd want to be Irish anyway? For crying out loud.'

The burn scene two

Headmaster Joe believes, has to believe, that the day is so packed with activities that the students have no time to get up to mischief of any kind. As far as he knows, they are always engaged in walking to and from the schoolhouse, in learning or playing or dancing, in singing or eating or sleeping. It is all mapped out and at all times a copy of the map is in his head, every pupil carefully spotted on it. But of course there are intervals, interstices, crevices in the edifice he has constructed that he can't afford to know about. Creases of time, worn patches and tiny holes that in the beginning seem too insignificant to be worth thinking about, but which are gradually expanding as the summer wears on. Slowly his map is cracking, and through the cracks the insects start to creep.

The gap between the end of swimming or ball and the beginning of the *céilí* is one crack. For the first few days, the afternoon sports ended at about five-thirty, giving barely enough time for Orla and Aisling to return to the house, get their tea, and get ready for the *céilí* at seven-thirty. By the beginning of the second week the enthusiasm of teachers for watching children play rounders and basketball is diminishing. And then it sometimes rains, or gets very cold in the late afternoon. The finishing time is pushed forward to five, then to four-thirty. On some days they pack it in before four o'clock. In addition to this development, the girls have speeded up their walking pace, so instead of spending an hour meandering up the road to Ceathrú (as the teachers call Caroo) they can get there in about twenty-five minutes. Headmaster Joe's time contracts and their own expands accordingly. He is not noticing this, or he is turning a blind and weary eye to it. What will they do anyway, in the bright afternoon, in broad daylight? Wash their hair, probably, or their clothes. Lie on their crumpled beds and talk English. Go to the sweet shop.

Orla is the first to go down to the burn.

It is the Wednesday of the second week, the Wednesday after the washing of the clothes in the walled garden. She has been playing rounders, although most of the students went to the shore today, to go for a swim, since it is a very fine day. But Orla has her own reasons for not going swimming, and instead she batted ball with a few others too lazy or too stupid to want to swim. Or having their periods. It is because they are aware that periods keep some girls out of the water that Headmaster Joe always allows a game of rounders, even on the hottest day. Máistir Dunne took it, lounging against the stone wall smoking his pipe while Jacqueline, who doesn't swim on principle, hating cold water as she hates anything uncomfortable, Orla and a few others ran lazily around the field. He let them off at three-thirty.

So Orla finds herself in the unusual position of being alone in the house. She lies on the bed for a while, writing to Elizabeth, as she still does regularly, although Elizabeth still has not yet replied, or sent on the extra pocket money Orla needs. She looks in Aisling's drawer then, touching Aisling's lemon Crimplene top with the white inset, which she admires. But she knows Aisling's clothes so well that there is no real thrill to be had from secretly examining them. It would be fun to go through Pauline's things but she decides against doing this – Banatee is down in the kitchen clattering around, and

Jacqueline may turn up. Orla last saw her sitting on the windowsill of the post office, licking a choc ice.

She goes downstairs into the narrow hall and slips around the back of the house. The garden she avoids. She does not want Banatee to see her, not because she plans to do anything illicit, but because she dislikes being watched even while she is performing some perfectly legitimate act. Some people – most people, especially if they are adult – love to feel the eyes of others on them. Reality is being perceived, condoned or condemned. But privacy is what Orla craves. The reality she is looking for is inside herself, hidden from all eyes.

The stone wall of the garden joins the house at the back of the east gable, and it is in that section of wall that the wooden gate is. The gate is standing open at the moment, as it usually is. Orla has a look. The garden is bathed in hot yellow light: the stream winks, a ribbon of glimmering mobile amber. She looks just for a second or two, then follows the wall around to the back. The sun beats strongly against the stones and she stands with her back against the wall, letting the sun-heat, which has penetrated the stone, seep back out again, through her shirt and into her skin. She listens to the babble of the stream, the other soothing sounds of the valley, highlighted by the background blanket of silence: larks twittering hysterically, blackbirds warbling, starlings mimicking one another in a symphony of whistles. Suddenly the harmony is shattered by a sound like a loud clock, or a raucous factory machine. The sound chops violently through the peace of the afternoon. It seems to Orla that it is coming from the lower end of the field, and she follows it across the grass, nimbly leaping over grass tussocks, clumps of thistle, yellow ragweed, until she is at the lower, eastern extreme of the large field. There is a stand of sycamores there, enormous trees mushrooming a canopy of lugubrious dark green over the grass. Their shade is so complete that she finds herself shivering. The clocking sound is louder than ever and is directly overhead. She is thinking. Bombs. A bomb-making factory for the IRA.

That is what this part of Donegal is renowned for, so says her father, laughing harshly and proudly. Dunsalt. One of the Coyles of Dunsalt Head is already in Portlaoise prison on an arms conspiracy charge. This is the suspicion, the reputation, that gives a *frisson* of colour and mystery to life in this otherwise sleepy place, with its dying language, its dying culture, the decay people suspect is endemic to such an area. Famine, poverty, emigration. The language changing, the thatched roofs torn down. Nothing to replace them, they think. The myth of the last is strong here. The last monoglot, the last Irish speaker, the last horse-drawn plough, the last fisherman. While people mourn the last of everything and have not accustomed themselves to observing the new firsts, the myth of the IRA, heroism, bravery, recklessness, lawlessness, sustains them. Bombs. Everywhere. In disused railway stations, in barns and byres, on the tops of mountains. They used to distil illicit whiskey, that was all the racket. Look. That's where it is. The still. Now they hide gelignite, manufacture bottle bombs for their brothers across the border. Every old shabby building may house a terrible secret. Glamorous, if you don't really know anyone who is directly involved. If you have not had to encounter in your own life the reality, the dull destructive time-consuming tragedy, of a death. You do not understand the futility of it, the uselessness of that kind of pain. You hear a strange sound and you imagine you have found something. Micheál, it would be, of course. An obvious candidate. Strong, sulky, not too bright. Stuck on this small isolated farm not fifty miles from Derry. He sits in a tree house here and makes bombs, of course he does.

It is a magpie. Just one, screaming and roaring blue murder. You would not imagine that one bird in a tree could make such a terrible sound.

Not a bomb-making factory. Micheál is perhaps just a boring country yokel after all, with nothing in his head but the latest prices at the mart and ambitions to drive a truck in England.

Orla laughs a bit, pleased anyway to have seen the source of the sound.

The burn is passing close to her feet.

Of course she was aware of this as she rushed down the field. It flows out of the garden under a low, nasturtium-draped arch in the wall and then down the field to the sycamores. There it passes through a barbed-wire fence into another, smaller field. Orla pushes down the wire and steps over the fence. This small field is overgrown with yellow ragweed and wears a bleak and sinister look, as if small, malevolent creatures were hiding under the umbrellas of the ragweed, spying. The yellow weeds gleam with a poisonous burnish. Orla steps onto a stone in the burn and leaping from stone to stone follows it further downstream.

The burn gathers momentum here as the gradient sharpens. It also gets deeper. The gaps between the stones widen and Orla suspects that soon she will not be able to keep up her game of leaping. The sun is hot but there is something about the harsh, glaring light here that affects her negatively. She thinks she should turn back, something tells her that the safe, good thing to do is to turn and go home. The others will be back now, it is time to start washing hair, thinking about tea. She should wash her yellow ankle socks.

Her feet keep going, however, as if they have a life of their own. They take longer and braver leaps, but they never miss. Even when she lands on a sharp pointed stone, or on a big round stone that wobbles terrifyingly, like a loose tooth, she remains upright. Her feet are sure and practised, they can cope much better than she would have given them credit for. They continue, leap by leap, to the boundary of this field. That is a thick hedge of brambles, dusty green and covered with white blossoms and with buzzing bees. Orla stoops, twists this way and that, under the brambles, because she is still in the burn, still following it. She thinks she will just cross this ditch and see what happens on the other side, and then turn back. The brambles fill her nostrils with the musky smell of blackberries, although only a few hard red berries are to be seen.

It is not easy to penetrate the thorny hedge but she gets through with just a few scratches. There is no field on the other side. Instead she finds herself in a verdant tunnel so green the air itself has a mossy green tincture, a delicate reflection of the thick solid green of the roof and the sides of the tunnel, which are made of hazels, brambles, willows, all tangled together. At first the roof is so low that she has to crouch, but soon it raises and forms a high green dome over her head. She stands on a rock and gasps. It is like being in a hidden green cathedral, deeply centred in a vast forest of shrub and bramble. The stream tumbles on through it but there is no patch of sky to be seen. It is completely enclosed, completely private. No fields, no cattle, no houses to be seen. Just green things: leaves, grass, weeds, thorns, moss. Water and stones and rocks.

Otters.

There will be otters here, Orla knows. This is the kind of place for them. And kingfishers. She thinks of otters, long and silky, slinking from the bank into the dark water, swimming silently through it. She pictures their swift silent progress, the furrow they leave in their wake, a line through the water as true and beautiful as themselves. She would love to see them. And she would hate it. Wild, graceful, sly, cunning. The thought of them thrills her and horrifies her. Now that she has allowed that thought into her head, the glaucous cavern seems not enchanted and protective but dangerous – or dangerous at the same time as it is more magically seductive than any place she has ever been.

She does not for one moment consider the real, superficial danger: that if she slipped, if something happened, nobody would think of checking this place for a long time. That does not concern her in the slightest, just as it has not crossed her mind that the burn may not be uniformly shallow and easy to traverse, that in its course it may include hidden depths into which a person could stumble. What worries her are fairies. Possible otters with possible vindictive purposes. Otters who, having never seen a human being before – and she believes that she is the only human ever to have come in here, the only tame creature, if not ever, at least in a very long time – will take fright and attack. The thought of otters is what turns her back.

As she turns, she catches sight of something glittering on the bank of the burn, gleaming red like rubies or garnets on a velvet cushion. In this case, green moss. She hops across the stream and takes a closer look. Crimson raspberries, tiny red berries on small delicate jagged leaves. That is what they are, she knows, although she has never seen wild raspberries before, child of the city, and she did not even know that they existed. Wild berries are so few in Ireland. Blackberries, fraughans, those she knows, but nothing else. She pulls a few of the berries and eats them. And of course they are as sweet and delicious as wild berries growing by a babbling stream that has not been visited by a human being or any domestic creature in hundreds of years can be. Sweet, tangy, cool, fresh, wild, tinged with an exotic flavour, like Turkish Delight, attar of roses, some flavour that is a perfume from a golden-covered volume of fantastic stories, a flavour that is a confirmation, for her, of the jewel-studded world that awaits exploration, that in all its richness is waiting for her to step into, to experience, sometime soon, when she grows up. That is what the berries seem to be: a taste of a wonderful future, not a residue of a wild world that is past, or passing. She picks and eats a handful and the red juice fills her mouth and trickles down onto her white T-shirt. Then she takes half a dozen and sticks them into the pocket of her shorts.

What does your father do?

After the visit to the burn, Orla is filled with courage. Something has happened to her, there in the chestnut water, in the green tunnel. She forgets about Elizabeth for a while. She stops worrying about the letters. She forgets about Auntie Annie, or forgets that she is a problem waiting to be solved.

Being down in the burn has made her happy.

In the burn, she was a part of whatever whole encompassed the water and the weeds and the raspberries and the drooping willows. Her heart beat in time with the babble of the burn down there, her feet gripped the stones as easily as a hare finds its burrow. Babble and rustle, bloodbeat and leaf, eye and water. Orla belonged with the river. She was nothing there, nothing more than a berry dipping to the water or a minnow floating under the surface of a pool. Nothing. And completely herself. Orla Herself. Not Orla the Daughter of Elizabeth, Orla the Pride of Rathmines, Orla the Betrayer of Tubber. Just Orla.

She feels it would be all right now to tell people who she really is — meaning who her relations are. What does it matter? They can tease her to her face or bite her when her back is turned. But who now has the power to harm her? Now that she has found her own place?

It should be all right to talk about her mother and her father,

her house. Her auntie. Maybe she could tell them about her auntie now, and go and visit her?

But when teatime comes the opportunity arises and she doesn't take it.

The topic of conversation is 'What Does Your Father Do?' It is a subject that raises itself constantly, among the girls themselves, in class, at school, on the street. What Does Your Father Do? Orla never wants to answer it, and usually she does not.

People choose their parents, so it is said. But would she have chosen hers? Maybe she would. Maybe she would. They are nice enough, Orla's mother and father; unthreatening for the most part, more comfortable to be with than anyone else she knows although it is getting harder to talk to them. Still, confronted with a shop windowful of parents perhaps she would still pick them out as the most suitable for her. Yes. I'll take those two, please.

But she would never have chosen their occupations. And somehow occupation is the defining feature as far as fathers are concerned. Nobody asks, 'Is your father nice?' (yes), What age is he? (don't know), What colour are his eyes? (blue), Can he sing? (yes, and play the mouth organ), Can he tell jokes? (not really). Occasionally someone will ask, 'Where does he come from?' meaning what county in Ireland. The one question everyone asks is, What does your father do?

What your father does is what defines your father, as far as other people are concerned. More significant, it is what defines you, if you happen to be a child. So it seems to Orla.

Her father is a bricklayer. That is what he is.

But Orla says, 'He is a building contractor.' It is what Elizabeth has told her to answer. 'What business is it of theirs, what your father does?' Elizabeth says, with a toss of her voice, and hard stone in her eye. Let them mind their own business.

None of the children know what a building contractor is. That is the beauty of it, perhaps foreseen by Elizabeth. But the children suspect that it is something not quite respectable, not the best answer. The best answer is 'teacher' or 'civil servant', it seems to Orla. Nobody she knows answers 'lawyer' or 'doctor' or anything like that. Aisling says 'journalist' which is confusing, although not confusing like 'building contractor'. 'Journalist' sounds glamorous: too glamorous. Having a father who is too unusual is almost, although not quite, as bad as having a father who is too poor. It marks you out.

All the very best girls, the girls with the whitest socks and freshest plaid skirts, the girls whose copybooks are neatly ruled with red margins and who always have the latest style of pencil case in their tidy zipped plastic schoolbags, are the daughters of civil servants or teachers. These are the girls who are cherished by the teachers, respected by the world in general. They get slapped less often than Orla, and much less often than the girls who live in the wrong parts of town, whose fathers have no jobs at all, or the girls – there are a few – whose fathers are dead, or reputed to be.

If Orla could choose her father's occupation, she would pick 'civil servant'. There is no dubiousness of any kind attached to those two solid, prim words. They are like an upright mahogany hall stand, Orla thinks, or a thick, painted hall door, opening, if it ever does open, onto a house full of polished and heavy silence. Elizabeth shares Orla's regard for these words. She has already decided that Orla will appropriate the respectability attaching to them when the time is ripe. She is to become a civil servant when she grows up. A Junior Ex is what she will be: the best job anyone could have. When Elizabeth says 'Junior Ex' a dreamy look overcomes her face. The soft *r* rolls around her mouth, reaching for the snapping shock of *x*. What does Elizabeth see in the words?

Certainly not the inside of a civil servant's office, something with which she is entirely unfamiliar, and which like all jobs people go to is obviously beside the point as far as Elizabeth, who has never had a job apart from a brief stint working for her own parents, is concerned.

What Elizabeth sees is the ship sailing from Dún Laoghaire on a sunny day. A new suitcase packed with clean knickers and nylons, crisp white-collared summer dresses. She sees Orla bringing her on holidays to Portsmouth where her two sisters, Agnes and Johanna, live. The two of them having a drink in the lounge on board, nodding and smiling in the honey morning light, as the sun strikes the blue waves and seagulls scream for sheer joy.

She sees Orla wearing a snow-white blouse and a smart tweed suit, purple or maroon, every day, not just on Sunday. She sees her installing new refrigerators, electric cookers, in the kitchen, and arranging to have a rich thick Donegal carpet laid in the hall which is now covered with slippery linoleum. Orla may even drive her own car: a gorgeous Mini, yellow or white or pale blue. She will be a lady driver.

Orla's father has a car but Elizabeth would never dream of trying to drive that. She belongs to a generation that catagorises her as wife and mother, not lady driver. Ladies drive, all right, in Dublin, lots of them. Ladies swim. Ladies run. Ladies wear shorts on the beach when the weather gets hot, and ladies are just beginning to go to the pub and drink sweet mixtures like vodka and orange, lager and lime. Some ladies. But not ladies like Elizabeth, who have set rigid boundaries to the march of their personal experience, as they have guarded their rebellious bodies in unbreachable roll-ons, rigid nylon stockings that no breath of air could penetrate. No shorts and no swimsuits and no swimming. Buses. No taxis. Holidays in the West of Ireland and dimming dreams of England. No drinking and no driving.

Men drink, men drive, men go to football matches, men go to the dogs, men bet on horses. Have jobs, responsibilities, pay packets. Cars. And so do some other kinds of ladies: ladies who are younger, richer, commoner than Elizabeth. Different.

The idea of driving Tom's car simply hasn't crossed Elizabeth's mind. Tom's car is like a part of his body; he has had it for so long that it resembles him, as pets look and behave like their owners. It is not exactly battered, his funny-angled Anglia. But stars of rust pock its bumpers, and its paintwork has the dusty, faded look of ancient cars. Subdued is how it looks, and long-suffering, and patient as a sad-eyed donkey.

Poor Tom, he works so hard, from six to six often. He works so hard and he earns so little, according to Elizabeth, who believes everyone else earns a lot. He works so hard but he is a nobody, an absolute nobody.

He has built or helped build half of modern Dublin. Bus Aras. Belfield. The new flats at Ballymun. Stillorgan Shopping Centre. Every big new building Orla sees around her, her father has worked on. The buildings are new and exciting, worthy of comment by all and sundry. And yet the actual work of constructing them is, for some reason, ignoble. Builders – all of them – are considered a shabby, uncouth lot. They are paid buttons. They work in undignified conditions, they go home dirty and dishevelled, smelling of cement and muck, because there is nowhere to wash on the sites where they work. They eat their sandwiches and drink their tin mugs of tea outdoors, in the mud, or in cold open sheds.

All of which means that they must belong to a lower caste of people than those who lick envelopes. They are paid less than men who stand all day in storerooms in city offices counting boxes of paper and keeping tabs on tins of pencils. The city grows quickly, thanks to Orla's father, but somehow no credit is given to him for any of this, for the roads or the churches or the schools or the universities. Instead he is derided by everyone, including his own family. Orla would respect him more if he were a licker of envelopes, a whey-faced man in a shiny suit with the tight, dead face some of her friends' fathers have.

A bricklayer! That's the answer Orla should give when the question is popped.

The same question is seldom asked about mothers. It is unnecessary. Most of them, almost all of them, 'do nothing', according to their children. And that is the correct thing. A working mother, no matter what she works at, is a bit of an abomination. 'Once mammy did some substitute teaching for a friend of hers. I really didn't like it when I came home from school and she wasn't there,' somebody – maybe it was Monica – had said in a classroom debate called 'A Woman's Place Is in the Home'. All the girls had nodded sagely, understanding Monica's profound point. I really didn't like it when she wasn't there. Monica's side, for the motion, won the debate hands down. A mother should be simply a mother, just as a child is a child.

But Elizabeth isn't. Oh no, no such luck!

Elizabeth breaks rank even in this regard, and has found an occupation for herself. She is a landlady. That's what she is. She keeps lodgers. That's what she does. Orla should say, 'My father's a bricklayer and my mother is a landlady.' But she doesn't. Not now. Not ever.

A surprise for Orla

The position of building workers in society has had repercussions that are more practical and devastating than blows to her pride could be. Tom's colleagues in the building trade staged a strike because their pay was so bad. The strike went on for months and months; the building contractors would not give in to the demands for twenty per cent extra pay, for pension rights, for overtime on Saturday, for holidays. The building workers, the scum of Ireland, were to be kept in their place. Poor and insecure and despised.

The Union of Saint Joseph the Worker, as far as Orla knew. Her father used to go to Mass on Saint Joseph's feast day. That was his only union activity before this, before he went on strike.

The union paid strike pay, but not much. There was no other pay either. The government was on the side of the bosses, not their workers. If the latter chose to strike, their families could starve.

They did not starve. But the year of the strike there were no clothes, no birthday presents, no sweets, no biscuits. The Crillys lived on potatoes and eggs and home-made bread. After five months, Elizabeth began to get cross for no reason at all. She screamed at Orla when she asked for a penny to buy a patsy-pop – this was summer. Luckily the strike happened mainly during the summer, the best time of the year for building. When Orla asked for money to go to the Blackrock Baths, Elizabeth hit her.

This is what happened next.

One day Orla came home from school, went upstairs and found that her bedroom was gone. The room was still there, of course, in its old place at the back of the house, overlooking the spreadeagling apple tree and the crisscross plaid of other back gardens, laid out like untidy beds full of mysterious growths and the debris of generations. The room was there, but changed completely. Instead of her iron bed the room held four divans covered with red and blue squishy army blankets instead of real quilts. Her clothes had been removed from her wardrobe. Her dressing table was still in its place next to the open fireplace, but it had been cleaned down and laid with a new lace runner. Her dolls and books and teddy bear were nowhere to be seen.

'You'll sleep downstairs,' Elizabeth said, from the landing. She said it in a neutral tone, as if she were saying, 'There'll be a fried egg for dinner.'

'Where's my bed gone ta?' Orla felt as if someone had scraped out her insides.

'Don't back answer me!' This was one of the phrases Elizabeth, and lots of other mothers too, used when they didn't feel like giving an answer to a child, which was frequently. But she sounded sad, rather than cross. 'You're sleeping downstairs.'

Orla did not even have her own bed any more. She had to share with her parents, sleeping at the bottom, with her feet up around their huge, stinky stomachs. It was a big soft mush of a bed, covered by mountains of hairy blankets topped off with a thick squelching eiderdown, purple silk. On the wall over the bolster hung a copy of the Pope's Blessing of their marriage: Elizabeth had moved this from the bedroom upstairs and got Da to nail it onto the wall, for protection perhaps. The Pope's hand, surrounded by faint red flowers, was raised over their heads every night as they slept, and their daughter's feet were raised over their legs.

That was the start of the lodgers. The two big bedrooms of the house had been given over to them – from now on they would share their house with six strangers. The one remaining room, the boxroom, was to be used by Roddy, who was three years younger than her and delicate. He got colds often, he had to be kept warm, he had to drink a lot of milk – which Orla didn't get, milk being too expensive for girls, according to Elizabeth. (Girls are so hardy was another one of her sayings. They don't need much food or attention, not like boys. God if boys were as easy to rear as young ones wouldn't we be blessed? Boys were boys or lads or fellas. Girls were just young *ones*: they did not merit a generic name of their own.)

There was no sitting room or dining room in the house after the lodgers came: just a kitchen and a hall and a bathroom. All the rest of the house was bedrooms. Orla did her homework in the bedroom at a card table which Tom got for her at an auction in Rathmines. She had an oil stove in the winter. It smelled strongly of paraffin, but its little blue-and-red wick gave out very little heat. Sometimes she had to go into the kitchen and sit in a big chair in the corner, doing her homework on her lap and trying to block the sound of the television out of her ears.

Ever since the day when she was eight and had lost her room, the house was more like a shop or some public place than a house where you go to find shelter from the outside world. The outside had come inside now. There was no escape from it.

The house was full of men. Elizabeth called them 'the boys' and loved them. Orla spent her life trying to stay out of their way. It wasn't easy. They were always coming and going. They were in the hall. They were queuing for the bathroom – one for the six boys and the four Crillys. They were seated around the big table in the kitchen, having their tea, smoking and laughing. Their smoke and their laughs rose on the air and spread all through the house.

Elizabeth was kept very busy, shopping and cooking, frying rashers and eggs, boiling potatoes. Making beds. She even made lunch for the boys, some of them, and this was one of Orla's jobs: slicing Galtee cheese and putting it on bread, six sandwiches per boy, also a packet for Da.

'I need the money if you want to go to Secondary!' was Elizabeth's reply, on the few occasions when Orla dared to question the need for the boys. She never directly questioned it, or asked why there had to be so many. Wouldn't four do? Instead of four Elizabeth upped the six to eight: Roddy had to move out of his boxroom; he got a divan in the family room. A boy moved into the boxroom and there was another, desperate, who slept on the landing without even a curtained screen to hide him. There was a dark tone in his skin, his hair was crinkly, so Elizabeth was doing him a favour. His parents were Irish, she was at pains to explain, he was not coloured, she would not have coloureds in the house although God knows they were probably often no worse than the rest of us. But you had to draw the line somewhere. And that was on the landing, with a half-caste – his name was Joe, and he was rather nice, in so far as Orla could allow any of the boys to be nice. Their niceness or otherwise was not her concern. Her concern was that they existed, and had taken over her house. Her wish that they were not there overrode everything else.

She could not admit to anyone that her house was a house of lodgers. She looked with longing at council cottages, at two-roomed flats. Even Sandra, whom she was not supposed to speak to because she lived in a flat, was luckier than her: she had her own room. Her own room. What Orla would have given her right arm for, what seemed to her more unobtainable, more inconceivable, than being the queen of England, Sandra took for granted. Sandra took for granted that her home belonged to her and her parents. When she came home after school, her mother would be in the kitchen listening to the wireless, smoking a cigarette. In private. That is what homes are: private places.

But the sacrifice paid off. There was enough money now for the Crillys to live a normal life, at least when they were not at home. They could try out the new foods that were advertised on television. They could go shopping in Dunnes Stores and buy clothes and household equipment. Tom could replace his car, which was twenty years old, with a new Cortina, only two years on the road and one lady driver. Orla could go to Secondary. There would be enough money for the uniform and the new bag and the bus fares and the books, for the hockey stick and the extra lessons and the pocket money and the dances. There would be enough for everything. And Orla would never have to take a part-time job or a summer job. She could concentrate on her studies. She would get an education, get the Junior Ex, or even go to university: suddenly that possibility became real. She could get well-off. Her life was going to be different from Elizabeth's. Of that they both were certain. She would be a lady driver.

So what did it matter that she hadn't got a bedroom of her own? That she wouldn't invite her friends home? That she darted around her own house like a thief, hiding from its strange transient population of young men? That she would be startled, more than once, when one of those young men stayed in her head when she sat upstairs on the bus and travelled five miles to school in the foggy cosy gloom of a Dublin winter, that the image of one or two of them hovered and lingered as she gazed through the misted glass at the glowing shop windows? Images of men who lived in her house but to whom she would never utter a word, men who did not just invade her bedroom, courtesy of their five pounds a week, but also had the power, unconsciously, to take up residence in her head.

Gemini at the
Hibernian Hotel

One morning every year, in late April or May, when the leaves on the trees in Herbert Park are a fresh, translucent green, as green as eyes, and there is a real stretch in the evenings, Elizabeth looks out the kitchen window and sees the blossom floating from the apple tree to the grass in the back garden. Angelically languid intimations of immortality. Omnipotence. Eden. 'Fancy a cream tea this afternoon, love?' she says, reverting for once to the idiom of her childhood. Orla squirms. She could say no but her answer is always yes.

That afternoon Elizabeth puts on her navy suit and navy-and-white straw boater, usually reserved for Sunday Mass in Whitefriar Street church, where the Crillys sit in the very front seat and where Elizabeth and Orla shout the responses at the top of their lungs, letting the priest and the congregation hear how religious they are. Vatican Two has given them a golden opportunity to show off in a new, vocal way. Little did Pope John the Twenty-third know what he was unleashing on the world.

Tom still mumbles his prayers under his breath, unwilling to open his mouth in church or out of it, no matter what the cardinals desire. Roddy is an altar boy. They gaze admiringly at his every move as he sways around the altar in a red soutane and white surplice, starched and ironed to be stiffer and whiter and superior to every surplice on the Whitefriar Street church's altar, to every surplice in Dublin, to every surplice that ever existed. 'Christ have mercy!' they yell, and their voices boom around the big, gloomy, empty church, like thunder on a grey summer's day.

Hats are no longer essential for Mass but Elizabeth has a selection in store, from the old days. No mantillas – mantillas were for another kind of woman. Hats, with high cocky crowns and turned-up confident brims. Pins, long and shining, sticking out of them like swords.

She pats herself into her suit, which gleams like a coat of armour, and sticks her pin in her hat. Orla gets togged out in her confirmation costume, purchased in Dublin's most exclusive children's boutique, The Gay Child – the most expensive and stylish confirmation costume any girl in Orla's school ever had. They walk into Dawson Street, saving sixpence bus fare. In the lounge of the Hibernian Hotel Elizabeth sits at a table in the window, where everyone can see her if they looked in. She puts on her snob accent and orders a pot of tea and a selection of cakes. You could have sandwiches as well but why bother?

'We'll just have time to slip into Brown Thomas's and purchase one of them new season's frocks before we meet Father,' Elizabeth says, as the waiter places the silver tea service on the white cloth.

'Yes,' Orla answers dully.

'I think that yellow colour would be most suitable for our holidays in Spain, don't you?'

'Yes, I do.'

'And you'll need another pair of Clarks sandals for the yacht. Clarks are the best. Remember the two pairs you had last year?'

Yachts, holidays, Brown Thomas, the Abbey, their cousin in Foxrock. Every year Orla knows this outing will happen. She knows when the evenings lengthen, and the birds sing as if there is no tomorrow, and the spring-cleaning of the house is over, that this afternoon will arrive and that she will have to collude with Elizabeth. All year she dreads the morning when Elizabeth looks out the window at the apple tree in bloom, and says, 'I think we should have afternoon tea in town today!' Still, every year it comes, inevitable as Christmas. And every year, Orla enjoys it much more in the execution than in the anticipation. Nothing is as bad as it seems.

Sava and her goings-on

Sava and the Dohertys have been displaced by Orla now, as Orla has been displaced by a gang of Micks and Paddys and Éamonns and Tommys and Noels and Seans in Dublin. Orla is the lodger, the one who pays for her bed. The family has been turfed out.

Sava, the daughter with the river-black hair, who waits on the table, has had to hand over her bedroom to Orla and Aisling, a room of dark and ancient moods, the sort of room many people have been born or died in, one suspects glumly, over several centuries. The black iron bars at the foot of the bed are what she has seen first thing every day in her life, until now.

The change doesn't bother Sava at all. She's delighted with it.

Now she sleeps on a narrow red tartan divan. When she opens her eyes she sees the roof of the caravan, white patterned with a pale yellow primrose, and then the sky. She loves the red Formica table that she bumps her head against when she sits up suddenly, and the tiny kitchen with its electric rings and little refrigerator. There is no refrigerator in the house, milk is kept cool in basins of water, meat in a wire safe, a thing that looks like a large gas mask, out in the garden. Sava keeps bottles of McDaid's lemonade, Football Special, in the refrigerator, and drinks it late at night, with ice, while her mother is still washing up in the kitchen and her father is at the pub at the Crossroads.

The Crossroads is where Sava works, at Kathleen Johnson's hairdressing salon, Kathleen's Place. In a way the caravan reminds her a little of the salon. It is in the same style, featuring Formica and plastic, bright colours, soft lights. It is as if the people who made the salon – Kathleen, really – and those who designed the caravan acknowledged women's need for an environment that looks soft and pretty, that is not completely utilitarian. Whereas the people who designed the house – the Congested Districts Board, and a few generations of Dohertys – did not know that, or could not afford to know it. Beauty existed in such houses by accident – a beauty born of harmony of materials with each other and with the landscape. In some country houses, a woman's strong desire to make her own mark, prettify according to her own will, allowed the addition of blue paint or green paint to the dresser, pots of flowers on the windowsills. But that was rare in Tubber, and mostly the only additional decorative objects took the form of crockery. Banatee had many fine cups and saucers, patterned with every kind and colour of flower, on her dresser and in her parlour cupboard. Sava longed for much more than that, for lightness of every kind, lightness of form and shape and colour and light itself. Dreariness was what she had grown up with, indoors, and what she was reacting against.

Hairdresser's are seldom truly dreary and Kathleen's Place is no exception. It is painted pink, and when Sava works there, washing heads of hair and sweeping cuttings from the floor, she wears a pink-flowered smock over her own clothes.

'That's a lovely shade you've got in your hair,' Kathleen said the first day Sava came into the shop, her two feet of hair shining on her back like some goddess's cloak. 'I wish I could find a rinse that looked like that!'

Kathleen is overweight, with a pleasant round face. Her hair is brown and curly. Both traits are natural, as far as Sava can tell.

'I'll let you in on a secret,' Kathleen confided, in a lowered tone, to Sava. She is the kind of woman who is always letting someone in on a secret, whose discourse consists largely of whispered confidences. To Sava this seems the essence of femininity, the secret code of the club of true women. 'I'd never let a drop of henna near my hair, not in a million years. It makes it fall out. Never tell a customer that.' She gave her a dig in the ribs.

'Do you colour hair a lot?' Sava was so shy that she could hardly get these words out. When she managed, they were almost inaudible. Kathleen had to strain to hear.

'Oh no, dearie, not a lot. It's mostly perms we do here, you know, and haircuts for the fellas. Perms for the old ladies. Sure all the young ones have their hair streeling down around them now, don't they? Rotten business!'

Sava has been with Kathleen for two years now. She can do perms herself, cut boys' and men's hair. She talks to customers in her subdued drawl: she always sounds as if she is on the verge of expiring from exhaustion, an effect that belies the truth, namely that she is endowed with exceptional stamina. She requires only five or six hours' sleep a night and spends a lot of time lying in bed, wide-eyed, pondering the events of her quiet but active life.

It was in Kathleen's Place that she met Sean, her boyfriend, one month before the Irish college started. He came in to have his hair trimmed, and Kathleen gave him to her to practise on. Sava knew, after she had snipped the soft hairs on the back of his plump white neck, and felt his neat, tender ears, that she would see much more of him, although she did not know how this state of affairs would come about.

Right now she is on a holiday, so-called. She took the first two weeks of July to help her mother out with the scholars, spoilt wee brats from Derry and Dublin. Sava barely distinguishes one lot from the other, since she spends little time talking to them. They all look similar: prim schoolgirls, overfed, seldom good-looking, who attend convent schools and will be teachers when they grow up. Lucky for them because who would marry them? Pauline is different, Sava admires Pauline's graceful figure, brown eyes. She reminds Sava of Elizabeth Taylor starring in *National Velvet*. Her eyes that same almond shape. She doubts if Pauline will become a teacher. She is the worst Irish speaker Sava has ever come across, and competence in Irish appears to be a prerequisite for professional success. That's why these people pay good money to come to a hole like Tubber, a place nobody ever visited before now unless they had relations there.

On Sunday, Sava dances at the Fairyland Ballroom in Glenbeg. The ballroom is a big wooden shed, set on the roadside in a flat and exposed plain. Glenbeg has no defining feature of any kind, not even a school or a church, apart from this ballroom, but it is within easy reach of several towns. Sava drives there with Kathleen and Kathleen's boyfriend, Denis Coll, and another girl called Mary Friel, a plain, fat girl who is an embarrassment to her in some ways and in others a protection. Sava likes her, however. Mary is an old friend, from Tubber, and sometimes she is glad of her companionship.

Sava has a white dress: white shiny satin with small turquoise spots, full leg-of-mutton sleeves. The skirt is lightly gathered and stops two inches down her thighs; her hair is slightly longer than the dress, and at the back it hangs over the edge of the hem in a fringe. She wears the dress with white tights and white platform shoes. The dress shivers and gleams as she walks into the ballroom, stepping from the warm evening into the dark, disco-lit interior already throbbing with song. Big Tom and the Mainliners, the favourite band of the time in Ireland, is playing and already there is a large crowd. Mary Friel wants to go to the Ladies – girls who look like that always do, they need to check their faces for shine, for lack of lipstick, for anything that will make them look even worse than they already are. Sava goes along with her out of a sense of obligation even though this kind of exercise bores her: for her it is unnecessary.

103

When they return, a new dance is just starting and the men are moving *en masse* towards the women. The tradition of women on one side, men on the other, is now considered *passé* here, but of course members of the same sex tend to congregate in little groups here and there anyway, preferring the comfort and protection of their own kind until they have to take their courage in their timid feet, take the plunge, face the music – join the dance. There is a jumble of groups, little huddles of men or of women, all around the edge of the hall. The old system was simpler: then you knew, literally, where you stood, and could examine all the men or all the women at a glance.

A man with brown hair, very thin, and a lined, red face approaches Sava and asks her to dance. 'No thanks,' she says. 'I've got a boyfriend.' A simple lie which she learned from Kathleen two years ago. He doesn't believe her, old faggot, and scowls, muttering under his breath, as he moves off. Sava shrugs and smiles. A young man with red hair invites her up and she goes. But all the time she dances, her eyes are checking the groups of men, and she does not lose herself in the rhythms of the music, music of which she is very fond. She cannot lose herself, she cannot relax, even though the boy is clean, smells of Old Spice, has a job with the county council in Letterkenny. He even manages to make a joke or two above the noise of the music. Sava loves jokes, believes that that is what men are for, making jokes. But she smiles distantly, her thoughts elsewhere.

Sean is not here.

She knew this one minute after she had entered the ballroom. Her instinct, her eager vision, sharpened by desire to spot him a mile off, even in a crowd of five hundred, tells her that. If he was here she would have seen him the minute she walked in the door. Her heart would have flipped and she would have felt perfect as a basin of cream, as a crystal well. This was the feeling she had anticipated all day, all yesterday and the day before that, since he had mentioned, in his offhand, meaningful, sexy way, that Big Tom was playing, did she like him? Like him. She was cutting his hair at the time, trimming small golden curls from the back of his big head and watching them float to the tiles. Yes she liked him all right, she had said, and took the huge step of adding that she intended to be there herself. That's good, is what he had said, looking her in the eye as he shook off his black gown – they'd black for the men – and rubbed his shaven neck with his hand thoughtfully.

It had not occurred to her, lying on the tartan divan while blackbirds and starlings sang, that he would not be there. She had imagined, in greatest detail, what would happen when they met, had imagined several possible variations of the meeting and its delightful consequences, but she had not imagined even one version of what would happen if the opposite occurred. The negative, the not seeing, is not so easy to invent, it is not the stuff of fantasy. But it is the stuff of reality, and now she feels it, a knife slicing through the skin of yellow cream.

The music stops, she slips away from the red-haired fellow – gangly, bespectacled, he looks surprised, did not want her to go – but quickly someone else swoops to invite her. She is remarkable, both for her looks and for the bright outfit she has chosen for tonight, which draws attention to her. She submits to their dances, their clumsy caresses, their inane invitations for lemonades. Every man she meets is gauche, lacking in charm, warmth, wit, lacking in physical attractiveness. She tries to keep her spirits up and tells herself that this one or that one is all right, is nice. But the image of Sean pops into her head and informs her that by comparison with him, they are worthless.

She is gloomily drinking a Coke with one of the thin, greasy-haired boys who are so numerous in this dance hall when he comes in, searching. Sava sees him immediately. She leaves the bottle half-drunk , abandons the boy from Rathmullan, and dances with Sean. The set is a fast one and they dance a few feet apart. She sways more provocatively than is her habit, swings her hips and thrusts out her breasts, which are small but well outlined by the empire line of the dress. He hardly moves at all. His feet shuffle back and forth on the floor, he keeps his arms bent, fractionally, from the elbow but they remain still while he dances. His eyes, blue, amused, observe her face, however, all the time. When the set is over he takes her hand quickly and rubs it against his cheek.

'Thanks,' he says, in a halting, choking voice, and walks away.

Sava stands still for a minute, not believing this has happened. Her eyes follow him as he walks away from her towards one of the flocks of women. As the next dance is called she sees him approaching one of them and then somebody, the old man she refused first time, asks her up. She dances, a slow set, in his scarecrow arms, trying to keep some distance between her white satin dress and the grey, smelly gaberdine of his trousers. She feels that the space between her neck and stomach has been turned to stone, and that if she lets that stone move or change its consistency in the smallest way she will collapse.

Where is Mary Friel?

Sava had lost her, forgotten about her, but now, once she is released from the old faggot's crazy and bitter embrace she goes in search of her. She is not in the ladies' loo or in the bar, however, and Sava cannot spot her among the crowds that hover around the edge of the dance floor. While she is engaged in this search, Sean approaches her again. He takes both her hands and pulls her to him, for a slow dance. She puts her head on his shoulder and rests her lips on the thin cotton of his shirt. Underneath, his skin is warm and soft – he is well-built, has a layer of subcutaneous fat, and soft cushions on his chest. His penis nudges her stomach through layers of cloth as she gives herself up to the moment, blends into him.

'Where were you last night?' Banatee asks Sava.

'Dancing.' Sava yawns. It is eight o'clock, a rainy Monday. They are frying rashers for the girls. 'One rasher or two?' Sava asks.

'One. They only eat half of them. You're exhausted.'

'Aye.' Sava is in her dressing gown, a quilted nylon housecoat, purple.

'Ye can't serve them in that!'

'Why not? You do it then, you're dressed.'

'So where were ye?'

'Out. Dancing.'

'Who brought ye home?'

'I got a lift.'

'Mary Friel?'

Sava considers lying, and does. 'Aye.'

'Be careful!' her mother says.

'Och ma, don't be embarrassin me.'

'I'm just tellin you. Young ones have little sense.'

Sava slaps rashers and mushed fried tomatoes on willow-pattern plates. 'Are yon ladies outa the bed yet?'

'I heard them half an hour ago. In the bathroom.'

'In the bathroom!' says Sava. 'They must be nearly washed away.'

'You're a fine one to talk anyway,' says her mother, as Sava picks up four plates and goes to the foot of the stairs, where she yells, 'Tá an bricfeasta réidh, a chailíní! Brostaígí nó beidh sé fuar!'

'Fu-are, beidh sé fuare!' says Pauline, sliding down the banister. It creaks under her weight.

Orla sees Micheál more often now

Orla sees him more often now than she did initially. Darting from the bedroom to the bathroom, slipping from the kitchen to the garden, crossing the farmyard back and forth, back and forth, carrying things, encouraging cattle to waddle from field to byre, she sees him. And she knows he sees her, watching him.

He is six feet tall, or thereabouts – the height of all men Elizabeth refers to as 'a fine cut of a fellow'. His hair is not dark like Sava's but reddish, and it curls. His skin is cream like hers, not red and spotty like that of most red-haired men.

Cowboys boots are what he favours for his feet, pointy-toed, light brown in colour, spattered with mud. 'Cool Hand Luke!' says Pauline, when she catches a glimpse of him. 'Hit the floor, dames. I don't want any of you ladies to get hurt!'

He has a dark green jumper the colour of fir trees, double-knit, cable stitch, its sleeves rolled to the elbow. His arms are a darker shade than his face, reddish-brown, broad, freckled.

Orla knows all this, watching him whenever she can.

Micheál works on the farm, doing the work his father Charlie cannot, which is all of the work. He fishes in the river and, when he can share a boat with other men, in the sea. At weekends he attends the dance in the Fairyland Ballroom. At this dance he does not speak to Sava or acknowledge that he is related to her. Nor does he dance, with anyone.

Urban foxes

Since the lodgers have taken over Orla's house, clothes are not as big a problem as they used to be, but Elizabeth still dislikes spending much money on them. What she loves is a bargain: any spare time she has is spent, with Orla, hunting down obscure small shops, spotting closing-down and end-of-season sales. Orla, although she craves designer clothes that never go on sale (meaning, in 1972, one thing: Levi's), shares Elizabeth's enthusiasm for the bargain. The red notices announcing 'Special Offers' send a rush of adrenalin to her brain. Some atavistic predatory instinct is aroused within her by the huge writings spread across shop windows, proclaiming 'Summer Sale', 'Spring Sale' or, best of all, 'January Sale': open season. Few experiences are more exciting than the scramble through the counters filled with richly scented leather shoes, the racks of fragrant coats and dresses, the thrill of finding something that is lovely, cheap and the right size. On your bikes! Tally ho!

Their love of sales explains Orla's possession of such a wide selection of mildly eccentric, off-key, occasionally beautiful clothes: a maroon anorak with a wide border of vaguely ethnic zigzag embroidery, when all normal anoraks are plain; green cord pants when the standard is blue bell-bottoms; blouses with wide Peter Pan collars or peculiar, heart-shaped buttons.

Dimpled tangerine shoes. She does not lack clothes, but hardly any of them are the kind of clothes ordinary, less adventurous, children wear.

Buying these clothes is one of the great joys of Orla's life. Shopping with Elizabeth is the highlight of her week. Every Saturday they set off, Elizabeth carrying the big brown shopper, into which are stuffed three string bags and a folded canvas bag. They walk from home to the bottom of Camden Street, as far as Whitefriar Street church sometimes, if they are early enough, where they catch Mass. This daily Mass is different from the Sunday Mass. Maybe it's in English, maybe Latin, but you can't hear it properly anyway, so it doesn't matter. One of the monks chants it in a low, sleepy murmur like the drone of a depressed bee, on a dark altar many yards away from the minute congregation. The congregation consists of the old, the maimed, the poor, the mad. They sit, one to a pew, in their ancient gaberdines, their tight, moth-eaten woolly caps, their long black coats, bent over long strings of worn-out rosary beads, murmuring or daydreaming. The church seems bigger and dimmer than ever; a greenish misty light shimmers across its vast emptiness. And it is given over to this soft mumbling, of people wrapped up in their own thoughts, lost in the caverns of their own souls. On days like this, Orla enjoys this church, a church full of strangeness and medieval superstition: relics of saints enclosed in silver boxes, notices advising of ceremonies, involving candles and oil, designed to ward off illnesses – sore eyes, sore throats. Novenas, retreats, special offers on absolutions – a hundred days off your stint in Purgatory, a right of appeal to your sentence to hell. It falls short of selling indulgences, but only just. The Middle Ages. Orla does not know much about the Middle Ages – in school they never did them, only history from 1800 to 1916. But she knows, kneeling in Whitefriar Street, that she is in a very odd, old world, a world full of a strangeness she has no name for.

On days like this, Elizabeth does not go up to the front. Why bother? The ones that are in are half-blind or in their dotage; they wouldn't notice if a lion walked up the aisle dressed in its Sunday suit. So she sits in the middle somewhere and mumbles along, a far-away look in her large eyes, or with eyes closed. She has no hat, just her old khaki gaberdine that she's had from before she was married – a coat such as girls wear to school, belted at the waist. On her head is not a hat but a silk headscarf or, if she had forgotten to bring one, a handkerchief – one of the large-size men's handkerchiefs, white with checked borders of brown or blue or red, which last longer than the small feminine kind, and which she prefers. You don't have to cover your head in church any more, but many women still feel edgy and nervous about going hatless, mantillaless, scarfless, or handkerchiefless. It is hard to accept, in your deepest heart, that a year or two ago it was sinful to display your head naked to God, but that now it is perfectly virtuous to do so. Many feel safer with a handkerchief, not necessarily perfectly clean, *in situ*. Just in case there's been some mistake.

After Mass, Elizabeth and Orla emerge onto the street, which is Aungier Street, pronounced, at least by them, Aynjer Street. Like the church it has an air of dark, Gothic mystery. It is a street defined by the monastery, by second-hand clothes shops, a café advertising dinners of green cabbage, sausage and chips for a shilling, a shop that sells Mass cards and gobstoppers. It is a ghostly medieval stretch of no man's land between George's Street on the left and Camden Street on the right. One direction leads to clothes, furniture, cafés, a rich and bustling shopping street, almost fashionable. In the other direction is food: Farrell's for eggs and poultry, Kattie for fish, many fruit and vegetable stalls.

Under the vaulting arch of the church door, Elizabeth stands and makes a decision. Which way to go? Orla hopes against hope they will turn down George's Street. That will mean a delicious hunt through the racks of dresses and coats in

Cassidy's, a complicated walk among the three-piece suites, the racks of wallpaper and paint in Dockrell's, possibly milky coffee and a cherry bun in Bewley's – her greatest pleasure. If Elizabeth wrinkles her nose and says 'No! We won't bother. Not today!' it will not be too bad though. All that means is feeling eggs and switches of bacon in Farrell's, where the eggs nest in baskets of yellow straw, as if laid there by hens, although the only hens are dead, hanging by their wrinkled long-nailed claws, three long rows of them, above the shopkeeper's head, their beaks prodding his bald head. Right means Kattie who shoves fish into Elizabeth's bag as Elizabeth protests, 'No no no, they'll all rot on me!' 'There ye are, maam, I'll give ye two dozen mackerel for half a crown.' And she stuffs in extra, wrapped in newspaper, stinking nevertheless all the way home. The vegetable sellers are not so pushy. Nor so red in the face, so scaly in the hands, so fat and old and wrapped in bloody, fishy aprons, as Kattie. A fishwife. The word does not link itself to Kattie in Orla's mind. Kattie is just Kattie. She doesn't have a surname or a place, only her table of fish and her pile of old newspapers, the first stall on Camden Street.

There are better treats there. Many of them. The fresh Vienna rolls, the flaky jam tarts, of the Kylemore Bakery; the racks of old-fashioned clothes in O'Reilly's the draper's, where money is still passed from till to till in canisters shooting along wires on the ceiling, wires like telegraph wires only noisier and more fun. O'Reilly's carries clothes you get nowhere else, for good reasons: it was there they got the red anorak with the little black squiggles and the gold chain at the front. The orange and brown jeans, in a leopardskin pattern. It's the drapery equivalent of Clover's, original home of Orla's tangerine shoes.

Urban delights. Shopping, church, coffee. Elizabeth.

They carry home half a hundredweight of stuff between them, distributed in the bags, which swell with their burdens. And then, arms dragged out of themselves, feet sore from the path, they dump everything on the floor of the kitchen and

Elizabeth says, 'Why don't you run down and get us some fish and chips.'

They've the house to themselves – Tom is at work, of course, and so are all the boys. Orla runs down and gets the fish and chips in the café on the triangle and she, Elizabeth and Roddy, just out of bed, sit around the big table, enjoying the delectable smell of vinegar and oil, munching the crisp batter-coated cod and the soft mushy chip-shop chips.

Elizabeth has to do it alone now. How will she carry home the weekly shop without Orla to help her? Roddy is around the house, he refused to come to the Gaeltacht. But he's out playing football a lot of the time. He's taken up pitch-and-putt. Elizabeth is alone for the summer, working herself to the bone, going to Mass and the shops all alone.

The truce is over
(but not to worry it's 1972)

They are eating salad because of the hot day. It's Banatee's version of an Irish salad: mountains of lettuce from the garden, scallions, a few slices of tomato. Sliced hard-boiled egg that has sometimes not been boiled through, so that one side is firm and good while the other, the side that did not hit the water, is runny. Even the albumen is runny, sliming out on the lettuce leaves like snail tracks.

Pauline shrugs and says, 'Everyone knew it wouldn't last.'

'What's this?'

'The IRA ceasefire. Don't you Dubs know anything at all? Did ye not even know there was a ceasefire on?'

'Well, we don't exactly spend all day tuned in to the newsroom, do we?'

'It started before we even came here,' Jacqueline pouts. Orla tries to wrap a piece of tomato up in a lettuce leaf, the way she has seen Monica Sheridan wrap fried mince meat in boiled cabbage leaves on television.

'So it's over, anyway.'

'William Craig said yesterday he could mobilise eighty thousand men in a minute if he wanted to.' Pauline does not know whether she should be pleased or upset about this. All it is is news, of the exciting kind, the kind they've been having for three years. What sort of news had they before that? The Queen is visiting Canada as part of a Commonwealth tour. Terence O'Neill has met the Prime Minister of the Republic for talks at Stormont. A woman was killed in a hit-and-run accident on Malvern Street. She was thirty-eight years of age, a mother of five. Now it's bombs, shootings, hunger strikes. Threats of all-out war. None of this excitement actually happens on her road, in her suburb. It happens on the news. That's what the girls from Dublin still don't understand. For Pauline, as for them, all this stuff happens only on the news.

But for Jacqueline the news is on her road, because she lives in a place on the news, the Bogside.

'They always shoot to kill. Shoot to kill shoot to kill.'

'Her da is in Long Kesh,' says Pauline.

'We know,' says Aisling too quickly. 'You told us that before.'

'Do you ... does she hear from him at all?'

'Her mother does, doesn't she?'

Jacqueline jumps up and runs out of the room, screaming at the top of her voice.

'Oh my God! What did I say wrong?' Orla looks guiltily at Aisling. Aisling looks at Pauline. They are all genuinely shocked but already beginning to enjoy the excitement and ready to analyse it. 'I suppose I should have guessed she'd be upset, talking about her father and everything. Is she close to him?'

'Och yes. Very close. She goes to Long Kesh to visit him in the prison and all. She misses him a lot.'

'It must be difficult, living in Derry,' Aisling says in her softest, politest voice. In fact she and Orla find it impossible to imagine what living in Derry or anywhere else in the North is like. Terrible, tragic, think of the stress. God help them. They hear people in Dublin making these comments all the time. But the words are remote and meaningless. Orla knows she hates them but she doesn't know why. They are just one part of a whole layer of adult expression that irritates her unbelievably, ringing false as toy pennies in her ears.

'It's not that difficult.' Pauline doesn't know what it is like to live anywhere else. The holiday in Donegal hardly counts as living. 'You just live there, you know, like you live anywhere else.'

'But the barricades and the bombs and everything . . .'

'Ah yeah. It's not as bad as people in the South think, you know. Not during the day, anyway, or out where I live.'

'Of course your father is a Protestant. Maybe that makes a difference?'

'I don't think so.'

Orla decides to take the plunge. 'So are you for a united Ireland or not, then?'

Pauline laughs. 'United Ireland? Are you?' she asks, picking a piece of lettuce up in her fingers and staring carefully at it as if it were a map of Ireland.

'Not really,' Orla answers. 'I think it's more fun having the North.'

'Being able to get Mars Bars and things, she means,' Aisling explains helpfully.

'Yeah, well it's like having a foreign country sort of on your doorstep,' Orla adds.

'Is it?' Pauline thinks of Italy, where her parents are. Italy is a foreign country.

'Yeah. Sort of.'

They pause and eat some salad. Sava comes in with a hot pot of tea, and overhears the conversation. 'There's after bein a terrible bomb,' she says, sighing.

'Where?'

'In Belfast. They don't know how many's killed.'

'Oh dear!' says Aisling, politely. She pauses before asking, 'Was it the IRA?'

'Aye surely.' Sava puts down the teapot and examines the milk jug, tilting it carefully to see if there is enough milk to serve a second round of tea. There is. 'The IRA surely,' she drawls, in her sad tired voice. 'Who else?' She stands and stares at the wall.

'The long hot summer!' Orla says brightly, to fill the vacuum and dispel the uneasiness that Sava's news has brought to the table.

Pauline gives her a sharp stare and Aisling shakes her head critically.

'Did I say something wrong?' asks Orla.

Jacqueline comes back into the room and they all stare at her in acute embarrassment.

'Jacqueline! Are you all right?' Aisling is the most grown-up of these girls when it comes to the crunch. She knows how to deal with surprises.

'It was just a bit of a shock, that's all. But my mind is made up. I'm going home tomorrow.'

Jacqueline has not had more bad news from Derry. She has found a large fat slug in her salad: that was why she left the room so suddenly. That night, before the *céilí* starts, she complains bitterly to Headmaster Joe about the Dohertys' primitive household, about her enforced starvation, about the lack of hygiene in the preparation of food, about her disenchantment with the Irish language and with the climate of Donegal, about her loneliness for her family, about internment, about William Craig, Whitelaw, Ian Paisley, and about several other things. She has surprising reserves of energy and vocabulary when her enthusiasm is ignited and her goal clear. He makes every effort to persuade her to stay. Even though he had marked her as a rotten egg – to any schoolteacher, Jacqueline would have been instantly recognisable as bad news – and he knows her presence in his college is unlikely to be advantageous to anyone, he desperately wants her to stay on. Nobody has ever left this college before. Nobody has ever been expelled either, contrary to popular belief. He would never dream of sending a child away, unless they committed some serious crime, for instance murder. Even then he is the sort of man who would say, There's more to this than meets the eye, so there is. His belief is that every child is a good child – rather a radical one for the time. Some Irish colleges have a reputation for authoritarianism, for strictness, for military discipline. They do very well: their waiting lists are long and their fees are high. Parents queue up to send their children there, where they will learn who's boss, where they will be licked into shape, taught Irish at gunpoint and despatched on the next bus if they utter even a single word of English. Headmaster Joe, although he can see that this is where commercial success lies, does not want to run his college along the lines of an army. His primary aim is that the children should enjoy themselves, although they never suspect that. Children going home he regards as the ultimate failure, the ultimate insult to himself as a headmaster, as the father of this college. He spends an hour talking to Jacqueline, seeking to persuade her to give the place one more chance.

But she goes. To everyone's surprise and subtle dismay she goes, and the next day is full of a grey feeling of failure and dismay.

Pauline is left alone
at the back of the house

Pauline is left alone in the room at the back of the house, over-looking the garden and the burn.

'Sandra could move in with her,' Aisling suggests.

'Yes.' Orla is not enthusiastic, but realises that the house will be different, lonelier, with one person gone. Three is not enough for a house. Three is not a crowd but a mistake.

'I'm going to tell her.'

'Does Pauline want to share with Sandra, though?'

'Sandra?' Pauline screws up her face. 'That girl you know?'

'She's in our class.'

'Share with someone from Dublin? I don't know.' Pauline can't imagine what it would be like. Dubliners. She thinks they are dirty: they don't seem to have enough underwear, and their socks are grubby.

'Sandra mightn't want to move anyway, now. I think she likes Carrs' and all that crowd there.'

'Monica Murphy and Noeleen Talbot, how could she?'

'Yeah. But she's used to them.'

Pauline moves around the little room, feeling it expand around her. The oak tree seems blacker and shiftier now that she's alone. The moon flits more dramatically in and out of the clouds. She pulls the curtains: darkness has always filled her with anxiety. She pulls her postcards from the bottom of her canvas bag, and examines them. Botticelli's *Venus*, says one. A naked lady, with a face a bit like Jacqueline's, rises out of a seashell, the kind you can use as an ashtray. Clams or oysters live in those shells, usually. The Duomo in Sienna, a dark, rusty red. Leonardo's *David*. The Duomo, Florence. The Duomo, Perugia. The Duomo, Pisa.

It's all churches. Are they Catholic or Protestant? Her mother doesn't say, but they look Catholic. All the pictures and statues.

'Tan deepening daily.'

'Sienna glorious, the colour of flowerpots, like a city on the moon. Wish you could see it!'

'Perugia unbelievable. Green and gold, old stone. A surprise a minute.'

It's not the first time they've left Pauline to go on a holiday together, without her. Two years ago they went to Malta, and before that to New York, to Vienna, and to Paris one winter for a long weekend. She stayed with her granny, in the Waterside, on most of those occasions. Twice her babysitter came and stayed at the house – that was after her granny died and after she'd got Shep. The babysitter is feeding Shep now, coming in twice a day, Pauline hopes. She hopes Shep is taken for a walk, at least occasionally, but doubts it. The babysitter, Nuala, doesn't like walking much.

Granny hadn't had a lot of time for Maureen, Pauline's mother. She never spoke about her at all, or to her: when Pauline visited, it was with her father or alone.

'Why?'

'Ah you know,' her father had said. 'Don't get on.'

'Lucky me!' Maureen laughed. 'One in-law less.'

But in fact Maureen has no contact at all with her in-laws. Blood is thicker than the law, as far as Douglas's family are concerned. And it is Pauline alone who dances the dangerous dance across the minefield that divides her mother's and her father's territory. The domestic borderland separating Stewart from Paddy, Myrtle from Eileen, is Pauline's special inheritance. All the adults in her life avoid stepping on it, and only one or two even acknowledge its existence.

'Them snotty relations of your da's,' Auntie Eileen said once, when Pauline mentioned that she and her father had Sunday dinner with their granny. 'I don't know how your ma puts up with it.'

So I don't.

So I don't.

Maureen puts up with it because she fell in love with Douglas when she was eighteen, working in a factory, a shirt factory, of course   of course, what else. The white shirt-tails, the starched collars, rolling down the conveyer belt: she machined on the collars, that was her job. She'd wanted to be an air hostess but her mother had laughed at her. Are ye mad? Sure there isn't even an airport here! Where would ye go to be an air hostess?

Dublin was where occurred to Maureen.

'They'll na take ye. I never heard of anyone from here bein an air hostess in Dublin, or anywhere else.'

Maureen applied. She wrote away to Aer Lingus in Dublin and got the application form. It asked if she had a fluent knowledge of Irish and she left that bit blank, although she knew a bit. They learned it after dancing on Saturdays.

They didn't answer the application at all. Not even an acknowledgement.

Maureen didn't tell her mother or anyone else about it. Until she met Douglas, who owned the shirt factory.

He stopped one day when he was walking through the workroom, nodding and smiling, lord of the manor. He stopped when he saw Maureen. Nothing unusual there. Everyone stopped, in their tracks, the first time they saw her.

'Hello!' he said.

'Hello.' Maureen broke a piece of thread with her teeth and

concentrated on her work, as any of the factory girls would have done in the circumstances.

'You're new here?'

'Yes. I started a month ago.'

It was the 'yes' that did it, Douglas thought. 'Yes' not 'Aye'. It proved something, he liked to imagine. It proved Maureen was different from the other factory girls, promising, individual. Thus he rationalised, when he had to.

His mother did not share his opinion.

'She's going to be an air hostess,' he had said helplessly, having heard the story of Aer Lingus.

'An air hostess,' his mother hissed.

'You're a bigot.'

'Don't you dare accuse me of any such thing.' She was dressed in red, a colour bossy people liked to wear. Her grey hair was coiffed and stylish, her lips creamed crimson. She had an air-hostessy look about her herself, he realised. In fact she had a Maureen look about her.

Sorry mother!

'You'll learn all about bigotry when you marry her and her filthy relations come to show their respects. What do they think about this?'

'They don't know yet.'

'You know what they'll do when they find out? Tar and feather, I believe, is their usual reaction. Cutting off the hair of the girl and . . . Don't do it.'

'I love her.'

'Love! It's not just that she's one of them, anyway. For Heaven's sake she works in the factory.'

'I know '

'You could . . .'

Have her. Without marrying. She was about to say that but bit it back. He did not hold it against her. Of course she believed it, that it would have been a viable way out. But she would not have believed it if she had ever deigned to meet Maureen.

They hadn't tarred and feathered her, or kneecapped him or tried to burn them out of their house. But his relations had frozen her out, completely. The wedding – in Paris – they had not attended at all. Eileen and Kathleen came to cheer her up, although they considered the whole thing a bad idea.

Still, Douglas was nice enough, when you got to know him.

And Maureen was getting a fine house on the Culmore Road, old but renovated, with a good kitchen. She would not have to work in the factory again as they had to, even though they were married.

Pauline was born at the end of the first year. Maureen would have liked to have her brought up as a Protestant. But even Douglas could not agree with her on that.

'It won't matter. She won't fit in,' he said.

'Why? You're her father.'

'Yes. But you're her mother and that's what matters.'

'I'm willing to make the sacrifice. My family won't like it.'

'They won't abandon her. But mine will. Even if she's Protestant. She'll be your daughter first and foremost.'

Maureen capitulated.

Douglas was wrong about his family, however. They ignored Pauline for about two months. Then his mother asked him if she could call and give her a present. He arranged it: Maureen went shopping. His mother had not had a grandchild before, and after that visit she could not keep away. Pauline became a regular visitor to the house in the Waterside. She preferred it, if forced to choose, to her other granny's house, a small red-bricked place in Ross Street. But the main difference between the two grannies was that one was rich and one was poor, not that one was Protestant and one was Catholic. She liked the house in the Waterside because it was big and elegant, and more exciting than the modern, stucco house she lived in herself. Her granny had treasures: a music box the size of a trunk, with a silver xylophone inside. You slotted in disks and it played 'It's a Long Way to Tipperary', Brahms's lullaby, and 'Rule Britannia'. She also owned a penny-farthing bicycle, stored in a shed at the end of her long, shady garden. There was a collection of hats in the attic. And many other things. The granny in Ross Street owned nothing at all: they had had to throw away everything because the house was so small. Two bedrooms, a kitchen and a sitting room the size of a stamp.

And she had had seven children. Three of them still lived there.

Granny Gallagher had only Douglas and his sister Myrtle, who was married in England. Their father had died when Douglas was young. Pauline used to think that meant he died when Douglas was seven or eight, but she has only begun to understand recently that he is much much older than her mother, fifteen or twenty years older. When she asked he would not tell her what age he was. But it meant his father died when Douglas was already grown-up.

On some Sundays, when Pauline was small, she had visited her granny in Ross Street, on others her granny in the Waterside. Since her Waterside grandmother had died she had given up Ross Street as well, although her granny there was going strong.

'So, have you thought about sharing with Sandra?' Aisling asks at breakfast.

'I don't mind.'

'It'll be better than being alone,' Aisling says.

'I'm used to being alone.'

'You're an only child?'

'Yes.'

'Are your parents having a good time in Italy?'

'Yes. They are having a good time in Italy. They write to me every day.'

'Don't you wish you were with them?'

' I'm better off here.'

Postman Joe don't go slow
be like Elvis go man go

Orla goes up to Headmaster Joe and asks if he has left something at the bottom of the bag, by mistake.

He looks at her impatiently – he is hungry for his lunch – but turns the white canvas bag inside out.

'I'm afraid not, *a thaisce*,' he says. Then he stares over the top of his black frames and pats her head. 'Tomorrow is another day.'

She manages to get to the toilet before she cries; it's the first time she has broken down; her patience is reaching breaking point at last.

'Why don't you ring them?' Aisling asks. Orla has not exactly confided in her, because this is not the sort of situation that Aisling could understand, or sympathise with. She would relegate it to the vast sea of difference that separates her and her family from Orla's. She would find it mildly embarrassing, that is all, and feel helpless.

'Is there a phone?' Orla has never seen one. That is the sort of place Tubber is, the sort of place where there isn't a phone in any house, not even in the school.

'I think there's one in the post office. You have to ask the woman there to let you use it.'

'Well . . . I've no money,' Orla says.

'Oh.' Aisling's mouth makes a small red *moue* and her cheeks flush. 'Well, you'll probably get a letter soon anyway.'

'I haven't had even one. You've had heaps.'

Aisling puffs her cheeks and blows out some air. 'I'll ask my mother to call yours. OK? And tell her to write.'

'Yeah.'

'What's your phone number?'

'We haven't got a phone.' Orla reddens, admitting a secret. The only way she can phone home is to phone Mrs Madden, the woman next door.

'Oh yeah. I forgot. Well. She can call around. She knows the address.'

Orla envisages Aisling's mother calling round to her house, talking to Elizabeth. The vision is too painful to bear. Pushing it out of her mind – and what else can she do about it – she changes the subject to Sandra. Sandra has said she would like to move houses, even though she's happy enough where she is. Aisling has promised her they'll talk to Banatee about it at lunchtime.

Lunch without Jacqueline is curiously quiet. Deprived of her partner, Pauline has little to say. She stares at her latest postcard and nods yes or no to queries. They are eating chips: since Jacqueline's departure, they have had them every day. Eggs and chips, sausages and chips, beans and chips, rashers and chips, potato cakes and chips, fish fingers and chips. Chips on their own. Banatee spends half the morning peeling potatoes, the potatoes grown by Charlie and Micheál, bockety brown Queens thickly coated with clay. She peels the spuds; Sava slices them into fingers, plunging the knife into the slippery cream flesh and listening to it swish through till it hits the rut of the wooden breadboard. She has cut her finger twice, and the bright red blood has ribboned into the watery potato flesh, colouring everything pink. Dangerous work, chip making. Next week Sava will have to go back to work at Kathleen's Place, to which she is looking forward. Cutting hair is easier than cutting potatoes. How Banatee will manage without her is anybody's guess.

'You go in and ask her. You can understand what she says,' Aisling orders, when they have pushed away their desserts: tapioca pudding, which is the one dessert she simply cannot force down. Even the sight of its glutinous texture, its myriad bulging eyes, revolts her.

'No way! We should go together!'

'OK. But what's the point? I can't understand her and she can't understand me.'

Orla goes into the kitchen alone. She looks around – she has hardly ever been there before. It is a big room, very hot, smelling of frying objects and baking bread. Banatee is at the table thumping a round flat pat of creamy dough. Her hands are floury and her glasses are dusted with a fine white coat of flour. She takes them off when Orla comes in, making them even whiter.

'Sea, a thaisce?' Banatee is alarmed. The girls never come into the kitchen. It has never happened before, even once.

'Mm.' Orla tries to find the words to say what she is supposed to say. Our friend Sandra wondered if she could come and stay here instead of . . . She wonders what the Donegal Irish for wonder is. She asks the question anyway, in the Irish she knows.

'Caidé sin?' Banatee has not understood.

Orla asks it again, in another way.

'Caidé? Abair sin arís, a thaisce?' Banatee puts her hands to her ears, indicating that she is a bit deaf.

Orla says, in English, 'Can I have a clean sheet for the bed?'

'Of course you can, dearie. Why didn't you just say that in English?'

'Well . . . I thought we weren't supposed to speak English.'

'Och, don't mind what them teachers do be telling you, *a thaisce*. Sure I'm from Scotland.'

'You are?'

'Och aye, did ye not know even that?'

'No,' says Orla. She considers telling Banatee that her mother is English, but decides against it.

'What did she say?' Aisling is on the stairs. Orla gives her a fresh purple sheet.

'She said maybe.'

'We know what that means.' Aisling sighs. 'Poor old Sandra!'

'Sandra's all right.' Orla feels cross, very cross, but she does not know why. She has got what she wants, after all. Sandra will never come here now and spoil things between her and Aisling.

Aisling changes for Outdoor Activities, taking off her skirt and blouse and putting on a T-shirt with shorts. Orla rifles through her suitcase until she finds an outfit that is similar. Standing in front of the wardrobe mirror, checking her chin for blackheads, Aisling watches Orla's reflection.

'Why are you wearing that?' She turns when Orla is dressed.

'Why? Why not?' Orla knows what she means but decides to pretend not to. 'It's a hot day.'

'You're copying me, Orla.' Aisling turns pink and her face contorts, not with anger but with embarrassment. Aisling is always nice; she does not accuse her friends of any faults.

'I am not!' Orla expostulates. 'I am not copying you. It is a very hot day.'

'So let's go for a swim then,' Aisling says. 'Why can't we ever go for a swim?'

'We can. We can go for a swim if that's what you want.'

'That's not the point.' Aisling runs out of the room.

Orla goes to the mirror and stares at herself in its misty surface. Her T-shirt is green and red, striped, a serviceable colour, and her shorts are khaki. Where did Elizabeth get them? O'Reilly's, that's where, close to Clover's where they bought the tangerine shoes which are on Orla's feet right now, contrasting vividly with her greyish-brownish socks. The socks were white, and new, when she packed them, but successive

131

washings with cold water and toilet soap have discoloured them. They are now the colour of the burn, a colour that is pleasant in rivers but nasty in socks.

Her legs are browner than they were, and also her arms and face. But she is too fat. She turns and tries to get a look at herself from the back. It's hard to get a good look, but she sees enough. Her bottom sticks out. It gets rounder all the time, no matter how much exercise she takes. Her legs too, although muscular, are thick.

'I look terrible!' Orla goes to the mirror and bangs her head against the reflection of her head.

Aisling is not as skinny as Pauline. But she is thinner than Orla, and taller as well. Her shorts are navy, a good crisp navy, and she wears them with a red and white T-shirt, navy socks, white tennis shoes. Her clothes, washed in the burn like Orla's, have survived much better – because they were much better to begin with, like everything Aisling has.

'Oh money no object!' is what Elizabeth says. 'The best of everything.' She says this with a strange look on her face, a drawn look, which suggests that she does not like Aisling, or her family, the people with the money. Why then does she insist that Orla be Aisling's friend, as staunchly as she discourages her from knowing Sandra? Elizabeth is drawn to Aisling and Aisling's mother even more than Orla is, and at the same time she disparages them, with subtle remarks and less subtle gestures, all the time. Orla knows that she is supposed to be like Aisling, that her mother wants her almost to be Aisling: that is her ambition in life. She is to be Aisling and then her mother will be satisfied. And yet, and yet, if she is Aisling will her mother curl up her face into a ball of resentment, and make sly remarks about her behind her back? Money no object. The best of everything.

Money is the key, Elizabeth teaches Orla, the key to everything that is good in life. Money is beauty and civilisation, money is refinement and flowers on the table, money is Chopin preludes on the piano in the front room and books on shelves in the bedroom. Money is low voices and gentle smiles. To Orla all these things seem complicated and many-faceted, life as lived by Aisling and her parents. But Elizabeth has simplified the complexities. They all boil down to one thing: money. The key to money is education, is the other part of the theory. You get an education in order to get money, and that is all you need to get, in this life. Get it. Orla's got it. She's got it that she's to get it, and then she'll get Elizabeth's approval. Elizabeth will lose that sour, hard, cruel, bitter look she carries on her face whenever she talks about her great friend Aisling, and Aisling's mother behind their backs, and replace it with the sort of look they have. Which is ... different.

Orla removes the shorts and replaces them with her one pair of denims, which are from Dunnes Stores, not Levi's. That means they are loose, and the denim is dark blue, not the pale, snug-fitting jeans that the best girls wear. She takes off her tangerine shoes. The heels are worn down, completely, from the constant walking. Rummaging in her suitcase she finds the schoolbag sandals, and these she puts on.

Without looking at herself she leaves the room.

The burn scene three

Aisling is with Pauline. Orla can hear them laughing as she passes Pauline's door, and her stomach contracts with jealousy. She wonders if she should go in, tell them she is off to Outdoor Activities. She decides not to; she hasn't the courage to face them. She knows if she speaks in their presence her voice will be strangled in her throat. Such jealousy she has hardly ever felt before and she does not know what it is. All she knows is that watching Aisling attach herself to Pauline changes the chemistry of her own body. It shrivels her.

But before she has reached the bottom of the stairs they come out of the room.

'Where do ye think ye're off to?' Pauline shouts.

Orla stops and looks at her, beaming. Her stomach regains its equilibrium.

'Rounders.'

'Sneaky article! You could've told us you were going!'

Pauline and Aisling come down and they swing out into the sunbaked yard. Micheál is crossing it as they go, carrying a lamb in his arms.

'What happened the wee lamb?' Pauline asks.

'It's broken its wee leg,' answers Micheál. The first words he has ever uttered in the presence of any of them.

'Och the poor wee thing. Isn't he lovely?'

Micheál says nothing. He smiles at the girls and doesn't move. An awkwardness falls over the yard.

'Baa baa black sheep!' sings Pauline. 'What will you do with it now?'

'Och, put it by the fire. Give it a drop of milk.'

'From a bottle?'

'Aye.' He looks puzzled, as if the implications of this were too much for him.

'Can I do it?'

'Feed it from the bottle?'

'Yes.'

'Why not?' He moves now, clumsily, to the door of the house. The girls stare at his retreating back and when he goes inside, they laugh.

'So where are you really going?' Pauline changes the subject, turns on Orla.

'Down to the burn, actually.'

'The burn?'

'Yes.'

'Why?'

'Just am.' She moves away, heading for the garden.

'I'm coming too so I am.' Pauline jumps up.

Aisling looks taken aback.

'Come on Ash, time for action!'

They follow Orla around the house to the garden and on into the field.

'Can't we walk along the bank? We'll get wet.'

'It's more fun this way!' Pauline yells, leaping from stone to stone. Aisling stands up to her knees in ripe grass and long-stemmed buttercups, watching as Pauline leaps rapidly from stone to stone downstream. Orla looks over her shoulder and waits for Aisling who, after a minute, steps into the burn and begins to make her way along its course with diffident steps.

They cross the second, ragweed field and come to the ditch where the burn goes underground.

'You can get through here,' Orla says, pleased to be able to surprise even Pauline. 'I'll show you.' She crouches and begins to creep under the wild hedge.

'I'm not going in there!' Aisling is red in the face and pouting. Orla hopes she won't cry. She finds a tiny smugness, a mean satisfaction, creeping into her. Aisling is not brave enough for Pauline.

'Don't be a fraidy cat!' Pauline looks at her crossly. Fraidy cat. Cowardy custard, Orla thinks, translating, but does not say. She just continues to crawl through the bushes. Pauline follows.

Aisling stares at them in dismay and irritation. 'I'm going back,' she says. 'It's nearly teatime. Banatee will be looking for us.'

'So long!' Pauline sings in a high neutral tone. 'Don't eat all the slugs on us.'

Orla and Pauline are in the glaucous cavern. It is a brilliantly sunny day outside, and here and there a flash of light penetrates the green roof of the tunnel, turning the dark amber water to gold.

'This darksome burn, horseback brown, his rollrock highroad roaring down,' announces Orla suddenly.

'What's that? This place is going to your head.' Pauline looks puzzled and annoyed.

'Nothing. Look.' Orla points at the raspberries. There are a few left.

'What are they?'

'Raspberries. Wild raspberries. I ate some the other day, they're lovely.'

'Maybe you're poisoning me? Maybe this is the last the world will ever see of Pauline?'

Orla steps across the burn and picks the last raspberries. There are about half a dozen left. She eats two herself and lets the red juice run out around her mouth. 'Here!' She hands the remainder over.

Pauline tastes one. 'Mirror mirror on the wall who is the fairest of them all?' she chants. 'Mm. Yum yum. Is that all there is?'

'Here anyway. Maybe further down.'

This is as far as she has come before. Pauline moves along ahead of her. The burn continues at much the same pace and size for a few hundred yards. They move easily along, their ears filled with the sound of it. It babbles, and at the same time there is a continuous loud hum, like the sound of a machine, under the babbling. On top of the burn sounds are the rustlings of the leaves, rustles made by birds and perhaps animals in the banks and overhead, and birdsong. Orla can let it sink into her head, along her bloodstream, even now, even in the company of Pauline.

The roaring becomes louder. After a while the burn runs deeper. It is harder to find stepping stones. Pauline, failing in one leap, steps into the water.

'Hey!' says Orla. 'Won't you take off your shoes?'

'No,' says Pauline. 'I'll be getting out again, sure.'

Orla follows suit, although she is wearing jeans and they get hopelessly wet. They wade through the brown, cold water, which in places reaches up to their thighs.

Then they come to the waterfall. The roaring is a thundering; they go as close to the edge of the fall as they can and look over. It is not very high, about six feet, and underneath, the burn widens into a generous pool. It is blacker than the water up here, and looks much deeper.

They stare at the pool for a while, and listen to the waterfall.

'I'm going down,' says Pauline.

'Mm. You can't, it's dangerous.'

'Doesn't look dangerous to me.'

'We don't know how deep it is.'

'I can swim. Can't you?'

'Of course.'

'You never come to the shore.'

'Well ...' One of Orla's little secrets. She is not going to divulge it to Pauline, of all people.

'Double dare you!'

'Hm.'

'Triple dare you. Don't be a fraidy cat!' Pauline does not say another word. She pulls herself out of the water and onto the rocks at the crest of the waterfall. Then she takes a jump – not a dive, just a clumsy, reckless jump, into the water below. Orla feels her heart stop. She watches Pauline descend – it is not so frightening, since Pauline is about the same length as the waterfall. Her feet are hitting the water below while her head is still just under the higher level. But her head disappears below the surface. The splash, the white spray, disappear, and the water closes over Pauline like a black skin. The violence of the falling water is all Orla hears. Pauline is gone.

Orla feels paralysed. Stands there at the top of the waterfall, staring. Her body has become, suddenly, totally relaxed. All the muscles spread pleasurably, the way they do after intense running or something like that. Her arms, tummy, thighs, legs feel soft, pleasured. They seem removed from her head.

Pauline surfaces. 'Hello there baby bear!' She can hardly be heard above the noise, but she swims around the black pool, her hair sleeked against her head, her brown eyes laughing.

'Come on fraidy cat!'

Orla closes her eyes and flexes to jump. But she can't. When the moment comes to give herself over to the jump, she can't do it.

'Come on! It's great! It's easy as cheese!'

Orla looks down at Pauline and thinks that it is easy, the water is deep and safe, the waterfall is not so high. All you have to do is close your eyes and stop thinking. Stop thinking! Stop thinking!

She closes her eyes and stops ... no she does not stop. She can't stop thinking. Every time she flexes her body for the leap her fear catches her, like a hand on her shoulder, and pulls her back.

The struggle goes on like a battle in her stomach and her head. She flexes, she blacks out everything, she's almost doing it ... But the hand clutches her and paralyses her. Her anguish is appalling.

'I can't,' she says. ' I just can't.'

Why can't she?

Pauline looks up, puzzled. But she recognises an impasse, or cowardice, when it stares her in the face from the top of a waterfall. She waves and says nothing. She swims around for another minute or two and then climbs up the side of the fall. Orla waits for her, wishing she could be so reckless, gazing at the black, dark pool. She loves to look at it, to skirt it on its banks, to find stepping stones across it. If she fell from one of those stones or from the slippery grass she would swim across the pool, loving the cold fresh water. It's the jumping she can't cope with, that sensation of free falling, being out of control.

Writing to yourself

Dear Mummy,

I hope you are keeping well and that your headaches are not bothering you. I am fine.

The weather is quite good now, coldish but dry, at least. We can go to the shore every day, or play rounders. Usually I play rounders. I am getting quite good at it. Yesterday our team won by fifteen rounds, which is really good.

Jacqueline, one of the girls from Derry who was staying in Dohertys' with us, went home a few days ago. She just couldn't stand the food we get here and wanted to eat some chips. The food is awful but it is edible. She was a strange girl! I think she was just homesick really. Her father is in prison in Long Kesh and her mother was not allowed to move into their new corporation house by the British Army.

Pauline the other girl from Derry is on her own now in the back room. It must be nice to have a room to yourself, but I suppose it is a bit lonely too. Aisling and I still share the master bedroom!

I am losing loads of weight. We walk for miles every

day and there is so much to do. But it is fun.

I have not visited Auntie Annie yet. I still have the present for her in my case and will call in with it as soon as I get a chance. It is hard to get the time. We are always busy doing something or other.

I hope you and Daddy are well. I wonder why you do not write? Is something wrong? I would like to telephone but I have no money left. Please do not work too hard and have a nice rest. And please write soon!

Much love,

Orla xxx.

Every day she writes now, recklessly buying stamps, hoping that a barrage of post will force a reply out of Elizabeth. As a strategy it fails.

And now Orla has no money at all, apart from the sterling Elizabeth has given her for purchases in the North. She hasn't enough Irish money to buy even one more stamp. So she decides to ask Aisling if she would consider being a *bureau de change*.

'No,' Aisling replies kindly, but without hesitation. 'But I'll lend you ten pence. You can pay me back when we get home.' She pauses for a second before adding helpfully, 'Maybe you could use the stamp to send a letter to your father?'

'My father?'

Orla cannot imagine writing to her father, to whom she has hardly ever said more than a few superficial words. She knows he loves her because he looks at her kindly and gives her a kiss before he leaves for work in the morning and before she goes to bed. His face crinkles up happily at these times and his eyes twinkle. But he is not able to talk to her. If she is alone with him, in the car for instance, an awkward silence grows between them and fills up all the space around them. Neither of them can do a thing about it. That is another difference between Aisling and Orla. Their fathers. Aisling has the kind of father who talks.

Orla knows they go for walks together, go to the pictures together. She has met Aisling's father at parties and outings, and he can talk to children as easily and naturally as a woman can. Aisling's father has light, smooth hair, long clean white hands. He wears a tweed jacket and fawn trousers. His shirts are pale green, pale yellow, pale turquoise, and seem to be made of some specially soft material. His shoes are suede loafers. Everything he wears is light in colour, to emphasise the cleanliness of his person and perhaps his occupation. In his smoothness, his blondness, his tallness, he seems to Orla to belong to another species from her father. Her small round father, with his red, weathered face, twisted, large hands with fingers as thick as thumbs. On work days he dresses in an old dark grey suit, a torn maroon jumper, huge creased black boots. A battered cloth cap. He smells of mortar, a sour wet smell, when he comes home late in the evenings from the building site.

At dinner he talks about the news, he shouts and rants about the North of Ireland. 'Let them shoot themselves to bleddy bits,' he shouts after his plate of ten potatoes and some meat, when he is drinking his cup of tea and eating a biscuit. 'That's good enough for them. Let them blow themselves out of it, that's all they were ever good for! Bleddy hooey!' he sneers, about something a politician might say. 'They're all the bleddy same, that crowd. Out for what they can get!'

He is vociferous in his condemnation of almost everything that is going on in public life, he distrusts everyone: politicians, public figures, the men who report the news on radio and television. All public life he regards as incorrigibly and inevitably corrupt. That seems to be his long-held and steadfast belief, and you would think he would be used to it all by now. But every day he is angered afresh when he listens to the news. Angered so that his face, relaxed after his meal, grows a fiery red and his usually low, gentle voice is raised in rage over the green tablecloth with a border of ducks, the potato dish and the plate of marshmallow biscuits. You would think he would stop listening to the news, but he doesn't. On the contrary he is addicted to it. The news must be turned on – indeed, the radio is on all the time, from when he and Elizabeth get up, early in the morning, until seven o'clock or later at night, when they turn it off and switch on the television set. He must be clued in to what is going on, in order, it seems, to be enraged.

His other interest is his own past. When he is not shouting about the North of Ireland, about Jack Lynch or Neil Blaney, he tells anecdotes about men he worked with long ago in England and Scotland. He remembers the smallest incidents in great detail, dramatises them and fleshes them out with dialogue. Every word anyone said twenty years ago he recalls. But he never talks about what is going on now, what is going on every day in his working life. It is as if he realises that it is of no interest to Elizabeth and Orla, that it is something they would prefer simply to ignore. Neither does he talk to Orla about her life. Closed books they are, to each other, although they are fond of one another. Or is that a myth, propagated by Elizabeth, who has no compunction about speaking up on behalf of other people? 'Orla is the apple of Daddy's eye,' she says. 'Oh yes, she can do no wrong.' Maybe Elizabeth has said this so often that they have both fallen into the habit of believing it, although no communication of any kind, good or bad, ever takes place between them.

The idea of him writing letters! Orla suspects, dimly, that maybe he can't, except in theory. Read, yes. He reads newspapers and books as often as he can, so slowly and carefully that he remembers them almost off by heart afterwards. But his life has little need or space for writing – apart from measurements: he always has a pencil behind his ear, a ruler in his breast pocket. But his hands are designed for other purposes: to lay stone on stone, brick on brick; to create houses and towns and cities, edifices that shelter and serve, buildings that endure in the landscape. Even looking at those hands, more like paws than hands, you know that they could not easily manipulate something as fine and flimsy as a pen, which is like a needle in a way, and requires the same slim delicate touch to create the same fragile webs as the needle. Orla's father belongs to another kind of humanity, the kind that makes tough, blatant, concrete things, things that are essential, that change the landscape and endure in it.

She can't write to him. All a letter from her would do is surprise and embarrass him. The idea is unthinkable. It surprises Orla that Aisling does not realise this. Although she keeps so many things a secret from Aisling, Orla expects her to understand such things. She even assumes that Aisling must know some of the secrets. She has been to Orla's house, after all. She has sat in the kitchen and watched Orla ignore two or three strange men walking through it to the bathroom, which is tacked on – by Tom, working on Saturday afternoons and summer nights – at the back of the house. Aisling watched them and said nothing, asked no questions. That means she must already have known not only who those men were, but that Orla was not going to talk about them. Orla expected a lot of Aisling.

She's met Tom. She should know that he is not the kind of father you write a letter to. 'Daddy is like Charlie,' she says by way of explanation. Charlie the Faratee she means.

'Like Charlie? Not really!' Aisling ponders this, comparing and contrasting. She likes Tom, although Orla could never believe this. 'He doesn't drink, your father, does he?'

'Oh no,' says Orla. They have seen Charlie swaying home, just once, one Sunday night, and been righteously indignant. Nobody they know drinks, at least unless it is a funeral or Christmas. Tom doesn't drink, or smoke. He doesn't go to the horses or the dogs. All he does is work, at work or at home, sit in front of the telly, and sleep. He's a perfect father in many ways, but Orla isn't satisfied. She wants another kind of father, the kind of father who would write letters to his daughter.

Orla does not stop writing. She has no stamps but she still has paper, wads of it, in her suitcase, blue letter pads and blue envelopes, and also several copybooks for the Irish classes. She writes letters, puts them in envelopes, but doesn't post them: she stacks them on the dressing table, waiting for the day she will have money to buy stamps again. After a while she stops putting the letters in envelopes; she just writes whenever she feels like it and then stuffs the letter into her suitcase, along with the dirty socks and underwear. Some she crumples up and throws out the window, or into the river. That nobody will read the letters no longer matters to her: she feels she is talking to her mother while she is writing them. Orla doesn't consider the matter logically. She stuffs her letters in the bin as she would stuff them in the letterbox if she could. What happens next . . . what happens next is that she starts the next letter.

Aisling sees the envelopes on the dressing table: five of them lie there, propped up by a plaster statue of a woman in a brown habit, some saint, perhaps Saint Thérèse of Lisieux, Aisling thinks. She knows about Orla's predicament but does not consider giving her money for stamps. She gets three pounds a week. It's just enough, really, and giving money to friends is not something anyone does. Orla wouldn't like it. She'd be embarrassed. So reasons Aisling, correctly.

The surprising past
of Tom and Elizabeth

Elizabeth loves Ireland and the Irish language with huge, often-expressed passion. It has never occurred to Orla to ask why. If asked, she would say that she loved Ireland too, and Irish, although ... although, how can she? What is this love, that people talk about? Love your parents, love your country, love your aunt, love your language. People keep ordering her to love them, as they order her to do well in school, to be the best in the class, to make something of herself. To get thinner, to polish her shoes, to set the table, to wash the delph. Love love love! Do it or else!

It surprises everyone to learn that Elizabeth is English. She speaks with a strong Dublin accent, she seldom refers to her past. But it is there, not a secret, just forgotten. Her parents have been dead for years.

She was born on the Isle of Wight of all places, in the village of Shanklin, a place which, in 1925, had as little in common with Tubber, where Tom was being born in that same year, as with a gathering of grass huts on the Trobriand Islands. Shanklin was then, as now, a busy holiday resort, known for its smugglers' chine, a shady path snaking down a steep cliff to the Channel, and a summer cottage, mullioned and deeply thatched, which had once been the property of Keats. On the Isle of Wight the nightingale can be heard. It is that much farther south than Tubber.

Elizabeth's parents had owned a small guesthouse on one of the streets of tightly packed, bay-windowed Victorian houses that link the coast of Shanklin and its old picturesque centre with the railway station inland. 'Mount Pleasant House', the sign in the narrow front garden proclaimed. 'Half Board and Full Board. All Rooms Cleaned Daily'. A separate sign saying 'Vacancies' or 'No Vacancies' dangled by a chain from the main sign. Elizabeth's job, one of many she had as a little girl, was to change the smaller sign as the need arose.

Her childhood was not spent swinging around lampposts on a Dublin street, as her accent and demeanour might indicate, but on a beach in the south of England. Breakwaters, bathing huts, Punch and Judy shows. Kiosks gaily striped like Arthurian pavilions displaying buckets and spades, shining rubber beach balls, spinning stars pink and yellow and blue: these were the pictures that filled her childhood. She worked the beach herself, from the age of thirteen, walking all day up and down carrying a tray filled with marinated mussels and pickled cockles, which she sold for a farthing a scoop to people sitting on the sand.

She was doing this in the summer of 1946. Portsmouth had been the target of heavy bombing during the war. The Solent was flecked with battleships, and mines were still being detonated regularly on the island coast, but children who had not been born when the war started built sandcastles and paddled as dark ships passed in front of their eyes on the summer sea, the donkeys plodded in the soft sand, the brass band played at the end of Shanklin pier. 'Rule Britannia', they played. 'It's a Long Way to Tipperary'.

Elizabeth had worked in the kitchen of the base in Portsmouth, as close as a woman would come to action if she stayed in England. She had had a boyfriend, a boy from Taunton. He had been killed in Avranches on the eighth of

June, just two days after D-Day. Since then she had not gone steady with anyone, and from Christmas 1945 she had come to live with her parents again. She knew she would leave the island and thought she would like to live in London, but for the summer she stayed to work the beach.

It was a fine summer, and the brilliant light of the sea and sun attracted her. Each morning her heart lifted, improbably cheerful, when she walked down the sunlit road to the quayside where she bought shellfish and stocked her tray. She had cared about Eddie with a light giddy love, which had seemed to float recklessly above the reality of its time. She had been sorry when the news came. 'Heartbroken', she had said – and acted, and, for a time felt. But that feeling had been as light as the love, and it floated off very quickly. Eddie had not made his mark on her in any way. He had had neither the power to impress her deeply nor the time to leave a mark, by devotion or betrayal. Elizabeth was just twenty when the war finished. Like all girls, she understood that the population of men of her age, in her part of the world, had been depleted. You could see, even in Shanklin, a distinct lack of males in their twenties and thirties. But she was not one of those who worried seriously about this sort of problem, being aware of her position in the sexual pecking order. Elizabeth had abundant black hair, a good complexion, a slender-enough body, by the standards of that time. Since she was thirteen all men had looked at her with careful attention. At almost any time since then, she had been aware of at least half a dozen who let her know that they desired her. Men existed for her, to be chosen by her, not the other way round. There were not so many, the choice was not so apparent now, but she could not believe that for her that would matter.

Tom Crilly had been a private in the 25th Regiment through the sheer bad luck that drafted thousands of Irishmen, citizens of a neutral country, into the British Army. In 1936 he had spent his first winter working in Glasgow as a brickie, and from there he had edged his way down through Manchester, Birmingham,

London as far as Southampton, living in digs, working for Irish contractors on the lump, always itching to move along and see some new place, the gratification of this desire to explore being his compensation for the life of the immigrant labourer. He worked, in those days and now again, from Monday to Saturday, seven in the morning until dark, whenever it fell. On Sundays he slept till eight and then explored his neighbourhood, whatever it happened to be. Edinburgh, Argyll, the Hebrides, the Cotswolds. York Minster, Westminster Abbey, Salisbury Cathedral. Folkstone and Dover, the Vale of the White Horse. The tourist spots of England, Scotland and Wales were as well known to him as to any well-heeled visitor from America or the Continent, motoring through the land in the mild summer months with baskets of chicken and strawberries in the boot, or travelling in first-class railway carriages, dining on roast beef with silver cutlery and crystal as the burgeoning elm trees brushed the windows of the train. He went on a bicycle, on Sundays spread over three years, to all the requisite places. How did he even know where to go? He read about them, in books bought at second-hand shops. *Know Your England.* Baedeker. Along with other books, collections of poetry, mainly romantic, always nineteenth-century. He had a special old suitcase for books, carted around the land along with his small cardboard case containing suit, work clothes, underpants. Wordsworth and Coleridge, Keats and Shelley. Lord Byron was his favourite. He knew *Childe Harold* by heart.

In so far as he had any political views he was with de Valera – neutral, listing towards Germany rather than England. English people as Tom had known them in Ireland were an overclass, superior, polite, dangerous. In Scotland and England his close associates were Irish expatriates, and the English he encountered in the shape of landladies or occasional tradesmen he could not connect with the political entity known as England, represented for him by the King, whom he could not take seriously, and by Winston Churchill, whom he disliked

149

because he was too fat, pompous, snobbish. It seemed to Tom, in so far as he considered it at all, that the few poor English people he met were more essentially Irish than anything else, had more in common with him than with the other English, who ruled the country and whose war it really was. He did not know much about Hitler until the war was half over. The prisoners of war he encountered he pitied. He was frequently in the guardroom being punished for giving cigarettes to German prisoners. He had not wanted to be engaged in the war and his record was inglorious. Some weeks before the invasion of Normandy he had a period of furlough. His sergeant gave him the nod, suggesting that he would be wise not to return. He deserted, staying in Donegal until the end of 1945. But in the spring of 1946, bored and short of money, he returned to England, running the slight risk of imprisonment. That summer he was working in Southampton, with a builder from Mayo called Healy, a risk taker himself, a crook, who had been in prison three times already on charges of burglary. Healy robbed meters, almost as a hobby — when he was not cutting corners, taking money for work not done, defrauding clients. Times were good for builders, however, just then, and for the moment he concentrated on work rather than crime. Since he was known to be unreliable in paying wages he had to take anyone he could get, and considered himself lucky to get someone like Tom Crilly, a skilled bricklayer but one whom it was an offence to employ.

Tom came to the Isle of Wight in order to look at Keats's cottage. He crossed by ferry to Ryde and then took a bus to Sandown. From there he walked along the cliff path to Shanklin, a walk of about two miles. (It was his habit, whenever possible, to build some sort of outdoor exercise into his Sunday afternoon tours, since he seldom had time to walk during the week.)

When he reached the end of the path he decided to go down onto the beach and eat his sandwich there before looking for the cottage, which is close to the village. This entailed walking down a flight of about two hundred steps, since the cliff is very high at this point. At the bottom of the steps he found Elizabeth, who sometimes stood here when she grew tired of walking up and down the sand. She was wearing a short blue dress, considerably shorter than the style dictated by the fashion moguls of 1946. Elizabeth had some long skirts but considered them too hot, and perhaps also too maidenly, for the seaside. Even then she had a mind of her own.

Tom stared at her hair, which looked as if it was on fire. Elizabeth felt his stare but paid no attention to him, not even shifting her leg or arm. She was used to being stared at.

'I'm looking for Keats's cottage,' he said, actually looking at the mussels in her tray. 'Do you know where it is?'

'Yes,' Elizabeth said. 'It's just at the top of that flight of steps. You go back up and then walk down the first road you come to and you'll see it.'

'Will you come with me, please?' Tom asked.

'Come with you? Up all them steps?'

'I'll carry your things.'

He kissed her in a secluded, shaded, almost damp spot, under a eucalyptus tree, at the bottom of one of the lawns that sloped gracefully away from the cottage on all sides, a spreading grass gown. His brownish face was dappled by sun leaking through the leaves, and his hair on that day was very crispy, very blond. He had let it grow after the army, and had washed it the night before. It was alive, electric around his head like a lion's mane, a halo. She liked that. Eddie had had ordinary brown hair, straight, not lively. She liked Tom's blue, smallish, humorous eyes, his bulky hard body, well-knit, his flat, huge, dinnerplate, bricklayer's hands. She kissed him back.

Thrushes, finches, starlings sang. The air was full of twittering. Leaves rustling, birds singing, grass creeping. The breaking sea murmured in her blood.

He gave her his address in Southampton, written on a

cigarette packet, and he told her where he lived in Ireland. Tubber, Donegal. 'I'll write a note,' he said. 'I'll come again next Sunday and meet you.'

He did not come the following Sunday, and he did not write. It was that – that he let her down – as much as his beautiful hair and his interest in Keats that inspired her love for him. Also that he was the first, not the first she had done it with, because Eddie had been that – it was your duty, almost, as a soldier's girl – but the first she had loved it with. The first time she had felt birds whistling in her own body. She did not believe he had forgotten her, knowingly abandoned her; she guessed there was some good reason for it. But she did not know the reason and therefore she was not certain, not absolutely certain, that he had not left her, as men leave women who are not beautiful. So, for the first time, she felt insecure of a man's love, and she began to yearn for him as other, less beautiful, women yearn for men who have grown tired of them.

She waited for a month and then she wrote to him at the address in Southampton. She got a reply, but not from him. 'Not at this address' was the reply, written on her own envelope. Then she went to the address in Donegal. Tubber. It was easier to get there than she had imagined. A long journey, of about twelve different legs, but once she started it was easy. One step after another. And when she arrived there, in Tubber, it was easy to find his home. He was there. Surprised to see her. But there. She found out why he had left England – to escape imprisonment, a long complicated story in which the criminality of Healy, from Mayo, played the major part – but she did not find out why he had not written to her to explain what had happened. She understood that much later, when she had been married to him for several years and began to understand his character – Irish, or masculine, or individual, or whatever it was.

Talking to a friend

On their walks, or at the meals, or in bed, Aisling and Orla hardly ever talk about problems, and this is one of the factors that distinguish them sharply from older girls, or women. To some extent they are like boys: they still use conversation for fun, or else to project whatever image of themselves they believe will make a favourable impression. Often these two objectives can be combined. Orla has decided, however, that she will best achieve her ends by remaining silent. There is too much in her life that she wants to keep hidden from Aisling, hidden from anyone that she calls a friend – she has not experienced enemies at all, does not understand that the line separating enemies from friends is blurred, or invisible, and constantly shifting.

Aisling has secrets, but they are not the same as Orla's. Orla never tells anything about her family because everything about them is too shameful. Aisling, on the other hand, uses her family constantly as raw material, for an ongoing stream of jokes and anecdotes. Aisling believes she is critical of her family. Her stories are peppered with sarcastic comments on every member of it. But Orla knows that she admires them. In fact Orla believes, in her darker moments, that Aisling is showing them off, her amazing, funny family.

She has a true gift for dramatisation. Everything that happens is transformed into a story. 'So at that moment Sean walked in with his plate of six cream crackers and cheese. "Where on earth have you been till this hour young man?" Daddy said. Daddy was really getting mad. "Oh," said Sean. "Were you worried or something?" "Well, just a tiny bit," Dad said in his most sarcastic voice. "I mean it is only two o'clock in the morning and we have been sitting up specially only for two hours and I do have to get up for a really important meeting at six-thirty today but no, no, of course we're not really worried. Now where the hell were you?" "Gosh sorry, Dad," said Sean, munching a cracker. "I was just down at the pub." "Just down at the pub?" "Yes." "But you don't drink. You've taken the pledge." "I wasn't drinking. I was nursing Seamas Barry. His head got chopped off."

' "Whaah?" we all screamed. "His head got chopped off?" "Well, you know, not literally. But he fell off his bike in town after the debate and was all cut up. I had to call the ambulance and stay with him and so on." ' Every day in Aisling's household is full of such events, such conversations, such battles of wit, usually between the two stars of the family, her brother Sean and her father Ciaran. To Orla, it sounds like the sort of life portrayed on *The Donna Reed Show*: eventful in a nice, always witty way, a way that reflects well on all concerned. Nobody in these stories behaves badly. Nobody has a serious row, or cries, or screams. Nobody is ever sad. A veritable comedy. That is what Orla finds herself saying to herself, as she listens, avidly, to the ongoing saga.

She feels she knows everything about Aisling's household, all their habits, all their jokes. She knows what they eat for their breakfast (muesli and orange juice) and their supper (cream crackers). She knows the names of all their neighbours and what they do for a living and what they talk about, and she knows who has a swing in their garden and who goes to France on their holidays. Although she has only met Aisling's family once or twice, she feels she knows them inside out. She wonders if they have so much information about her. Does Aisling go home and report on life outside, life in school, in the same way that she does the opposite? Orla can't imagine this other side of the coin. She can't imagine being a character in one of Aisling's stories, a character with amusing habits and lines of hilarious dialogue, rather than a listener. She can't imagine, doesn't want to imagine, a fictional existence for herself, separate from her real self, the kind of wonderful but curtailed life that Sean and Ciaran and Nuala have in Aisling's tales.

Aisling knows so little about Orla. (But maybe that wouldn't stop her? Wouldn't stop her inventing a character called Orla, based on lack of knowledge, or on what she sees that Orla does not see? Orla skips away from the terrifying and tantalising thought, scuttles into the privacy of her burrow when the suspicion crosses her mind.) Orla offers no stories in return for the wealth of gossip, of information and invention, that she gets from Aisling. How could she reciprocate? It is not that life in her house is uninteresting. In a way, even she can see that it offers as much in the way of fodder for chat as Aisling's, more even. The lodgers, for instance, their looks and their histories and their habits, give her plenty to think about and could give her plenty to talk about too. And they have their own stories, ready-made, packaged, ready-to-shoot. Every day one or another has something to report, something big and dramatic from the adult world of work, of men, even of love. The lodgers come from all kinds of places; they have experienced marvels. One of them knew a murderer. His own brother killed his father with a hammer on the day before St Patrick's Day four years ago. Mad. The brother was mad. He'd been let out of the asylum for St Patrick's Day as a special treat and that was how he used the holiday. One lodger fell in love with a nurse in London but she did not fall in love with him. He followed her from London to Birmingham, and from Birmingham to Cavan, where she was from, where she had

155

gone on a holiday, or to escape from her suitor. Elizabeth and Orla were party to this chase, to his desperate, terrible love. They were in on all of that, the only two women in his life that he could turn to for sympathy. They gave him his breakfast and brushed the shoulders of his sports coat the day he took a taxi the whole way from Dublin to Cavan to plead with this girl to marry him. And they were there the next day when he came back on the bus. She'd said no. That is all he told them. No. They could see the deflation in his eyes, his red skin, all the hope and fight gone out of him. They could taste the tragedy. Even Orla cried for him.

And nearly all the lodgers confide in Elizabeth readily, turn to her for advice and comfort. She is like their mother, as well as being Orla's mother. More useful to them in a way than their own mothers, objective, more of a friend.

Other things go on too where Orla lives, on Orla's street. It is close to Aisling's place but it is another world. Another world. The long-haired good-looking woman in the wheelchair who lives in the biggest house on the street had got compensation because a sailor threw her off a ship in Dublin's dockland. That is what Orla has heard from Elizabeth, but Elizabeth has not explained why. Why did a sailor throw her off a ship? What was she doing there? She bought her house with the money she got after the court case, the compensation. The like of her getting compensation! Elizabeth has set up a group on the street and the aim of this group is to get rid of that woman. Why? Orla does not know, she does not even know where to begin suspecting, she is that innocent. All she knows is that Elizabeth hates the woman in the wheelchair with a terrible vengeance.

Then there is Old Joe across the road, the road's character. Nobody minds about him, or wants to get rid of him. On the contrary, they are rather proud of him. He is ninety years of age and never takes off his coat. He lived during 1916 and all, and his house is full to the roof with old, rotting newspapers. The front garden, and presumably the back, is piled high with brown beer bottles. Rats and mice run around his bed as he sleeps. They run across his face and he just raises his big old hand and brushes them aside as if they were flies. How do people know this? Who has seen it happening? His windows are so dirty, so thickly grey with dust and cobwebs, that no light gets into the house and you can't see in from outside. He has not washed his windows, or washed anything else, in thirty or forty years. Once he was a rich man, a bookie. He had a bookie's shop on Camden Street and another in Rathmines, and went to the races at Leopardstown and Fairyhouse and the Curragh. Even as far afield as Cheltenham. The road's only once-rich man. The woman in the wheelchair is rich, but that is not enough to redeem her. Money from a claim. Not honest money, like Joe's once was, from a betting office.

Later, when Orla grows up, she will remember some of this stuff and use it to spice up dinner conversations or to amuse lovers in the early stages of relationships, while they are still interested in her personal history. But now she can't. It is unspeakable. Too raw, too shocking, it reveals much, much more than she is prepared to reveal. All Aisling's neighbours are cute little families just like her own, or else widows with cats and genteel habits, or old men whose most outrageous adventure is a weekly trip to the public library. Orla's life belongs to another genre, of dubious morality and questionable taste, a genre labelled ADULT. Aisling's is a shiny paperback novel for children under the age of ten. Aisling is an open book, and no wonder.

A lot of the time their talk ranges over safe, easy, neutral ground. They talk about people they both know in school, or now in the Irish college. Who is beautiful and who is not is their main preoccupation.

'Alison is gorgeous, isn't she? She's got that lovely smooth skin. She's as brown as a berry already, I'd love to be like that.'

'Some people are lucky suckers. Pauline looks nice too, doesn't she?'

'She's a very attractive girl,' Aisling says primly.

'She's a bit too tall,' concedes Orla.

'Yeah. I wouldn't like to be that tall.'

'It's nice in a way' – they always qualify every criticism with some comment of this kind, anxious to soften the blow they have inflicted on an absent person and anxious also to appear to be kind and nice. Their intense desire to be nice people, liked by the universe at large, is in constant tension with their equally driving need to criticise everybody in the world. They are always sticking a knife in somebody's back . . . and then pulling it out and caressing and bandaging the wound.

'She'd be a good model,' Aisling nods. 'You have to be very tall to be a model.'

'And she's so slim!'

'Yes, she's really lucky in that way. She eats like a horse too, it's not fair.'

'Some people have all the luck. I'd love to be skinny. Most of the girls in this college are skinny actually.' Orla glances at the jagged line of blue jeans, pastel T-shirts zigzagging between the hedges of lugubrious fuchsia, the wheeling barbs of bramble.

'Apart from us.' Aisling sighs, but not because she is bored. Discussions of the shape of girls' bodies never bore her. This subject, in all its intricacies of hair and complexion and bones and features, colours and decorations and coverings, fatness and leanness interests her and Orla more than any other in the world. They seldom discuss boys' bodies, or boys. Their sexual talk, if that is what it is, is all focused firmly on themselves. To be attractive, to learn how to present the perfect Orla or Aisling, with gleaming hair and glossy, slender limbs enclosed in the most alluring and correct garment, is such a huge preoccupation that it is as yet an end in itself. The goal of it all is as vague and distant as the dream husband. Orla and Aisling and all the girls know that all this effort is in no way connected to the boys who are even now thumping and biffing one another as they straggle or run or kick their way down to the shore. Those boys will not notice whether their hair is washed or greasy, whether they weigh ten stone or eight. They can spot star material like Pauline or Jacqueline all right. But the subtleties of feminine beauty to which Orla and Aisling devote so much thought and energy, so much amateur contrivance, are beyond them.

'I think our problem is that we eat too much,' Aisling laughs, then grimaces. This is not a joking matter.

'*They're* always eating too, as far as I can see.'

'I bet they don't really. I bet they just pretend. Well, I can't do anything about it. I was born with a healthy appetite.'

'Maybe it's the best way to be.'

'It's not. I'd love to have no appetite at all. I'd love to be like Jacqueline, thin as a lamppost and eating nothing.'

'She liked chips.'

'Chips. I don't believe it. I think she just used that as an excuse to get away from here.'

'She was peculiar, wasn't she?'

'God. She was the most peculiar person I ever met. Thank goodness she's left.'

'She was really awful!' Aisling pauses and reconsiders, as if aware that someone might be eavesdropping and finding out that she is not as nice a girl as she should be. 'Of course she was nice in some ways.'

'Oh yes, she was nice in some ways and she looked gorgeous, I thought. That fair hair!'

'I'd love to have fair hair!'

All in English of course. You couldn't, really, have this kind of completely enjoyable and intimate conversation in Irish. Irish was for quite other matters, mostly related to school.

The experience of time passing in the Gaeltacht is a microcosmic version of how time feels throughout life. The first week is interminable: the walks from the house to the school are arduous, the meals are slow and horrible, the lessons drag out. The second week is enjoyable; a routine has been established. Journeys that were painfully long during the first week are manageable now. Compromises have been reached regarding food; expectations on all sides have become realistic. Headmaster Joe knows that the scholars are not going to speak Irish all the time, and that many of them are going to learn none at all during their stay. The scholars understand that they're not going to get delicious food for every meal, that dinners are not to their taste but the suppers are excellent. The banatees realise that they're not going to make a fortune and a lot of little friends from Dublin or Belfast or Derry. Everyone is more or less happy. It is that easy time, which occurs in every enterprise, when the end is comfortably far away, and so is the beginning.

Then the third week comes. Some students have fallen in love, some have made new best friends, one has gone home. Most are very happy. By now, students and teachers know one another quite well, and a teasing relationship exists between them. It is conceded that the college is a success. The students know that no one is going to be sent home for speaking English or for anything else, and the teachers know they won't have to send anyone away. Time moves along at a steady, cheerful clip; it is hard for the children to imagine that there was another life before this, before the Gaeltacht. They don't want to imagine it. School, the city, home become faint memories, shrouded in unreality. The norm is this: living communally, chanting sentences and songs in class, playing games, dancing every night. The norm is your friends and banatee and Headmaster Joe like the pin at the centre of a spinning top. The norm is the green valley, the smell of brambles, the shining lough.

By the third week, Sandra has settled in so happily to her house that she hardly even talks to Orla and Aisling any more. They see her hanging on the arms of Monica and Noeleen, those common, gawky girls, chewing gum and giggling. Monica, who makes up the songs or knows them, seems to keep everyone in stitches all day long. When Orla says 'Caidé mar?'

to her and Sandra, Monica mutters something under her breath ('Cuddy Marley broke her hurley sliding down a heap of shite', actually). Then Sandra, Monica and Noeleen burst out laughing, and laugh until Orla goes away.

Orla feels hurt, and also something else, when this happens: she feels stupid. Sandra was fun, she was a good friend. Now that she's gone – and she's gone, something in her eyes, the blue eye and the brown, indicate that Sandra has had enough – Orla realises what a good person she is, and feels the loss. Elizabeth flits through her mind when she looks at Sandra, her strange hair floating down around her waist. Elizabeth and her 'She's nits!' Elizabeth and her 'They live in a tenement!' What was wrong with Sandra really? She's good enough for Monica, and everyone knows that Monica's father is a doctor (unbelievable as it seems – Some doctor! Aisling says, suspiciously). Still. She's loads of money and three pairs of Levi's so it's probably true, her foul mouth and mind notwithstanding.

Sandra. She's gone. And Auntie Annie is still there, waiting for her stockings. And Elizabeth still hasn't written. But Orla, battered down by all her problems, is beginning to feel comfortable nevertheless. She is beginning to feel liberated from the comparisons that rule her life in Dublin; she feels, almost, the same as everyone else, what she yearns above all to be. She lives in the same sort of house as her peers, eats the same food, is governed by the same regulations. There is a kind of equality here that isn't possible in Dublin, land of 'What Does Your Father Do?' This is the Gaeltacht, a land of the child. What matters is the length of your hair and your skirt, the sweetness of your smile and your voice and your Irish, the lightness of your step, your ability to make friends.

But of course Orla is not entirely free from her family, not like the other children for whom Tubber is a holiday camp only, a haven removed from every adult connection. Orla relishes the freedom and happiness she senses burgeoning all around her, but she feels these feelings under threat. Try as she will she's not an ordinary Gaeltacht scholar. Tubber still contains her relations. And her Auntie Annie.

Most of the relations are all right; they've seen Orla, even said hello to her as she walks the road to school. They don't require much contact; they're busy with their students and they probably realise that Orla would rather be left alone, for now. But Aunt Annie is a different story. She hasn't any students to keep her busy. She won't understand Orla's wish for privacy, her wish not to acknowledge her aunt: how could she? Orla knows she is the focus of her Aunt Annie's attention. She feels it, like an evil eye, staring at her all the time, as she romps and plays and learns Irish.

The only reason Orla has escaped for so long is that Aunt Annie lives miles from the Dohertys' house, far away at the other side of the valley, and Aunt Annie seldom goes out anywhere, except to Mass. Orla has had a hard time avoiding her there, but she's managed to do it so far – she stays at the back of the chapel and dashes out as soon as the priest leaves the altar.

Aunt Annie hobbles up the aisle, hunched like a hedgehog, in her black suit and black hat, her face grimacing and one of her eyebrows ticking, her eyes peering anxiously around, looking for Orla. Orla watches her cautiously, then escapes before she can be caught. Even though she knows that in the end she has to see her Aunt Annie – because she can't go home to Elizabeth if she doesn't – she continues to avoid her. Into the third week, the best week, she does that rather than take the plunge. Take the plunge and get it over with. But what would the consequences of that be? Aunt Annie is not the sort of plunge you can take and get over. She's not rational, she'd want another visit. That Orla is a child is not something her Aunt Annie would understand, or pay any attention to. Elizabeth, who is intelligent, possibly brilliantly so, does not understand this. If she does she has no trouble dismissing it. Orla has no right to be a child. Nobody

162

has or ever had; that is the thinking. Children are there to carry out adults' orders, first and foremost. Their feelings, and adults do not believe they have any, simply don't matter.

Tubber is small. Orla knows she can escape for a while, but not for ever. She is amazed that it has gone on for so long, her avoidance. Every minute, except when she is either safely ensconced in the schoolhouse or hidden deep in the tunnel that covers the burn, she expects to feel the hand on her shoulder. She expects to turn a corner and see Aunt Annie's peculiar face jerking and nodding at her, and her voice squeaking: 'Orla! Is that Orla? And how are ya?' Then Aisling and Sandra and Pauline and the teachers will know. They will know that Orla, whose connections in Dublin are as bad as anyone could wish, has an even worse connection here in Tubber. And they will laugh at Orla behind her back. In their estimation she will sink down to the bottom of the midden, there to remain for ever and ever.

Auntie Annie lives alone in an old farmhouse near the shore: she is the custodian of Orla's ancestral home. This is the house and farm where Orla's father grew up, where the Crillys have lived for perhaps centuries, farming and fishing, spinning and weaving, eating and drinking, living and dying. Dancing, telling stories, singing. Crying. From here Crillys have walked to Derry and taken the boat to Scotland, to New York, to Australia, to Gros Île. To Normandy. To Vietnam.

Crilly men have built the house: they have been masons and carpenters for centuries. Almost every chair and bed and table in it was made by their hands. The old clothes that fill the wardrobes were made by the women: Orla's grandmother, great-grandmother. With wool from their own sheep they spun and wove, dyed and sewed. The house is full of history, it is full of the history of work and creation.

Now it is Auntie Annie's house.

It is here that Orla's family has always taken its irregular holidays. Elizabeth, in her more reckless moments, when she is

163

blind with pride or backed up in some corner of snobbery, calls it 'our holiday home in west Donegal'. There is only one true word in that phrase, namely 'Donegal'. The house is not even in west Donegal, but in the east of that county. 'East', however, is not a good enough word. It is not a tourist word, so Elizabeth, travel agent for the nation, would eschew it automatically. Or perhaps her ignorance of locations is partly real. Lots of women, lots of other people too in those days, could be vague on geographical distinctions of even the most basic kind.

Elizabeth also ignores Aunt Annie, or is ignorant of whatever it is that is wrong with Auntie Annie. There is plenty wrong with her that Orla can see: she is out of kilter, not plumb with the world. Her face is crooked, her mouth is crooked, and she walks with a clumsy and awkward gait; her feet cannot be relied upon to meet the ground at every step. What we would say now is that she lacked co-ordination. When she sets a cup or saucer on the table it often misses and falls to the stone floor. She grabs the handles of red-hot saucepans with her bare hands and gets burnt. Her voice emerges not in the rhythmical singsong of the native accent or the flat tones of Dublin, but in a jerking staccato, screeching one minute, inaudible the next. Observing Auntie Annie you understand that normality consists in being even. Normal people are people who are more or less identical to everyone else, and who fit, tongue and groove, foot and slipper, into their time and place. Normal people are in tune, and the most normal people of all are those who hear the latest air split seconds before the majority and set the tone, beginning to sing in time to it, split seconds ahead of the posse. Everyone in Tubber, almost everyone, is out of step with Dublin and Derry, and by extension the rest of the western world, but on the whole they have their fingers on the pulse of their own region. Its norms, however complex and strange, a mixture of old and new, are known to them, consciously or otherwise. They are not known to Auntie Annie. She is in Tubber but positioned at

164

an oblique angle to it. There was a crooked woman and she had a crooked house. And that woman is Orla's aunt.

The people of Tubber do not mind. They can deal with the strangeness that crops up among them, especially if it is a strangeness bequeathed by nature. If somebody among them walks crooked they will try to prop that person up so that they can survive in the symmetrical world. Their ethos is that of the neighbourhood more than of the clan or of the family. Networks of friends other than relations or neighbours are completely foreign to them. Because Auntie Annie is either their distant cousin or else their neighbour they look after her, keep an eye on her, do the work that the members of her own family don't do or won't or can't do because they have moved away to another neighbourhood. The more go-ahead people in Tubber, people who have made the transition from the older rural values to a new set not unlike those that prevail in the city, realising that Dublin is not an unsurmountable distance away, might frown and say, 'The Crillys should do something about Annie Crilly. It's not right that they leave her there alone and depend on the neighbours to look after her. She's their responsibility.' But the others ask no questions. For them connections and responsibilities are ordained by physical closeness more than by ties of blood. 'Ar scáth a chéile a mhaireann na daoine,' they believe. Meaning that neighbours must rely on one another. This is a neighbourhood where most people's closest relations live in, say, Philadelphia and come home once in ten years on big holidays, celebratory, boozy, disruptive. Those who stay behind, the survivors or the abandoned, feel more kinship with one another than with those who went away, even if they are their own brothers and sisters.

Their own nephews or nieces.

Orla mutters to herself that she hates Auntie Annie. What she feels is not hatred, however, but the feeling that is much more familiar to her, and that is worse. Shame. She is so ashamed of

165

her aunt that she wishes she did not exist, which is further than you usually go with hatred, that being reserved for people you once loved, probably quite a lot. And what is this shame if not fear, born of a suspicion, an acknowledgement, that Auntie Annie is of no use to her? Is, in fact, a most serious threat? Some relations are an asset because of their good looks or their charm or their money or their success. Lucky relations, their luck spreading from them through the blood of the family. And others are a hindrance. As a relation, Auntie Annie is a disaster. Orla knows that if her friends see her aunt she herself will lose whatever status she has in their eyes, which is not very much. Auntie Annie, even more certainly than the lodgers, will pull her down, down to rock bottom, where she will be left alone, alone and unloved. That is what she fears.

She feels frustration, too, that Tubber, the idyllic village of her history and her dreams, has to be spoiled for her by Auntie Annie. Paradise Valley, and her closest relation in it is the valley simpleton.

Orla knows people who have handicapped brothers or sisters, children with big smooth troll-ugly faces and short plump lopsided bodies. There are plenty of them in Dublin. They are different from Auntie Annie. They are labelled. 'Handicapped' is the label of the time, although like all such labels it changes every twenty years or so. These children – and it is the children one sees mostly, rather than the adults – go to special schools or workshops, often on special marked minibuses, white minibuses with windows full of their strange, broad faces, minibuses that position them firmly on the outside of ordinary society, since all ordinary children travel on double-decker buses or on foot. Their families, although they suffer terrible practical depriva- tions and terrible emotional worries, do not, or so it seems to Orla, suffer from damage to their pride. (She is wrong about this.) The handicapped children are distanced from them to some extent by the label that is attached to them, as they are dis- tanced from everybody else by the special little buses, the special schools, the special jobs. Everyone knows that they are an accident, something that is separated from the family norm. Everyone knows that now. They occur because their mothers were too old or because some chromosome got pushed out of place or because they were deprived of oxygen in the birth canal. That is probably what happened to Auntie Annie but nobody in Tubber would have noticed it or known. None of the Crillys have ever mentioned it, discussed it, even thought about it, as far as Orla can see. They have always pretended that Auntie Annie is normal, or else they actually believe that she is normal. And how can that be? How can people look at someone who is so odd and acknowledge nothing? Maybe because so many people in that community have twisted bent faces, as if the God who had made them had suffered from a shaking hand, or a malicious sense of humour. Or maybe because they think it would be unkind to mention any flaw, as it would be unkind to point out that a person was exceptionally ugly, or had a bad portwine stain, or, even, a limp or a crippled leg. Unkind because these things were caused by bad luck or bad behaviour and also because nothing can be done about them. Because they themselves feel powerless to do anything about them. That is it probably. 'What can't be cured must be endured,' they would say, with a deep, resigned sigh. 'It's the will of God. Ours not to reason why.' All their proverbs tell them to shut up and accept whatever has happened. Their religion tells them that. Also, that deformed people are in the world for a reason, and are dearer to God than the ordinary, robust run-of-the-mill.

Mainly, though, they turn a blind eye to the flaws and lend a helping hand because their deepest instinct is to be kind and charitable to any underdog. People in cities, it is rumoured, love the rich and successful. People in places like Tubber love the poor and the failures.

The unfortunate thing is that Auntie Annie isn't bad enough to need acknowledgement even by people who come from another kind of place, from the city, people who know better.

Like Elizabeth. Auntie Annie doesn't have a big head or a deformed body. She is well able to perform all basic domestic and farm functions adequately. She is almost there but not quite, not quite the full shilling but certainly about eighty per cent of it. She can talk and walk and cook and clean and milk the cow and feed the chickens. She can sell eggs to campers or visitors, if they want them, and she can go to the post office to collect her disability pension (so someone had acknowledged something – when? who? the doctor, maybe, or the district nurse). She can dress up in her good clothes – of which she has wardrobesful, masses of silk and crêpe and fine flowing jersey, in the dark and plummy colours and clumsy, jerky shapes of decades gone by, sent in brown parcels over the years from England and America and never thrown away – and go to town, if someone gave her a lift, and to the chapel every Sunday. That is all she needs to do to survive, to live. It is not necessary to go to school or take an exam, to clock in at a job. With her tiny pension and tiny farm she manages, she is a completely self-sufficient person, not even, it seems, poor or deprived. Her house is comfortable: warm as an oven, clean as a cat. Beautiful, since nobody has ever bothered to change it in fifty years. And she looks almost like anybody else.

As a matter of fact she looks like Orla. At least that is what people in Tubber say.

'You're the image of your Aunt Annie!' They see the same colouring, the same shape of face and feature, and ignore the differences of age and expression and fashion, which to them are an irrelevance. They do not seem to know anything about children, or perhaps they know but do not care. They do not know that children want to look only like themselves, or else, perhaps, like the most glamorous person they know. Orla would not mind being told that she looks like Mary Quant or Twiggy, but she does not want to look like her mother or her father or any of her relations, and she certainly can't bear to be told that she looks like Auntie Annie.

It is another reason for wanting to avoid her, not wanting to look at her twitching strong unadorned face, her sometimes sour and resentful face, and think that that, and not the familiar and, it seems to Orla, pleasant if flawed image that appears in the mirror, is what she looks like.

So the package containing the used elastic stockings lies in the corner of her suitcase, a repulsive reminder of her duty, a mark of her guilt. Because she knows she should be kind to Aunt Annie. She knows she should acknowledge her. This has been impressed on her by Elizabeth, who for some reason wishes to force Orla to face this demon, to confess it, to show her aunt to her friends, to her girlfriends. Maybe because Annie is not Elizabeth's own relation and does not tarnish her image in any way, she would like Orla, superior intelligent educated, rather standoffish Orla, to have to face the fact of Aunt Annie. Orla's aunt, Orla's blood, so much so that Orla looks like her. That, Elizabeth thinks, will be good for Orla and force her to see where she fits into the great order of the universe, lest she begin to feel she is superior to Elizabeth.

Or maybe it is not so vindictive. Maybe Elizabeth wants to place Orla side by side with Aunt Annie so she can show Orla off. Look, she might think. That is where my husband comes from. This is his sister. And look what I have done for him, see what I have created. Orla. A pretty and normal child, clean and nicely dressed, with a smooth face and clever eyes. Spot the difference! Elizabeth, like all mothers, uses her child to demonstrate to the world what she once was. I am old and ugly now, they say, but look at this, look at this. As she is now, so was I. And also to say, I am out of touch with things but look at her. She is with it. She is in the right place and the right time. Deal with me through her because she is the one who represents our family now. She is the family future, the embodiment of its achievement so far. She can speak grammatical English and fill in forms, she can make telephone calls to authoritative figures and remain cool. Thus far have we advanced. Maybe this is

169

how Elizabeth sees it. Whatever the reasoning behind her insistence that Orla show Auntie Annie to her friends, she does not do the same herself. She has never, for instance, considered inviting Auntie Annie to stay with them in Dublin, not even for a weekend, even though the Crillys are regular visitors to the house in Tubber.

The road to the shore

It is because Aunt Annie lives near the sea that Orla avoids swimming, although she loves swimming more than anything else. Aisling, who suspects something, nags her. 'Why don't you ever go swimming? I'm sick and tired of rounders every day. This is supposed to be the summer, our summer holiday, for heaven's sake!'

Orla always makes some excuse. It is surprising how many excuses she can make up, when pushed. Her powers of invention know no limit. She is sick, she is cold, she is tired, Monica laughed at her swimming togs. She is afraid of Killer Jack.

The worst thing that could happen for Orla is a spell of good weather. But this so seldom occurs in Donegal that it would be a miracle if it did. Miracles occur, though. Even Ireland has an occasional heatwave and in the third week in July, until then one of the coldest Julys on record, the summer weather arrives, like a film star suddenly pulling up in a silver Rolls-Royce in the muddy farmyard and halooing to the farm folk, as they emerge, blinking, from their dark byre or barn: 'Yoo hooo! I'm here! Surprise surprise!' A blue and gold day, a glamorous day of satin water and azure sky. The temperature is twenty-six degrees. In the eighties, people said then, meaning as hot as abroad, as hot as they could stand, as hot as America or Spain.

'There'll be no games today,' Headmaster Joe announces after An Post. He feels as happy as if he had sent in an application for the good day himself, and was now pulling it out of his sack of letters to present to his charges. 'We'll all go to the beach and stay there until eight o'clock. We're going to have a barbecue. First I'll barbecue myself and then Máistir Gallagher!'

There is a loud cheer. (Which is a different thing from saying 'everyone cheers'. Orla doesn't, and neither do some others for reasons of their own.) By now, students know that although Headmaster Joe has to play gruff and threatening, it's skin-deep: he's not the expelling type. But still, he rules the roost. When she hears the announcement Orla's stomach crumples up and she feels she would like to fall down, to wither up in a little heap on the floor. But she doesn't. Sturdy body, sturdy mind. Later she thought she should have done it. Faked it. Faked a faint. She realises, all of a sudden, that probably many fainting fits, and other physical manifestations of psychological shock, are faked, and that the world is not filled with strictly sincere people as she has been taught by her schoolteachers, although not by her mother. And a faked faint at that point would be enough to get her off the hook, for then and perhaps for ever. But Orla cannot do it, she cannot put on an act – she has one of those stiff natures that cannot bend itself to another role. It is not a virtue: rather a mixture of gaucheness and slow-wittedness that has rendered her the way she is.

So she goes to the beach, a lamb to the slaughter, and for decades afterwards she will metaphorically go to the same beach. Do things she hates doing, see people she would rather not see, sacrifice herself. She will go on believing that she must do what she is asked to do, not what she wants to do herself. She will do this so often and so systematically that eventually she will not know what it is she wants, one way or the other – and that will become a problem too. That is how it is for girls, in 1972. Doing what you are told is ethics, philosophy, morality, religion, all rolled into one. It is the key to happiness and peace of mind, to every kind of success. This is what girls believe. What other people tell you to do is always right. Other people are adults, teachers, the Church, the government. Or anybody else really who has ideas to force on girls. Trust them all, they know what's best for you.

It's easy when you get the hang of it, easier than any other system of getting through life. Most of the time. Most girls will be reluctant to abandon it as a way of life. Many never will. How can they? They've been taught, from babyhood, not to think or ask questions, to turn their backs on their own souls.

The students walk in a straggling broken line from the schoolhouse to the beach, a curling meandering snake about half a mile long slowly moving through the valley. Some of them carry damp striped hand towels, in which their swimming togs are rolled up. Others have sports bags, or plastic bags, or string bags. Lucky students, like Pauline, chew gum or even lick chocolate, while most snatch fuchsias from the wayside bushes and suck from them, desperately and optimistically, the pinpricks of sweetness. Mostly the flowers taste of nothing, but once in ten sucks you could get the faintest suggestion of watery honey.

> 'Tá an bláthóigín ag fás i lár an fhraoigh
> Goirtear di
> Erika!
> Bíonn na mílte beach ag dordán leo de shíor!
> Goirtear di
> Erika!'

Thus sings Headmaster Joe, in a sweet clear tenor. It is his favourite song from their songbook, *Abair Amhrán* – a rousing Nazi march, but nobody knows this, except maybe the people who compiled that songbook. It is a wonderful song, cheerful and rousing, about heather and bees and walking in the hills. The children sing along with him for a while, joining in the chorus with a shout that reverberates around the valley: 'Goirtear di Erika!'

Aisling and Orla talk about their futures.

'I'm going to have a cream dress.' Aisling's voice is serious. She is discussing her wedding, a matter to which she periodically turns her most concentrated attention. 'A silk cream dress, with lilies of the valley in my hair. I want it to be really simple and natural. The bridesmaids will wear long pink dresses.'

'I hate pink,' Orla says, forgetting to be cautious, carried away by the fascination of the topic. 'Mine are going to have green.'

'I never heard of bridesmaids wearing green. I hope to God I'm not one of them. I don't mean a kind of ordinary pink, I mean the very palest sort of pink, a sort of creamy peachy pink. And I want them to carry tiny pink roses and have white straw hats.' Aisling changes her mind about the details of her wedding almost daily, but there are always a lot of details all the same.

'That sounds nice enough.' Orla is unconvinced. The wedding plan is not as preoccupying today as usual, because of the imminent danger.

'I don't know where I'll go on my honeymoon, though,' Aisling muses, moving along.

'I think I'd like to go to somewhere really different.'

'Like Siberia you mean. Like Outer Mongolia. I'm going to Paris. That's where Mummy and Daddy went, actually. You know Daddy said to Mummy, which would you like a week in Paris or a house, and she said a week in Paris. Where did your parents go?'

'I'm not sure,' Orla lies. 'I must ask them. I think Spain or something boring like that.'

'Oh yeah. Well Marie Fitzgerald went to Spain. They went to Spain. She liked it. She brought us back this lovely tablecloth with a long yellow fringe and bullfighters on it.'

Actually Elizabeth and Tom went to Bundoran. They brought back a teapot, one of those teapots like a yellow house, with *Present from Bundoran* across the side.

'What is your husband going to work at?'

'I think he'll be a journalist, like Daddy. Or a lawyer, maybe. Mummy says lawyers are richer than journalists and I'd like him to be rich. I want to have a huge house and a servant.'

'Me too. Though nobody has servants really.'

'Tell us another. Of course they do. Denise Murphy from Monaghan, they have two servants. She's always talking about them. Showing off. Not showing off actually, I don't think she means to show off but mentioning them, you know. Just mentioning them about a million times an hour. Haven't you heard her?'

'I don't really talk to her all that much. I want my husband to be a teacher.'

'A teacher?'

'Yes. I think, you know, it would be nice with the holidays and everything.'

'But men aren't. I mean, it's an OK job for a woman, being a teacher, but it's not a good job for a man. Did you actually think being a teacher was a good job?'

Orla does. She thinks it is one of the best jobs in the world, because Elizabeth has told her teachers are very well paid. The life of Reilly they have, she said, huge salaries and long holidays, sure they have it all sewn up.

'Well, maybe a doctor then.' An image passes across the window of Orla's brain: Micheál, in his green jumper, pushing the cows across the yard. She pushes it away without lingering on it for a moment.

Aisling is offering advice. 'You should do medicine then, if you want to marry a doctor. You know what Sister Veronica says: on your honeymoon you have to be able to talk about what he's interested in, otherwise he'll get bored with you. And you know, not like you any more.'

'I could do nursing. I don't think I'll be bored on my honeymoon anyway. I think we'll be busy, swimming and looking at things, and going shopping. I'm going to leave lots of things for the house until I go on my honeymoon so I can buy exotic stuff in the bazaar. Silk cloths and little things made of copper and brass.'

Orla envisages her husband on his honeymoon, the husband who will accompany her on her swims and to the bazaar, and he always looks the same to her. Bridegroom Man. He has thick smooth black hair and a regular face, with a shy, honest, wide-awake look in his eyes. A quiet, observant, intelligent face, is what he has. And he is dressed in a dark jacket and white shirt. His skin is sallow and he is so clean, so clever, so handsome that she defers to him all the time, treats him as if he were made of china, or as if he were a precious pedigree pet. Which he is, Bridegroom Man. Delicate and highly strung, refined, clean. She has never seen a man like this and she does not know where her picture comes from. When he touches her – brushes her arm, places his warm, dry hand on her cheek – he treats her as she treats him. They are both exquisitely sensitive, delicate people. There he is, waiting for her, waiting to love her and marry her and bring her to the bazaar.

> 'They say that in the Gaeltacht
> The boys are very fine
> You ask for Elvis Presely
> And they give you Frankenstein ...
> I
> don't want no more of Gaeltacht life ...'

It is Monica Murphy, chanting behind them. 'Talkin about fellas, girls?' she taunts.

'Shut up, Monica.' Aisling is prim, hot, embarrassed.

'Ooh aah, ooh ah ah, I left my knickers in my boyfriend's car!' responds Monica. Sandra, who is linking her, joins in.

'Ná bígí ag labhairt Béarla!' warns Killer Jack, carelessly, patrolling the outside of the line.

Monica smirks at him and says, 'Nílimid ag labhairt Béarla, a mháistir! An mbeidh tú ag an chéilí anocht?'

'Och tusa,' he says, and passes on. It's too hot to care about Irish or English today.

Monica strikes up again.

> 'Aisling and Seamas sat under a bush
> Says Seamas to Aisling "You're my little thrush!
> I'm only a boy but I'll soon be a man
> And I'll make you Mrs Seamas as soon as I can!
> Tooraloo! Tooralay!
> I'll make you Mrs Seamas O'Meara some day!"'

The crocodile has reached the bend in the road where Auntie Annie lives. The house is concealed by trees, right on the corner where the main road is joined by the lane leading down to the sea. You can see the slated roof and, at the back, the window of the small bedroom where Orla usually sleeps when she stays there, a room lined with cream timber, a smell of mothballs pervading it. On the main road there is a gate to Aunt Annie's yard and then, around the corner, another small entrance without a gate. Two ways in and two ways out. Orla fixes her eyes on the blue, sweating tar, considering the implications of this. Aisling's voice continues, the buzz of the thousand bees, the singing of Headmaster Joe, the lower singing of Monica and Sandra and Noeleen. Alison from Terenure, who has a loud soprano, belongs to some special choir or other, has burst into an operatic aria. 'I dreamt that I dwelt in marble halls,' she sings, loud enough for the world to hear. She sounds like an angel, so good that they let her sing in English. The teachers, that is. The students, a lot of them, mock her, accuse her of showing off.

> 'With vassals and serfs at my side
> And of all those who walked within those walls . . .'

'That I had the biggest backside!' adds Monica.

Orla is giggling, choking on the giggles, the fear, as they round the bend. She knows that even if Aunt Annie is not at

177

the first gate she could be waiting just around the next bend, at the back entrance.

She needn't worry. Annie is at the first post. She has come up from the house to the top of the street, and she's sitting on a big stone that stands near the gateway. Lying in wait. Her face is all smiles, festooned with them. She is wearing her navy-blue overall and her old white runners, unlaced, muddy from slapping around in the chicken shit. Her legs stick out from the stone like sticks, white and gnarled with varicose veins.

She smiles and waves at Orla.

Orla waves back. But it is a tiny wave, an excuse of a wave, meant to suggest to anybody watching that she is one of the crowd.

'Who is that?' Aisling has stopped giggling. She is a little shocked by Auntie Annie, who would shock anyone from Aisling's background, just by her appearance.

'Oh some local person,' says Orla, her voice prim and low. She can hardly get the thin, mean lie out. Above all she does not want Monica to notice what is going on.

'Well I gather that, Orla,' says Aisling, not too kindly. 'I mean I didn't think she was a tourist from New York or something.'

'Orla.' Auntie Annie calls her name in a surprised tone. Orla and Aisling have passed her by. She is looking after them, at their backs, as they approach the corner where the road turns towards the shore.

Monica hears. 'Somebody's looking for you,' she says to Orla. Orla's stomach turns to water. Her legs weaken. Monica looks back and sees Auntie Annie, who is standing up on her wobbly feet, whose face is not smiling now, but stunned.

Orla looks at Monica looking at her Auntie Annie and waits for the insult, waits for her world to collapse.

But Monica says nothing at all. She looks at Orla, her cheeky face puzzled, and then at Sandra. 'Race you to the beach!' she says to the latter. 'Last one there is a rotten tomato!'

Aisling is not so easily deflected. 'That woman is calling you,' she says. 'Why don't you talk to her?'

'Why should I?' says Orla.

'Well, it's normal to talk to people who say hello to you.'

'I don't feel like it,' Orla says. 'I don't even know who she is. Some sort of village idiot. She knows me because we stay near here when we come on our holidays.'

'Where do you stay? Which house?'

'You can't see it from the road. It's over there, behind those trees.'

Alison is still singing. She has smooth creamy skin, sallow, as few Irish girls have, and a wide mouth, a shining, happy face. All this as well as her glorious angelic voice, a voice like the summer sun. Such girls must be happy.

> 'And best of all as I walked those halls
> I knew that you loved me still.
> I knew that you loved me still.'

The sun, the sun, the sun

The heatwave continues. Every morning when they wake up, the sun is pouring into the room, butterscotch hot. The sky is a clear plane of milky blue, unthreatened by any cloud. The lough twinkles at the bottom of the valley like a flashing turquoise star. Very soon you begin to feel that the place has always gleamed like this, that it has been this palette of fresh green and gold and heartbreaking blue for all eternity.

Walking down to the schoolhouse makes them sweat. The backs of their necks burn, their arms and legs bronze. Within days almost everyone looks healthier and more beautiful. It is as if nature ensures that their bodies blend in with the perfect landscape, the light of the brilliant summer. Most of the children look as elastically smooth as spring leaves. Even those whose skin turns red instead of tan give off a nutty electric glow.

Morning lessons are cut by an hour to allow the students to get the benefit of the fine weather. Every afternoon they go to the beach and spend three or four hours there. After the day when Orla denied her, Aunt Annie has not come out. Orla wonders vaguely if she is offended, and hopes, crazily, that she is not. But she does not care very much. The relief of not having to worry about her is greater than the burden of guilt. She would like, she realises, Aunt Annie to be dead. This is such an un-nice wish that as soon as it enters her head she pushes it back. Of course you don't, she says to herself. Of course you do, she says to herself. Think how easy it would be if she simply did not exist at all. Then you would be free to go to the shore whenever you liked. You and Elizabeth and Tom and Roddy could come to Tubber for holidays and not have them spoiled by her. The house would really become a summer home, and not what it now is.

The heatwave is too hot for fat people and old people, but Orla loves it. The afternoons on the beach are perfect. For ever after, this will be her vision of paradise: a rocky cove, a silver beach, a crowd of children scattered across it like oystercatchers under the faithful blue sky. The diamond swords glinting in the waves, the terns diving.

She likes to change rapidly, to rush down and jump from a dark grey rock whose tiny pointed barnacles bite the soles of her feet into the softness of the water. The water is always cold, even though the air temperatures are high, but she doesn't care about that. She succumbs to the silky softness of it, feels protected like a moth in amber. The clarity, the coolness enrapture her. She likes to swim with her face just under the surface, watching the rippling trellis of gold that the reflected waves cast against the sand. She likes to see the darting shoals of tiny fish, quick and nebulous as clouds of dust, shivering around under the water. She likes the hanks of yellow-brown kelp, and waving elf-green fronds of sea grass, the black jungle stiffness of sea rods. She does not often lift her eyes to the rounded hills, pale in the descending sun, at the other side of the lough, or to the boathouse, or to the silhouettes of noisy figures perched around the beach behind her. All her concentration is on the water. It pours over her, it redeems her.

Afterwards, she roasts on the sand, working on her tan. Nobody worries about ultraviolet rays, nobody realises that children should not get sunburn. Headmaster Joe encourages it! 'Nothing does you as much good!' he says. 'It'll set you up for

181

the winter. Off with those clothes and let the sun get at you.'
Some of the children are red as lobsters, their skin peeling from
their hot backs and chests in white flakes, like snow or dandruff.
They show it off. They revel in it. Look at me! Nobody has
cream, or protective lotion of any kind. Not even Nivea or
Pond's. The sun is perceived as the friend of children, not
another enemy to be warded off and defeated.

The hot weather and the trips to the beach liberate everyone.
Teachers sit together beside Lynchs' black boat, which is tied up
at the back near the river. The students scatter all over the strand,
spill over into the boathouse. A teacher is always supposed to be
in the water, making sure nobody goes out too far. But in fact
this does not work. The children want to stay in for hours, and
run in and out, and no adult can stand it for that long.

Pauline has found another liberation. She has found an escape
route, and has commandeered none other than Gerry – teacher's
pet, star student, Irish speaker *par excellence* – to be her partner in
crime. Gerry doesn't want to escape. He is happy where he is,
surrounded by the comforting forces of law and order. But he
fancies Pauline, and there is a price to be paid for that.

Now is the moment for the bold to assert their independence.
The tide is right. Pauline knows it. The atmosphere is so relaxed,
everyone is so drunk on summer, that teachers have ceased to
keep the constant watch they kept during the first week or
two. They have learned to trust their charges. This is the
dangerous time.

Pauline noticed that she needs to stay on the beach at the
beginning, when each teacher is still connected to his own class
and would notice if anyone was absent. And she needs to be
there at half past five for the walk home. But between half past
two and half past five there is no way of watching her. She could
be in the water, she could be in the boathouse – in the glare of
sunshine, the distinctions between the children become blurred.
They all look the same in their swimsuits, a darting shoal of fish.
It's easy for one or two of them to slip away unnoticed.

The girls use the old boathouse, crumbling and delapidated, as their dressing room – they are much too modest to undress out on the open beach, where the boys and the teachers are. The boathouse looks like a small church. It is long, dark, musty, damp. It has a cobbled floor which hurts your feet, and it is pervaded by the smell of rotten fish. The girls tend to cluster just inside the doorway, distrusting the darker corners at the back of the building. It seems empty; not even boats are kept in it. But a few old hanks of rope lie around, looming in the dimness. There's a black tyre under the high narrow windows. The dark, the fishy smells, the sandy crunchy floor, are subtly alarming. Nobody dares venture into the murky back of the stinking boathouse. Nobody wants to know what hides there.

Except for Pauline. She ventured down there on the very first day she came to the beach, picking her way over the stinking cobbled floor in her long flip-flops. 'Yuck! How can you?' the others had said, wrinkling their noses. 'You'd never know what's on that floor.' Excrement, they meant. Human and animal. They could smell it, mingling with the sea smells. From that day a tacit commandment was made. Do not go to the back of the boathouse. Pauline chose to ignore it. She walked barefoot on the stinking cobbles. She checked out the one old broken boat, the lobster pots, the hanks of rope. She peered through the windows: two high narrow Gothic openings in the sides of the building, and one larger one, with stone frames though lacking glass, at the back. Behind this window, behind the boathouse, a high overgrown bank looms, stretching from the beach to the fields above. Now Pauline is standing on the slipway, letting the sun burn her back. She is staring at the clotted tangle of bramble, dog rose, hazel and willow. She notices a faint indentation traversing it, zigzagging from top to bottom.

'You can get up that thing!' she informs Orla.

Orla confirms this for Pauline. She tells her a secret: the way from the beach to the top of the cliff is called the Seven Bends, it could be a title for an Enid Blyton book, which is why Orla feels it's a secret which can be shared. Her father has often pointed out this path to her but warned her not to use it. 'Why not?' Elizabeth has said. 'It's just like Shanklin Chine that is. Where the smugglers from France used to carry their ill-gotten goods.'

'Let's go up,' Pauline whispers. 'Let's just try it. Nobody would know we were gone even.'

'No,' says Orla. 'We're not allowed. And anyway I want to swim.' She looks at the boathouse and the cliff with deep dismay. She has managed to get past her great adversary – her Auntie Annie, in order to gain the beach. She won't give it up now just to satisfy a whim of Pauline's.

'All right then.' Pauline pulls off her shorts and runs down the slip, jumping into the freezing water without a second's hesitation. She spots the head of Gerry, head of the star boy, cutting a straight furrow through the water parallel to the shore, and marks him as her victim. Thrashing the water with her long arms she swims towards him. Meanwhile Orla picks her way thoughtfully over the golden stones and slides into the water very slowly, like a fish being poured from a green net back into the sea. Once in the water, she spends time with her eyes closed, swimming away from the slip to the middle of the bay. When she opens her eyes, Pauline has left.

'I've something to show you,' Pauline says to Gerry. 'Go around to the back of the boathouse.'

'Hm,' says Gerry suspiciously, shaking water out of his eyes, since he has been pretending to be a deep-sea diver.

Pauline wears a red bikini. Her eyes sparkle and her skin sparkles. Her breasts push against the thin red cotton. Water drips from her hair and runs in shining rivulets into her cleavage. The clear green water laps against her brown thighs.

'Well, OK,' he concedes, placing his hand in front of his swimtrunks as casually as he can, to hide what is happening there.

They leave the water separately and dress quickly. Pauline

slips to the back of the boathouse and climbs out the window. He is standing at the corner.

'You can climb to the top of this cliff,' says Pauline. 'Do you see the wee path?'

'Yes, quite clearly.'

'It's called the Seven Bends. Smugglers used to use it.'

'That's very interesting. What did they smuggle?'

'Wine and silk.'

'I wonder what use the inhabitants of Tubber had for wine and silk?'

'Tubber wasn't always like it is now, you know. Did you think it was?'

'Well . . . I see no evidence to the contrary.'

'Are you on then?' Pauline eyes him with an amused smile.

Gerry clears his throat and puts his hand to it, to straighten his tie. He isn't wearing one, of course, but he is the sort of boy who is always, psychologically, wearing a tie.

'Of course,' he says. It is one of the phrases he uses very often, a phrase he thinks sounds grown-up and self-assured. 'Of course,' he repeats, with greater emphasis. His eyes shift uneasily.

'Come on then. Follow me.'

Pauline begins to scramble through the undergrowth. She pushes willows and brambles out of her way, unconcerned about the scratches they inflict on her bare arms and legs. Gerry follows a few yards behind, his body torn by reluctance and desire. They traverse the hairpin bends, stooping under the level of the growth so that there is no chance that anyone could spot them from below even if they were looking, which they are not. The students are all in the sea, the teachers are stretched out on the sand at the other side of the beach.

Gerry hates it. The undergrowth has the same dank smell as the boathouse, as if many things have decayed in its shelter over the years. He kicks against dried cowpats. 'Wouldn't imagine cows actually climbing up here, would you?'

'They would if they had to,' says Pauline blithely, clambering on. She is graceful and nimble, even when bent double in a tangle of weeds. 'But nobody has been here for a long time. We are the first, maybe in hundreds of years.'

'Of course,' says Gerry, disbelieving. 'Will we have to go down again, immediately?'

His tone includes a *soupçon* of sarcasm. Pauline picks it up. 'You can do what you like,' she says shortly.

Fee fie fo fum

At the top of the cliff is a wooden gate covered in flaking pale blue paint. It opens easily and then, to their surprise, they find themselves on a neat, trodden path which passes through a field of short thick grass – different from the parts of Tubber they are used to, which are pastoral rather than rugged.

'It's nice here.' Pauline gives him an encouraging smile. Gerry looks around, surprised by the contrast between this and what they have just left behind. The grass is sheep-cropped and reminds him, comfortingly, of a golf course. The flora is of the pleasant, seashore kind: flimsy windblown pinks and dark blue scabious, elegant translucent harebells, which sway like dancers in the light breeze. Here is no smell of danger or decadence, but a fresh salt tang, a hint of roses.

'Aye,' he lapses. 'It is.'

She runs along the path, which is on rising ground, leading over a small protuberance. Over its brow they find a cottage – the traditional whitewashed thatched kind, of which there are still half a dozen or so in Tubber. The door is open and Pauline walks inside. Gerry follows.

'We shouldn't be here.'

'Nobody's home. They'd never care anyway.'

'How do you know actually?'

'Who do you think owns this place? The Wicked Witch of the Western World? Maybe she'll put us in a cage and fatten us up for the *céilí mór!*'

The cottage is obviously lived in, although it is not clear what sort of person could live in it. Renovation of the original design has occurred. The floor is covered, wall to wall, with a turquoise and black carpet, brilliant and crackling with static. The interior walls are papered with cream paper embossed with huge sprays of silver grass. In one corner is an electric cooker and in another a television. Fireside chairs, brown and beige plush, are placed at each side of the hearth, in which sits an electric fire. Against one silver and cream wall stands a small bookcase.

'Hm.' Gerry walks down to look at the books. 'Very interesting.'

The air is fragrant with the aroma of old fried onions.

'*An Analysis of Capitalist Theory,*' reads Gerry. '*Keynsian Economics Made Simple. The Fortunes of the Irish Language. The Death of the Irish Language.* Who lives here?'

'He likes books, whoever he is.' Pauline is snooping, opening cupboards, sniffing. 'That's a lovely smell, isn't it?'

'*Lolita.*' Gerry is still reading spines. 'The *Kama Sutra.* Hm.' He pulls out the volume.

'What's that?'

She must know, he thinks. Pretending. 'Nothing.' He glances through it. 'Something about India. Let's go.'

'Wait a second. We just arrived.'

'Time is getting on,' says Gerry, still turning the pages.

'Never mind. Look!' She pulls a packet of Tayto out of a press. 'Look! Lots of crisps.' She rips open the packet and tastes one. 'Not even stale!'

'Don't eat it!' Gerry looks up, alarm dragging him away from a riveting page. He slams the book shut angrily, and replaces it on the shelf.

'Och it's not going to poison me.'

Pauline opens a door and peeps into the room into which it leads. 'Look!'

'Let's go,' says Gerry. But he does not go. He follows her into the room.

It is a bedroom. The walls are white, and on one of them a stone carving of a monster hangs. There is a wide wooden bed in the middle of the room, covered with a red-striped quilt. The crooked wooden floor is cluttered with books. Leaning against the end of the bed is a guitar. Pauline picks it up.

'Let's go!' says Gerry. 'Before the owner comes back!'

But Pauline has sat on the bed, and is strumming the guitar. 'Are you going to Strawberry Fair,' she sings. 'Parsley, sage, rosemary and thyme.' Her voice is strong and clear. Gerry sighs and goes to the door of the cottage to keep watch.

The céilí must go on

That night, the schoolhouse throbs with sweet, scratched music and the thud of feet on floorboards. The yellow stream of sunlight is still hot, but that doesn't change anything. The *céilí* must go on. Everyone knows the dances perfectly by now, and the *céilí* swings through its repertoire of six dances without a single hitch. The children hop and swing. Killer Jack operates the record-player. Headmaster Joe stands at the end of the room in his black suit, barking out the orders.

Gerry dances only once with Pauline, towards the end of the evening, to pay her back for her boldness during the day. She is furious but she smiles her sweetest smile and waves. 'See you tomorrow. Same time same place!'

He can hardly hide his anger, walking back to his bench by the wall. Damn the girl, he thinks to himself, in his old-mannish way. He knows he will be there, a lamb to the slaughter, tomorrow.

Orla swings her way through the dances with Alasdair, with Damien Caulfield, with Seamas Brennan. Sandra dances with Seamas Brennan, Damien Caulfield, and Alasdair. Aisling dances with Seamas Brennan and Killer Jack and Máistir Dunne and a new partner called Kenneth.

Sava takes a big risk

Sean invites Sava to walk with him in the pre-Cambrian hills. It is so hot he wants to take some time off, take advantage of the summer while it lasts.

Sava is taken aback. They have been together for three weeks and seen each other almost every night, but they have never before met during the day.

'It won't be so easy to get away,' she says. But it is not true. It is easier to get away in the afternoon than at night. All she has to do is get the after-lunch washing-up done quickly and then she will be free until teatime. She runs in and out of the parlour as quickly as she can, scraping the plates of mashed potato, faded red corned beef, glutinous cold gravy, into the pigs' bucket before her mother can begin to lament the terrible waste – every day, most of every dinner finds its way to the same destination. It takes two hours to prepare and two minutes to throw out. 'What would they eat?' Banatee groans. 'They eat bread and jam,' says Sava. 'We can't give them that for dinner. They'd take them off me if I did.' Today she is not in the kitchen but out in the byre with a sick cow. Sava hardly gives the girls a chance to eat even if they wanted to. She puts down the plates and takes them away again one minute later. She washes everything in double-quick time. She doesn't bother to put them back on the dresser, just leaves clatters of delph on the table for Banatee to deal with.

He meets her at the end of the lane and they drive to the foot of Knockeany, a hill about six miles from Tubber. There is a lake at the top of the hill, an old glacial lake, the reservoir for the local villages, the lake referred to in the brochure for the Irish college, upon which the students should go boating.

They haven't walked very far when Sean asks Sava if she would like to take a rest. And she would like to take a rest. They sit on the rough, scratching heather, admiring the view: patchwork of multicoloured fields, little blue roads with a few cars winding along them, the lough.

'Donegal must be the most beautiful place in the world,' says Sava. Not an original sentiment, but for her quite a momentous sentence.

Sean is not listening. His mind is on other things: he is wondering if he could possibly afford to buy a television set for his bedroom. This question has been preoccupying him for almost a week, ever since one of his colleagues in the office started bragging about the new colour set she has recently acquired for herself and her mother. Colour set! He doesn't want that. They cost almost twice as much as black-and-white and what is the big advantage? Ninety pounds for a new twenty-inch black-and-white. You could have a month in Majorca for less. And you couldn't even get RTÉ here, just Ulster and the Beeb. Such is the train of his thought, on such pathways does his mind inexorably wander, through the crowded passages of little electrical shops and the blank dark surfaces of banks, when Sava jolts him, first of all by saying something, anything at all, unsolicited, and second by saying something romantic, poetic, involving feeling, even if it is only feeling about place, the emotion all people living in the scenic West of Ireland are programmed by history and the tourist board to register as the primary human emotion and the one most suited to spontaneous expression. He pushes the problem of the television, TV or not TV, aside temporarily, and turns the full focus of his attention on Sava, who is lying, stretched, on the ground. White skin, jet hair, purple heather. It is a good colour combination.

'You are lovely,' he says. It is saying a lot, for him, and it is the immediate effect of his recent excursus into the world of television.

She is luxuriating in the sun. She yawns and stretches, stretches her legs, letting the hot sunbeams warm the shins. She is thinking that if she keeps this up she will have a tan that lasts into October or November. But when Sean bends over her she banishes the tan from her mind: it spins above them, up into the azure, along with his television set, and they concentrate on one another.

Pauline gets her own back

At the *céilí* that night, Killer Jack, the most sought-after teacher at the *céilí*, and the one for whom many girls nurture a tender, painful crush, asks Pauline to dance first thing. And then on the third dance he approaches her again.

'Oh my God.' He brushes his forehead in mock dismay. 'I'm losing my memory in my old age. Or maybe . . . have I danced with you before sometime?'

'Thank you, I'd love to,' says Pauline, winking, actually winking, at him. She glances over her shoulder to see if Gerry is observing this. He is.

Then at Lady's Choice she asks him up herself, not making a joke of it, just using the formula. 'An ndéanfaidh tú an damhsa seo liom, a mháistir, más é do thoil é?' He hasn't got a choice, according to the rules set by himself, although according to his own personal set of rules he never dances with a girl student more than twice on one evening, no matter how much he wants to — and in some cases he wants it very much. He is attractive, and sexually promiscuous — like a surprisingly high proportion of men in Donegal — but the college girls are out of bounds. The rule has never been spelt out: Headmaster Joe, in common with the world at large, has not allowed himself consciously to articulate the dangers inherent in the situation:

194

nubile girls, young male teachers with heaps of authority and, occasionally, charisma. A month in the country. But not articulating them does not mean he is unaware of them, or unable to communicate his awareness. They all know the rule. Hands off.

It does not mean that you can't flirt, and Killer Jack does this as a matter of course, considering it normal and nothing short of the girls' due. Most of the girls share his point of view, the plainer ones unfortunately with more enthusiasm than the beautiful, who become puritanical at an early age as a reflex strategy for self-protection. Pauline he does not even fancy. She is objectively good-looking but she is not his type at all – there is something hard about her that he mistrusts. She is different from most other girls. He, and everyone, can intuitively sense this, although they cannot put their finger on what precisely this difference is. It is not that she is rich and beautiful. It is that there is some part of Pauline that is never available, to anyone. Maybe it is secreted inside her and she guards it carefully. Or maybe she is simply a bit odd. Wired to the moon, that sort of thing. Maybe there is a bit of her floating in outer space, out of her reach altogether, which means that when you look at her or talk to her, she is not all there, not all there for you anyway and maybe not all there for herself.

Still, he, Killer Jack, is pleased when she walks down the schoolroom to the corner where the on-duty teachers congregate and says, in the hearing of the other two, 'An ndéanfaidh tú an damhsa seo liom, a mháistir, más é do thoil é?' She says it quite well. Her accent is faultless. It is the first piece of Irish he has heard her say without stumbling.

The dance is an old-time waltz. Every evening, since the beginning of the third week, they have had one of these at each *céilí*. Killer Jack instigated it, after much dispute with the headmaster. He didn't introduce it so that he would have an opportunity to hold the more desirable girls in his arms. He didn't need that, since every evening after the *céilí* he headed off to the Fairyland Ballroom, or the Texas Saloon, for more sophisticated pleasures. He argued, forcefully, that so many couples in the college had now formed, so many boys and girls were deeply infatuated with one another, yearning for love, that allowing them to waltz might prevent more serious attempts to breach the main unwritten rule of this as of all Irish colleges: 'Thou shalt not get pregnant.' 'Be realistic. They need to let off a bit of steam,' he said to Headmaster Joe. Who nodded his round head and wondered if there was an old Strauss LP somewhere in the parish (the parish priest it was who had one, and lent it after being given one small whiskey in the Texas Saloon).

And now the bodies of the students glide around the classroom, cling to one another as tightly as they can while still transcribing the obligatory circles and shifts from one side of the floor to the other that the dance demands. It is, after all, a much less formal dance than any other they have to do. All you have to do is sway about, pulling your partner with you.

The couples who are uninterested can be relied upon to make the more sweeping and dramatic movements, whilst the dancing lovers cluster at the end of the schoolhouse farthest away from the record-player and the master of ceremonies, and press bodies, hungrily, deliciously, to the sickly sweet tunes – 'Danny Boy', 'Buachaill ón Éirne', 'Tabhair dom do Lámh' (always the same three) – that egg them on.

Pauline does not exactly seduce Killer Jack in the middle of the schoolhouse, but she comes close. She musters all her meagre store of Irish in an effort to talk to him. Translating the clichés of dancehall conversation to Irish, especially to her brand of Irish, sounds funny.

'An dtéann tú anseo go minic?'

'Ta an banna music go maith.'

'An maith leat dansáil?'

Funny, and charming. Especially since she wedges her long fleshy thighs firmly against his crotch, lets her breasts bob against his shoulders – she is taller than him, by about six inches. He didn't fancy her. Until now.

The seductress. How can a girl aged fourteen and a half know what to do? Pauline knows.

'An maith leat an ceol sin, a mháistir?' she asks, rubbing his shoulder through the thin material of his shirt. It is a turn-on to be called 'a mháistir' by a girl who is doing something, anything, to your body. She even knows that, injects the words with all her sexuality. He shrugs, mentally, and gives himself to the moment. The dance is halfway over anyway. Soon enough she'll be gone, and what can he do anyway? He suspends good sense and squeezes her waist, pulling her even closer to him. She draws him down the room to where Gerry is dancing with a little drip of a girl from Dublin – Orla, actually. She does not look at Gerry at all but circles slowly, very slowly, around him. When the dance is on its last legs, she lays her head on Killer Jack's shoulder, and when the record screeches to a halt, like a car stopping suddenly, she kisses him on the side of the neck.

The cottage on the clifftop

Pauline returns to the clifftop cottage, alone, the next day. The door is open and the cottage seems to be unoccupied. She steps inside. The spicy onion smell hits her nostrils and a peaceful emptiness, tangible as still water, fills the room. The light admitted by the little window is dim, but one bar of gold light lies along the stone floor, a path of promises. She breathes deeply, loving the smells, the quiet mixed with mystery. Loving being an intruder, while beginning to believe that this is her space.

She goes to the cupboard and pulls out the packet of crisps.

'Who's that?' asks a familiar, robust voice.

'Um!' Pauline turns.

'Can I help you?' he asks, in a humorous but unfriendly tone. 'Although you seem to be looking after yourself.'

Pauline looks at the door. She drops the packet of crisps and makes a run for it.

He chases her and catches her T-shirt.

'There's no need to be afraid, Pauline.'

'I'm not afraid!' she says, trying to shake away his hand.

'I'm glad to hear it!' He smiles a thin, mouth smile but does not release his grip. 'So what are you doing here, Pauline? Indulging in a little petty burglary?'

'I'm sorry.' Pauline doesn't know what to say. She wishes he would let go of her T-shirt. That is all she wishes.

'Did you take anything, apart from the potato chips?'

'Oh! No!'

'Got you just in the nick of time.'

'Will you please let go?' Pauline asks. She begins to feel hopeless. She knows he will not let go and she does not know what should happen next.

He looks at her appraisingly and smiles. 'I think we should have a chat,' he says. 'Come back inside.'

He propels Pauline into the cottage, which looks different now that he is in it. Once inside he lets go of her, and invites her to sit down. Pauline considers making a run for it again, but decides there's no point. She wonders, if he will murder her, or do some worse, nameless thing to her. The air in the room vibrates with potential danger.

Killer Jack's mouth forms a sardonic, twisted grin. His eyes glitter like Dracula's before a deadly bite.

Pauline, numb with terror, awaits her fate.

A glass of orangeade.

A rattle of crisp packets.

The air in the cottage settles back to normal banality. Killer Jack yawns, displays boredom.

Pauline thaws. She is not to be a hapless victim after all. She is not to be a mangled corpse, a girl child wronged.

She is to be a nuisance. That is all.

'So this is what you do in your spare time? Have you visited other houses?'

Pauline is not at her most talkative. She wishes she could be away from here. She wishes she could turn the clock back half an hour and simply not have come. It's funny, how you can't do that, is what she is thinking. You can't undo anything that is done. You can't bring Maureen back from Italy. You can't make your mother and your father not have all the fights they have. You can't tell Jacqueline she is a nitwit and really should

199

just eat the food and stay in the Gaeltacht because if she doesn't she'll be classified as a loser, incorrigible loser. You can't make yourself never have climbed the Seven Bends once you have climbed them. She strains her ears. The sounds of laughing and happy screaming reach them, faint and unbelievably tantalising. Oh to be back down there and not up here!

'How did you get here?' he asks.

'I came up from the shore,' she said.

'I see,' he drawls. 'Well, I could do with a visitor now and then. But hasn't anybody told you, it's an idea to knock first?'

'I thought there was nobody here.' She looks around. 'It's a nice house.'

He doesn't answer.

'You stay here on your own?' Pauline doesn't believe it. In a minute someone else will walk through the door.

'Alone, yeah. I'm fond of solitude. You wouldn't think it, would you?'

'Wouldn't know now,' says Pauline. 'I better be gettin on home.'

He looks at her, not smiling. 'Don't go,' he says. 'Not yet.'

She looks at him. His skin is sallow like her own, even though his hair is fair. He has small eyes creased at the corners with many little wrinkles, and very light blue irises. There is a thin film of sweat on his cheekbones, and one of his big teeth is capped with gold.

'I'll have to, soon,' she says, carelessly. He's deferring to her now; she knows where she is with him. She gets up and walks to the window.

'They're all at the shore, having a swim.'

'I know.'

'Is it your afternoon off?' she asks.

'Aye.'

'I've never heard you speaking English before.'

He smiles, but wanly, and says nothing.

'I've got to go.'

He nods.

'You're dead right!' he says. 'Go, and don't come back. Do you hear me now? And we'll say no more about it.'

Neither of them says goodbye, and as she walks out she can feel his small crinkled eyes staring at her back.

A most surprising visit

Most of the scholars do not see their parents for the whole month of the Gaeltacht: it's too awkward to get to. There are no trains to the Gaeltacht. The old railway lines were ripped up by some 1950s government which decided nobody would be going anywhere much in Ireland for the foreseeable future, so there was no point in wasting money on trains any more. You're as well off staying at home. Most people don't own cars.

But Aisling's parents do. Own a car. And Aisling's parents visit her for the last weekend. They arrive at Banatee's house at six o'clock, just as everyone is sitting down for tea. Nuala and Ciaran are several steps ahead of Elizabeth and Tom in onomastic matters: their names precede them like badges identifying the specific nature of their rung in Irish society.

Orla and Aisling hear them exchanging some words with the Banatee. Her rapid unintelligible gunfire is punctuated with Nuala's musical, rather whimsical tones. Then they come into the parlour.

To the children, they look like creatures from another planet. Their fashionable summer clothes, their city hairstyles, are outlandish in the brown country parlour: it is as if Marilyn Monroe dropped into the classroom in the traditional Irish schoolhouse to take the choir practice. And by now Aisling and Orla feel they belong in the brown parlour, not anywhere else. They have been here for three weeks and already they have lost their accents, their affiliation to Dublin. Already they belong to Banatee and this country farmhouse and the valley and Headmaster Joe and the college.

They stare at Nuala and Ciaran, clutching the edges of their wonky chairs defensively. Ciaran stands in the doorway, Nuala walks into the room and looks around, lopes around, imperiously, curiously, slightly mockingly. For a minute, neither of them say a thing. In that minute Orla sees the parlour with their eyes, fresh from Dublin. Seeing this image of it superimposed on her own makes her angry.

They start to talk then, in their confident, bossy, adult Dublin voices. Their Irish sounds strange too. After the Donegal Irish – straggly, glottal-stopping, somehow as untidy and wild as the countryside – it sounds foreign and artificial.

'Hello there!' They are all smiles and *bonhomie*, of course, as they look, themselves perplexed, at the little group seated around the big dark table. 'Sorry to butt in on you like this but we thought we might whisk you away for supper, you two!'

Orla and Aisling look at them in some amazement. The idea of not sitting here eating tea as they have done every night now for twenty nights! The routine has become so entrenched that any disturbance of it upsets them. They smile but remain silent, not knowing what they are supposed to do.

'So,' says Nuala. 'Wouldn't you like that? I've told your *bean an tí*, it's fine with her. Would you like to . . . eh, maybe change your clothes?'

They look terrible, is what she is thinking. Sunburned and freckled but scruffy, untamed, like tinkers. Their hair is matted and thick with salt, their clothes are badly matched, dirty. They look like orphans! Like children who belong to nobody: they've got that wildness.

'Do we *have* to change?' Aisling has picked up the unvoiced criticism and resents it. She looks at Orla. She realises that she is dirty and unkempt, in spite of all their best efforts in the bathroom, in the burn, in spite of their aspirations for the *céilí*. God knows they've done their best, but the result is pathetic by grown-up standards.

'Yes I think you do, darling.' Nuala is firm, and looks at Ciaran for support. He looks away.

He is wearing light fawn trousers, a white open-necked shirt, a beige linen blazer. Nuala is dressed in a white cotton dress, snow white, with a navy blazer and golden sandals on her feet. Both of them were at the hairdresser's yesterday, and both are goldenly tanned, the weather in Dublin having been considerably better than in Donegal. It is hard to connect these two groomed and smart people with anyone sitting at the table in Dohertys'.

'Can Pauline come too?'

'No,' Pauline says quickly. 'Thank you very much but I'm all right. I want to go to the *céilí*.'

'Will we not be going to the *céilí*?' Aisling pouts at her parents.

'Well, when is it on?' Nuala is beginning to lose patience. They have been driving for six hours, were held up at the border post at Aughnacloy for half an hour. You'd think Aisling would express some pleasure at seeing them. You'd think she could have washed her face and changed her clothes.

'Half past seven.'

'I don't think we'll make it. It's six already, darling. Don't you want to come out? I thought it would be a treat.'

'Well.'

'We'd like to,' says Orla politely. In a way she would. She has only eaten at a restaurant on four or five occasions in her life.

'Hurry up then. Brush your hair and change into something clean.'

They don't have anything clean any more, so they change into something dirty. Nuala sighs when she sees them and smiles at Ciaran, but says nothing.

Nuala asks Banatee for advice on a good restaurant. Orla squirms as she overhears their conversation. It seems so typical of Nuala to enter into a discussion of this kind with someone like Banatee. It seems typical of her not to realise that someone like Banatee probably never ate in a restaurant in her whole life and knows absolutely nothing about them.

But she does. She knows about Mary Anne's, over the hill in the next parish. And there they go, in Aisling's father's sky-blue Cortina, collecting Sandra *en route*: her hair is wet, a black seaweed down her back. She's washed it for the *céilí* but it takes three hours to dry, she says, with pardonable pride. That's because it is so much thicker than ordinary hair.

Mary Anne's is the strangest restaurant Orla has ever seen. It does not look like a restaurant at all, but more like somebody's front room with the three-piece suite taken out and a lot of kitchen tables added. The tables are draped in sober and sobering oilcloth, the kind of oilcloth that reminds Orla of human mortality. On each table is a silver stand containing salt and pepper, red sauce, brown sauce, and mustard. The sign on the door would say MARY ANNE'S EATING HOUSE if there were a sign on the door, but there is not: you have to ask for directions. Luckily Aisling's father is good at asking, and he remembers what he is told.

The surprise of Mary Anne's is the view. The narrow, country-house windows look out on a beach just under them. Beyond is a pier, the sea, the other side of the bay, all that. You can sit at a table looking at children jumping from the end of the pier, people fishing, the odd sailboat.

Nuala and Ciaran and Orla and Aisling and Sandra sit by the window, and Orla's heart, which had sunk when she caught sight of the place, lifts. She senses that whoever built Mary Anne's – Mary Anne, perhaps? – had a giddy streak in her, a sense of holiday. A boy dives into the sea from the side of the pier, and she laughs.

The smell of the place, too, is appealing. It is the smell of frying: crispy and greasy and sweet. The smell at Banatee's is mainly of boiling. Boiling potatoes, boiling cabbage, boiling clay. A sad and sour, a watery smell. Orla loves fries, as who does not?

'Isn't it lovely!' Nuala sings. 'Such a wonderful view!'

'It's a quaint little place,' Ciaran says, reading the menu with satisfaction. Salmon, mackerel, pork chops, sausages – beans and chips with everything. 'I've never seen anything quite like it. It's amazing.'

The girls eat chips and sausages and mushrooms and onion rings, served with tea and bread and butter. For dessert there are things like jelly and ice cream and fruit cocktail and ice cream.

'You've certainly got good appetites,' Nuala says, with her grown-up habit of stating the obvious. 'Don't they feed you at all?'

'Oh yes,' says Aisling, reluctant to be disloyal. 'They feed us corned beef and cabbage.'

'Yuck!' Orla doesn't care. She has no fealty to anyone. 'One of the girls actually left because she couldn't stand the food!' She is anxious to make some contribution to the conversation as a thank-you gesture for the meal, which she has enjoyed enormously. Her stomach feels as if it would burst, and she can feel that her face is flushed from overeating. She gazes happily, drunk with food, at the terns and at the boys plunging into the water.

'Really,' says Nuala. 'How strange.'

'Well, she was a bit odd actually,' says Aisling. 'Wasn't she, Orla?'

'She had problems at home, in Derry.'

'Was she one of those kids they send out to get them away from the Troubles? Poor thing. They probably can't cope, after all they go through.' Nuala sighs and sips some tea.

'She lived in a corporation house,' Aisling adds, glancing round. The room is full of northerners: the clipped crispy twang of Belfast and the dry drawl of Derry are the sounds, as fry is the smell. The restaurant has an intensely Ulster feel to it, Aisling thinks, feeling that she is in another country. It is a feeling she savours.

'Really? What's wrong with that?' Ciaran asks.

'She had loads of money. She bought sweets all the time and her clothes were quite nice too actually. She didn't look poor to me.'

'No, well . . .'

'The Brits wouldn't let her family move into their new house.'

'What?' Ciaran seems interested, although why is not clear.

'They were moving into a new house and the Brits came along and kept them out. She was upset about that.'

Nuala shrugs. 'Oh yes. Gosh, yes, I read about it in the *Irish Times*. Well she is just unfortunate. The two communities, you know Aisling what I mean by that, the Catholics and the Protestants, seem to be trying to keep their own areas completely to themselves now. All the Protestants are forced out of Catholic areas and all the Catholics out of Protestant areas. It's amazing. I can't really understand it.' Nuala shrugs again, and turns her gaze to the window. In the little harbour two men in striped jumpers are clambering down the side of a boat into a rubber dinghy.

'The IRA should be all hanged. They've started all this. I don't know why it has taken the government so long to see that it's all a terrorist plot.' This is Ciaran's contribution. Orla looks sharply at him. He has such modulated, educated tones and he looks so squeaky clean, but this view sounds just like her father's. Let them all bleddy blow themselves to bleddy hell. Crowd of bleddy bastards!

'Jacqueline thought . . . it was different. She said they couldn't get a house because they were Catholic. She said Protestant bachelors got houses more easily than Catholic families of ten. Like hers.'

'Ah, she sounds like a bit of a moan to me,' says Nuala. 'Look, that man nearly fell into the water!'

They all look out of the window at the man in the stripey jumper, who is being pulled back up to the deck of the boat.

'Who forced them to have ten children anyway?' Ciaran says in a low furious whisper to Nuala. Orla's ears prick up, but she pretends not to hear.

'Ciaran!'

'Well honestly, that sort of thing . . . You'd think there was someone standing at the end of the bed pointing a gun at them!'

Orla thinks of the Pope's blessing at the end of her parents' bed. Framed and smiling Pius. He hasn't had much effect on her parent's productivity, there's just the two of them. But he does try.

'Would you like more ice cream, girls?' Nuala makes a face and seems to kick Ciaran.

'Yes. Yes. Yes.'

More ice cream! Ripple, banana and neapolitan, a scoop of each, again.

Aisling's parents drop Orla off at Banatee's, but they are taking Aisling with them to have a look at the guesthouse where they are staying. Nuala has a key: Aisling can get into Dohertys' later. Just before Orla gets out of the car Nuala hands her a parcel.

'Your mother sent you this. I forgot about it earlier.'

'Oh!' Orla takes the parcel and begins to get out of the car.

'She's very well,' Nuala continues. 'She misses you a lot, though. She said to tell you.'

'Gosh.' Orla wonders if she should say 'I miss her too.' But she can't bring herself to. It sounds so show-offy. 'Thanks for the tea,' is what she manages instead, adding, 'See you later, Ash.' Then she goes into the house and upstairs. She rushes into her room and pulls the paper off the package. Surely it contains chocolate and biscuits, like everyone else's packages? And something to wear, since it feels soft. Money as well, probably.

The brown paper falls onto the bed, followed by two packets of chocolate goldgrain and a hank of wool. No money. Orla roots through the wool, wondering if it could be secreted there. She examines the wrapping paper carefully. Nothing. But there is a note from Elizabeth:

Dear Orla,

Thanks for all you letters. I hardly get time to read them, you write so often Still its nice to know you are well we are fine here Daddy working away and me busy as usual with the boys Tommy Byrne left last week found a flat I put an add in the Press for a new boy but so far no luck its the wrong time of the year i suppose please God someone will turn up soon. How are you hope you are well and Aisling it will be nice for her to have a visit from her mam and dad and maybe theyll bring you out somewhere too you neer know. how is Annie did you give her the stockings she'll need them with her bad leg here is something else you can give her when you call in next its wool for socks she will knit some for tom and send them in the post theyre much better than the ones you can buy in the shops and much better value too well thats all for now be a good girl looking forward to seeing you next week dv say a prayer for me and daddy love Mam.

That's it.

Orla gazes helplessly at the white wool and brown wrapping paper littering up the bed. She gazes hopelessly at the beige walls, at the broken wardrobe. Never has the place seemed so cheerless and menacing. The tree outside the window shakes mournfully in the night.

Orla takes a packet of chocolate biscuits, and goes down the landing to Pauline's room. A chat would be nice. A chat in exchange for a few biscuits.

There is no reply. She opens the door and looks inside. The light is on, but Pauline is lying in bed fast asleep. 'Pauline!' Orla calls in a loud whisper. 'Pauline!' She goes over and looks at Pauline, who is lying flat on her back, her hair blending in with the brown nylon pillow. Orla nudges her shoulder gently. But even that doesn't arouse her. She appears to be in a very deep sleep.

Orla goes back to her room and digs in her case for an illicit English book she has secreted there for dire emergencies: there is a rule against reading English books in the Irish college; you are allowed to read Irish books, of course, but Orla possesses none of these. There are a few in the library in the school back in Dublin, but she has never read one of them, although she reads voraciously in English. The book tucked into the bottom of her suitcase is a copy of *Heidi*. She had this copy from Elizabeth when she was six years of age, and couldn't even read properly. Elizabeth read it aloud to her and Roddy over what seemed to be about a year, a couple of pages every night. When the book was finished, Orla took it to her bedroom (she had a bedroom then) and tried to read it herself. Tried, and soon succeeded, since she remembered so much of the story anyway. Since then she has read it about a hundred times. It's an old, battered red volume, with a black magician or chimney sweep embossed on the spine over the inscription 'Blackie's Children's Classics'. The spine is breaking, and the yellowed endpapers are covered with silly illustrations she made herself when she was eight, thinking that blank pages were left between the cover and the title page so that readers could provide their own pictures (there were none in the book, and the dust jacket, which had shown a very tiny, sweet girl sitting on a rock beside two goats, disappeared a long time ago). Now there are Heidi and Alm Uncle and Peter and Clara and Fraulein Rottenmeier scrawled all over the book in red biro. She didn't try to do the goats, or the old blind granny. Oh gonny!

She decides to start at the beginning of the book and read it right through. By page 3 she is feeling very happy.

Sava and Sean
have it off again

Margo and the Country Folk. Paddy McDevitt and the Northern Lights. Roly Daniels. Jerry Bland and the Seasons.

Sean and Sava have picked the Northern Lights, playing at the Texas Saloon, as their aperitif tonight. They are still in the ballroom, turning each other on in the hot sweaty embrace of the dance. The warm night wraps the hall, and waits for them.

The stones,
the trees, the water

Orla and Aisling are asleep in their lumpy bed. Outside the window of Pauline's room the sycamore is shivering in the dry summer night. Pauline looks at the moon, a thin sliver, a silver canoe in a navy-blue sky so crowded with stars that it looks like a dark bowl full of blue sparks. The dog barks in the barn. Pauline glances behind, at the room. Her bed is hot, the blankets tossed into a sticky sweaty twist that will allow no sleep. A statue of the Virgin stares down from the top of the wardrobe, upside down – someone, Sava, stuck it up there out of the way.

Pauline slips downstairs and out into the yard.

'Have some.' Gerry hands her a can of beer. They are sitting on the slip outside the boathouse. The black water laps against the stones, squelch squelch squelch.

'I thought you didn't drink.' Pauline takes the can and pulls it open.

'I found these in the yard of our house. Thought you'd like one.'

'Thanks very much.' She takes a slug of beer and looks up. The dark blue sky is still crammed with stars. 'Have you any fags?'

He shakes his head and puts an arm around her shoulder. 'No. I didn't think you'd like them.'

Pauline considers making a glib remark, but restrains herself. She feels sorry for Gerry tonight, for some reason that has more to do with the surroundings than anything rational. The landscape is so intense at this time of night. The plash of the waves against the slip, the occasional murmur of the trees on the cliff behind them, the continuous winking of the stars, a winking that has no beginning and no end, make her feel that everything is alive. The stones, the trees, the water. The dark solid purple black mountains on the opposite shore. The canoe of yellow moon, floating above them. Everything that is simple and familiar during the day has been transformed.

'It feels weird here, doesn't it?' is how she expresses this feeling to Gerry.

'Weird, but lovely but,' he agrees. Of course he agrees. He feels it more than her, but he'd agree anyway.

'Are you looking forward to going home?' she asks, wondering more or less for the first time what 'home' means for him. Out here you know nothing about anyone.

'No,' he says simply.

'Me neither.'

They stare at the sea. He tightens his grip on her shoulder and she snuggles closer to him.

'Your mam and dad . . . they're away?'

'They're away in Italy. But they'll be back next weekend. They'll be there when I get home so they will.'

'That's nice, isn't it?'

Pauline doesn't reply. How could she tell him everything? About her mother and her father, the way they fight.

Gerry is trying to find some way of keeping the conversation alive. It's not easy. He can hardly believe that this is him, sitting at the boathouse in the middle of the night with a girl.

'My parents split up last year,' he says. It's the first time he has told anyone, any young person, this.

'Oh my God!' Pauline throws off his arm and faces him. 'That's . . . too bad. That's terrible.'

'Och. You get used to it.'

'Which one do you live with?'

'I live with me granny actually,' he says. 'For the minute. For the minute I'm with her.'

Pauline puts her arms around him. They tumble down onto the uneven slippery surface of the pier, and kiss for about an hour.

A sack in the darkness

Saturday is not different from weekdays here, as it is in the rest of the ordinary world. The round of classes, singing, games, swimming and *céilí* is played out on Saturdays as on all other days. But this last Saturday is an exception. A few people, like Aisling, are absent (her parents have taken her away on a long long drive; others are tired or sick or pretending to be sick), and there is a general relaxation of discipline. This means that nobody notices that Pauline has not turned up for classes. She came home sometime very late last night and did not get up at the usual time. Sava, serving breakfast, was too exhausted, after the Texas Saloon and its aftermath, to notice or care. She stumbled bleary-eyed in and out of the kitchen.

'Where's Pauline?' she asked at one point.

'Asleep,' Aisling answered. 'She's not feeling well today.'

'The poor wee thing, I'll bring her up some tea,' Sava said. But she didn't bother. Pauline stayed asleep till midday.

After breakfast Aisling leaves with her parents and Orla goes down to the schoolhouse alone.

The wool and the stockings.

She knows she will have to do something about them now, at last, since Elizabeth will find out eventually if she fails to deliver the wool. No wool no socks. How would Elizabeth find out?

215

She'll write, she'll write to Annie herself or to somebody else, when the socks fail to arrive.

It is harder now to visit Annie than it would have been at the beginning. On the other hand, even if she had visited her earlier she'd have to go again now anyway, with the wool. So ... maybe. Maybe she should just skip off alone this afternoon and do it. Alone, without telling anyone, would be easier than with Aisling or Pauline. It would be more terrifying, and Aunt Annie, with her jerks and her winces and her erratic voice, was terrifying, as everything that is different can be. But it would not be shameful.

She thinks she has made a decision although a nagging voice suggests to her that perhaps she has not, that maybe this so-called decision is temporary and, until the action is over, it can be postponed at any time. Orla is radically different from Pauline in this way, a way that determines character. With Pauline, word and even thought are action. With Orla words are words are words and the link with reality is always in question.

Still, she walks with a lighter step along the little road, which by now is familiar to her in every detail. The two little council cottages at the corner of the Dohertys' lane, where the women wore wellington boots and blue overalls all the time, and the children either wellies or bare feet as they scamper around the road. There is a pump, painted blue, on the road outside those houses and that's where the children always are, messing around in the puddle of water at its base. Then the donkeys in the rushy field, their huge penises sticking out obscenely and fascinatingly, among the spikey rushes and the orange montbretia. The Scallan, the old Mass rock where they said Mass in Tubber in the penal days and where there is now an elaborate grotto, modelled on Lourdes or somewhere: grey stones in a sort of mound shape with a plaster statue of Our Lady in a little niche in the middle of it. It is close to the burn, actually, to the place where the burn breaks out of its cover and meanders for a while in a flat pastoral style. That is where Alasdair and his friends stand and fish all the time. They are there even now, as she passes, getting in a little fishing before school. Alasdair stands, fat and fair, squarely in the middle of the burn, his eyes glued to the riverbed, a model of intense, fishermanly concentration. He hasn't got a rod any more but a gaffe his faratee has given him as a special present, an acknowledgement of his status as an obsessive fisherman. He holds it with both hands, poised, ready to trap anything that moves. In the house he stays in they don't eat bacon and cabbage any more – most days they have young salmon, or a couple of fried trout for their tea, courtesy of Alasdair.

'You'll be late!' she calls. She'd never spoken to him off the dancefloor before.

'Shut your mouth you wee whore,' is what he says. 'You'll scare off the fish on me.'

She does not take offence, recognising enthusiasm when she sees it.

Orla walks on down the blue road, through the straggling village. It is called Tír an Laidin, which she thinks means, appropriately, the Land of Latin. She has already found out that names often do not mean what they first seem to, however. Bun na Toinne, where her aunt lives, does not mean the Bottom of the Wave, but something about the family at Ton. Nobody knows what Ton means. Names, Máistir Dunne has explained, are often more ancient than any other part of the language. They are so ancient that in some cases they are not even Irish, not even Celtic, and nobody knows what they mean. There are layers in language, as there are layers in the earth. Rock and clay and bog and growth and then more clay and bog and growth. You dig and dig and sometimes you don't recognise what you find.

The Land of Latin is asleep in the lemon morning sun. Some doors stand open. Chickens scratch in the dirt on the roadside, cats sunbathe on the little windowledges. But no human beings are in sight. The schoolhouse is closed and empty, classes will not start for an hour yet. Orla feels a wrench of the heart as she passes it: it is such a nasty building, like all those country national schools, with its unfriendly high windows. It looks as it was when it was built: a mean bossy terrifying place, where children learned to be silent and frightened along with anything else they learned. Where they learned that life was hard and horrible and that you got beaten if you didn't conform to the demands of whoever held power over you. The schoolhouse was domineering in every line of its architecture. When Orla learns later, not much later, of such buildings being bought for a song by Dubliners and converted to holiday homes she can't believe her ears. All schools are the reverse of holidays but these are the sternest in their design. And empty, the schoolhouse is left with nothing but its stern tall structure. It is so dead and so boring, the building that has been for the past few weeks the repository of so much life and fun and feeling. She is sad, momentarily aware of the transience of everything, sad enough to forget momentarily the task in hand.

On she goes, along the road traversed last night by Pauline, a road that is as well-known to her as almost any other in the world, and that in the morning is a romantic idyllic ribbon, winding its way through a green-and-gold patchwork of fields, past hedges dripping with roses and fuchsia: here is the well, here is Marley's shop with the old HB pennant hanging from the tree as the only indication that a shop is there, hidden down a lane. You have to knock at the door to get Mrs Marley to come and open the shop and serve you. The shop smells of flour and grain, there are sacks of them lying against the back wall. And just a small wooden table covered with boxes of chocolate bars. Dairy Milk. Whole Nut. Turkish Delight. No Mars Bars. It's not the North of Ireland. But Orla feels a huge surge of desire for the goods on offer, nevertheless. She aches for a slab of Whole Nut. She can taste, almost, the deep satisfying chocolate, the dryish slightly bitter nuts. If she had some money she'd get one on the way home as a reward.

She sees a few people she knows as she walks along – it is inevitable, since she knows everyone who lives along this road, and most of them are in some way related to her – close cousins or distant cousins, she never knows which, since Elizabeth likes to acknowledge those who are better-off and pretend that the others don't exist. She sees her cousin Denis Black cutting hay with a scythe in the field in front of his house. Denis lives in a thatched cottage, perfect in every detail, on a farm that is probably run along the same lines as it was a hundred years ago, or maybe even a thousand years ago. Well, he has a tractor. But otherwise he is growing hay and corn, potatoes, cutting turf on the side of the mountain and bringing it home on a donkey, raising five cows, and farming sheep up in the hills. He lives with his sister. That is the only flaw in the ointment. His sister, Orla's cousin also, Maisie, who is fresh-faced and beautiful, quick and lively as a kitten, the perfect Irish farmer's wife. She is the sort of woman who never perms or dyes her hair. It is cut in a snow-white bob. She is the sort of woman who always wears white next to the skin, at least when she is dressed up, and who in the house has a clean overall. Her big hands are always busy churning or cleaning, baking bread, feeding their flocks of chickens and ducks and geese and turkeys. They are the sort of farmers who have a duck pond and ducks as well as boring old chickens, the sort who have a pony as well as donkeys, the sort who have busy lizzies on the inside windowsills (at this stage, nobody in Donegal, perhaps in Ireland, puts potted flowers on the outside windowledges) and a rambling rose, palest most translucent most heartbreaking pink, around the door. The half door. They are the kind of people who still have a half door, a settle bed in the bed outshot, a crane hanging over the open fire, a big black kettle always boiling. Stone floors, white walls, that smell of grain, a dry clean nutty smell. They could be in an open-air museum, everything is so spic-and-span and perfect. But they are not. They are living here, efficiently and economically, and doing well enough, apparently, although it takes a lot of work to keep the whole enterprise going.

Charming. Denis is six feet four, brown, with a long face, a bit simian actually, large-jawed like those cartoons but unlike them very handsome. And very Anglo-Saxon in his wiriness and height. He could be American. He could be from Nebraska or Nevada or Minnesota, a weathered farmer of the grainlands. Or from Massachusetts or eastern Connecticut. And Maisie could be a star. Little house on the prairie. She has a Laura Ingalls Wilder face, rosy and clean, wide-smiled, blue-eyed, a *Sound of Music* face.

Never married. That is a problem, but they are just a statistic, a brother-and-sister arrangement, common maybe in these parts of Ireland in the past. A kind of economy of incest operated, although probably not real incest, not in their case anyway. Their libido, their sexuality, must have found its outlet in work. You have to work eighteen hours a day, hard, to keep that little cottage and farm in perfect shape. And it is in perfect shape. It is, even Orla can realise, perfect of its kind, a monument to the way of life that is just ebbing away now from Tubber. The tide going out. Willow basket making and the bed outshot. Duck ponds. Scything hay, that long graceful stroke, the strength and endurance required to do it. Hay ripening in the July sun, lying in swishing delicious pale swathes on the ground, stacked, the shape of Christmas puddings, the colour of the sun, in the corner of that field opposite the door of the cottage, the home field, the kind of little field close to the house all farms have. Where the haystacks are, the calves, the ducks, the carthorse, the home field where the house and the land meet and mingle. Muddle: there is the old coulter, the ploughshare no longer used.

The rural idyll, real Ireland. You sense the wholeness walking through the door, or imagine that the neatness and activity and beauty and naturalness mean wholeness. Maisie and Denis don't seem to worry about money. They have enough. They don't seem to worry about anything, but they obviously have high standards. Living up to their high standards, which are different from anything else in this valley, keeps them happy. They must have sad moments, at the end of dark winter days when there is not so much to be done and nothing, after work, to occupy them. But these moments are apparently few, and visitors would never be aware of them.

Denis and Maisie. It would be nice to acknowledge them, it would be nice if they were her true aunt and uncle instead of her third cousins, and if the house she stayed in with her parents were their cottage instead of Auntie Annie's dour grey stone house. Orla is not ashamed of everyone in this place, just of Annie. But still she has not visited Denis and Maisie either. She hasn't even been ordered to do that. It is as if everyone knows that they have enough common sense not to expect a child to pay a call to them. And Annie has not got that much sense.

Maisie and Denis don't speak Irish either, for some complicated reason to do with a mother from another area, something like that. They didn't speak Irish to their mother, and when they were nine or ten they were hired out as farm hands to farmers in Tyrone. Hired girls and hired boys, they were. And of course everyone spoke English in Tyrone, only English. That was where Denis and Maisie had learned to be such excellent farmers, such neat housekeepers. Professionally trained by the hardworking Presbyterian farmers of the Lagan, and their neat thrifty wives. The thing about Denis and Maisie is that their place is perfect because it is not, strictly speaking, typical of Tubber. It is a Protestant farm on a Catholic hillside. Its influences manifest themselves in the cut of the kitchen, the neatness of the yard, the clean worn ancient utensils. The tidy golden thatch. Keeping things, acknowledging and cherishing what you have rather than abandoning and replacing it, is the key to the ethos. Most people Orla knows are constantly reinventing themselves and their environments. But the old Protestant country attitude is to conserve. So Maisie and

Denis's farm is the only one in Tubber still to look exactly as it must have looked a hundred years ago. It looks like that but still remains in pristine condition. Hard work is necessary to stand still. The result could be an exhibit in a folk museum. Someday this house will be lifted, stone by stone, and rebuilt in a park near Belfast. But for the moment it is the home of Orla's cousins, safe in its niche under the hills.

Orla waves at Denis and he waves back. But he doesn't really recognise her. He would wave at any stranger. Country manners. Orla walks on, not unrelieved, and hopes she doesn't meet anyone else.

She doesn't.

It is not such a long road, maybe a mile long, and soon she is turning the corner into Aunt Annie's street. It spreads before her like a framed picture. Balm of Gilead is a phrase that comes into her head. She does not know why, or even where it comes from. Not from the Bible, with which she is totally unfamiliar, at least directly. She has read this phrase in some novel, maybe *Little Women* or some novel like that. Spreading eucalyptus trees. There are no balm of Gilead trees here, or eucalyptus, of course there are not. But there are spreading trees of some kind – sycamores – at one side of the street, and at the other, where it bends and goes out to meet the road again, a cluster of Scots pines, dark as green can get before becoming black. In between are the byre, white with red wood trimmings, the cobbled street, with the hens and a few ducks scrabbling among the stones, the house flanked by the stables on one side, the barn on another, like two arms reaching out. It looks, Orla sees for the first time, quite nice. Quite large and generous and old-fashioned and nice. Nicer than the Dohertys' house, if not quite as nice as that of Maisie and Denis. She stands and looks at it admiringly. Maybe, once, there was a buzz of life around this house. Warm family life: nice-looking women and children, tough, competent men, moving across the yard, in and out of the barn and stable. Action, laughter, talk. Song. Even song.

Even music. Nobody in Orla's family, now, sings or plays an instrument or even listens much to music. Maybe . . .

It is all so empty, like the schoolhouse, although much more appealing, even empty, than any schoolhouse. What dwelling house would not be?

She walks, without too much effort, down the street to the door of the house. The house is whitewashed now, and the door and windows are painted red, the favourite colour for doors and windows in the locality. There is no knocker on the door, just a latch. Usually you open the latch and walk in. But when she tries the latch it doesn't engage. The door is locked.

She rattles on it a few times and then knocks on the wood with her fist. There is no response. She goes to the window of the kitchen and peers in. Through the curtains she can see most of the kitchen: the square stone floor with a bit of worn linoleum in the centre, the black range, the electric ring, battered pewter or tin, with its coils of tubing like a spiral drawing in the Book of Kells, on the table just inside the window. The red chest for layers' mash. But no sign of Annie.

Irritated, disappointed, she bangs once again at the door, with a stone this time. But she knows it is pointless. If Annie were at home the door would be open – she knew the minute she lifted the latch and felt it flop back limply against the door that the fateful encounter was not going to occur.

She puts the brown paper package of wool, and the paper bag containing the stockings on the stone slab beside the door. She notices the texture of the slab: grey stone, a sort of grey sandy concrete, with small pebbles and stones mixed through it, not rough but soft and bumpy under her knees. It is surrounded by a border of grey slate. Somebody bothered, once, to go to the trouble of setting this slab outside the door, and decorating it. And then there is a path of stones from the door to the byre, where women go to the toilet and where they also milk the cows. The path is not cobbled but made of stones set on their sides like half moons and cemented into the ground. Not comfortable to walk on but interesting to look at. Somebody had gathered the stones, hundreds of them, probably on the beach, and set them carefully one by one into this path, which is the kind of path a child would like to make. It is like the work of setting shells in the sides of a sand castle. And somebody has done that too, on the portico surrounding the door. It is carefully encrusted with barnacle shells and oyster shells, so that the entire surround is shining and shimmering. A bit silly-looking, Orla has often thought. A bit childish and a bit in bad taste.

She looks at the packages standing on the stone and on second thoughts removes them and places them on the windowsill. The scrawny cat, a cat without a name, so unimportant is she, comes along and rubs her legs, and then jumps up on the windowsill to investigate the parcel.

Orla walks away from the door through the street, which is the name given to the farmyard. Orla is not planning to go to the beach but she walks out by that way rather than doubling back on her tracks. She feels disappointed, and this feeling shocks her. Why should she be disappointed at evading what she dreaded so much? She walks slowly along the cobbled street, feeling the round edges of the stones bite into her sandals.

Passing the barn she hears a small sound. The big red door is ajar and she looks inside.

Dim, dusty, smelling of dry hay and leather, the barn is dominated by a huge old threshing machine, which looks like a clumsy Cinderella coach. It hasn't been used in thirty or forty years but it lies there, with some bits of hay around it, along with the old harnesses for long-dead horses, the broken donkey cart, the rusty plough. The cats live in the barn. When Orla played there she was often surprised, frightened even, by the sudden appearance of a cat or a kitten, skinny and half-starved, emerging from some secret nest and peering at her with curious eyes before dashing away again. They were half-wild, the cats, hunting animals, terrified and terrifying.

There was something else in this barn. The chemical toilet. A plastic bin that you sat on in the middle of the huge dark room, much too big for comfort. Toilets should be small and hidden, even cats know that much.

Orla can't see much through the crack in the door. She can see the big outlines, though, the thrashing machine, the cart. She can see, since her eyes travel to its position quickly and automatically, the toilet, in its central position.

On the floor a figure, lying.

The figure is just a heap, a heap in the darkness. It might be anything. It might be an old sack. It might be a bag of rubbish or a bag of turf or a sack of potatoes. There is no reason to believe that it is anything else, nothing in its shape or movement to indicate that it is anything other than one of these, or something else entirely. The dog, Murphy the dog, asleep.

Except that Auntie Annie wouldn't keep sacks of turf or potatoes or even rubbish there, in the barn, next to the toilet.

And Murphy would not choose it as a place to lie down, for more reasons than one. The cats. The smell. The dryness. The dark. None of these things appeal to him.

Orla shuts her eyes and then she closes over the door, just a little. She doesn't fasten it up. Usually when Auntie Annie leaves the house it is fastened, locked with a stick which you pass through a loop. Orla looks at the big stick, dark grey with tiny bits of red paint still clinging to it. She sees herself picking it up and passing it through its loop, something she has done often before, and something she always enjoyed doing, passing the big heavy stick through the loop, feeling its lovely smoothness, hearing the little almost inaudible click it made as it slotted into place, firmly fastening the door. (Why? Anyone could open it from the outside, there was no lock. What it could do was prevent any animal or any person inside the barn getting out.)

She sees herself performing this action.

But maybe she does not do it. The picture of the stick passing through the loop is in her head as she runs down the lane, out onto the road to the shore . . .

The burn scene four

The burn runs by the side of Aunt Annie's road, wide and quiet here, a deep sweet thoughtful river, not a burn any longer, although they still call it the burn anyway. The same name, or non-name, sticks to it right along its course, no matter what it looks like.

There is a bridge over the river just by Aunt Annie's, a humpbacked stone bridge, and Orla has often played on this bridge on holidays with Elizabeth and her father. The same game always. Putting sticks in the river on one side of the bridge and catching them at the other, trying to catch them as they floated out. It wasn't always easy, since the current got stronger just after the bridge and then they got borne swiftly downstream. Lost. But usually she caught them. It is one of the best games she has ever played, she thinks now, crossing the bridge. The stick game, a game without a name but one that all children who ever come near a bridge must play. The sticks were like her happiness, thrown onto the stream and floating along underground in dark damp green places. Elusive, darting like little animals, little fishes. Little birds. You had to catch them, you had to stand and wait and catch them as they surfaced, and you had to be quick or you would lose some. But you could always go back and try again. As you watched one

226

stick bob off, disappear in the river, you could turn and go right back to the bank at the far side of the bridge and throw in another stick. There were lots of them and each one had the potential to make you feel great as you sent it off on its precarious journey, as you waded in the deep cold water and retrieved it. Dogs must feel like that when they catch ducks, cats when they catch birds. Catching sticks, catching anything, is catching joy. So it seems.

Micheál is standing in the burn. She doesn't see him at first he is so quiet, standing there close to the bank with his eyes on the water, waiting. Like Alasdair further upstream. But he does not look like Alasdair. He looks like the playboy of the western world or something, the hero of some historical romance about Ireland, or even Italy. Orla looks at him standing there and realises that he is the most beautiful boy she has ever seen. He is tall and well built, with brown eyes and brown skin, brown from being out of doors all the time. His mouth is full and red, and his hair is dark red and glossy, curling over his head and down over the nape of his neck. He is wearing a white shirt rolled up at the sleeves, and blue jeans which are not rolled up and must be wet through. When he steps onto a flat rock for a minute she sees that his feet are bare, and she can see the shape of his feet on the flat golden rock – they look bony and golden, long narrow graceful feet, unlike any male feet she has seen before. She stands on the bridge for a few minutes, two or three minutes. Then he glances up and sees her. He is obviously taken aback: it must be clear to him that she has been staring at him for a while; now that he catches sight of her he remembers that he felt eyes on him all the time, as his eyes were on the fish he is stalking. But her eyes have forced him to take his off his quarry, something he never does. He stares back at her for a moment: he recognises her immediately, he has known her for years although she has never really spoken to him. They look at each other and Orla smiles and raises her hand a fraction from the bridge in something that is about one tenth of a wave. He doesn't smile or make a gesture.

The salmon leaps.

It had been lying under the bank, a long fat tapered roll of fish flesh, still as a rock until he moved, and then it darted deeper into the bank, out of the bank, out of his reach. He'd been stalking it for an hour, and it had eluded him, it had teased him. All the salmon like to tease him; it is as if, he feels, they know him at this stage, know what he is up to but maybe think it is some sort of game, cannot know what the outcome will be for them if he wins. They know about him, his long arms and hands, his long legs and feet. But they are not familiar with frying pans.

He catches it as it leaps. It is almost impossible to do this and he has not done it before, although he has taken fish from the murky water under the banks as they lurk in the mud. To take a fish leaping is a miracle, but he has done it. The silver slippery fish is in his arms and it will not escape now – fish do not escape from his hands, they are not like other people's hands. He has to concentrate totally, grasping the big heavy silver thrash, and struggle, walk along the uneven but familiar riverbed to the bank, stone the fish until it understands what the end of the game is.

She stands and watches. A boy in a white shirt catching a salmon with his hands. She knows it is not a common sight but she has seen so many boys fishing in this burn that it does not seem as unusual then as it will later. She watches him catch it and she thinks he will look up and wave, look up to see if she is watching. And he wants to do that but can't. Until the fish is stone dead he cannot take his eyes or his mind off it for a fraction of a second. When it is stretched, its body twisting in the last, insignificant death throes, he looks up.

She is there. She does not stare into his eyes, though, any more. She waves, a full wave aloft, and he waves back. Then she walks on.

Pauline in love

Pauline gets up at about noon. The room is full of hot sunshine, and she feels depraved as she stretches and glances at her watch. Depraved, because she had slept late. But an extraordinary sense of well-being also fills her. It takes a minute or two before she remembers why.

She dresses very quickly and dashes out of the house. Taking the road at a trot, she gets to the schoolhouse just as the last pupils are straggling out. She sees Orla and avoids her. Killer Jack spots her.

'Pauline!' he says, winking. She winces. 'You're looking well. Did you enjoy class this morning?'

'I'm in a hurry.' She says it as nonchalantly as she can, and keeps the chill she feels towards him under control. He seems to know too much. But could he?

'Did you see Gerry anywhere?' she asks, thinking honesty will baffle him.

'Gerry, did you say?'

'Yes.'

'He's away down the road ten minutes ago.' He looks at her quizzically, screwing up his eyes. What is this? Innocence?

'Be seeing you!' She runs off down the road in pursuit of Gerry.

He hasn't gone far, exhausted as he is. About five hundred yards down, near the old well where children often stop to mess in the water, she finds him. He's alone: the others are far ahead.

'I wanted to say hello!' says Pauline. 'How are you?'

'I'm fine. Why weren't you in class?'

'I slept in.'

He looks cross. 'You're ... they noticed. They wondered where you were.'

'What odds? I was at home in my bed. I could have been sick or something.'

'That's what that girl ... the one from Dublin ...'

'Orla.'

'The fat one. She told Killer you were sick.'

Pauline nods. So he knew all right. 'That's good.'

Gerry sits down on the stone wall which surrounds the well. 'I'm wrecked.'

'Here, have a drop of water. It'll freshen you up!' Pauline bends to the well, a square of water set in slippery grey flags. She scoops up some of the cold water in her cupped hands and splashes it over Gerry's head.

'Ouch! That's freezing!'

'You need more of it!' She douses him again.

'OK. I feel wide awake now.' He pats the wall beside him and she sits down. He takes her hand in his. 'Can we do it again tonight? Like last night?'

'Yeah,' she says. 'We can surely.'

They stare at one another intensely, and Gerry kisses her, just for a second.

They have pulled apart and are walking along by the ditch when Killer's car passes. He honks his horn and shakes his head ironically. Pauline waves at him. 'Might as well act friendly,' she says.

'I wonder if he saw us?' Gerry looks anxiously at the cloud of dust that the car has made.

'None of his business, is it?' Pauline tosses her head. 'You're still on for tonight?'

'Oh yeah!' Gerry's voice is worried. 'A few of the lads might come along.'

'The lads?' Pauline is taken aback.

'Midnight feast sort of thing. They noticed me slipping out before. I think . . . We'd better let them come along too. Maybe not tonight. But they want to come along, some night soon.'

'Well . . . all right.' Pauline doesn't care. She's in love with the night, with the sea, with the risk, more than she is with Gerry. 'Maybe I'll round up some girls.'

'The fat little ones from Dublin?'

'You'd be surprised. There's more to them than meets the eye.'

'I hope so!' laughs Gerry.

The burn scene five

Lunchtime. Sava is not at home, Pauline is not at home, Aisling is not at home.

'Where is she?' Banatee asks Orla. She is referring to Pauline. Aisling is accounted for; Sava has not been at home as far as Banatee knows since yesterday, but she guesses she is at work now, and she postpones worrying about her until this evening – Charlie has gone to the Crossroads to see if she is at Kathleen's. But Pauline. Banatee does not know that Pauline has not been home during the night, she does not realise that she has hardly seen her in a week.

'I don't know,' says Orla. 'I think she is probably down at the school still. I think they stayed late today.'

She believes this. When she passed the schoolhouse on her way back home the scholars were still inside. She heard them singing. 'Bheir Mí Ó', everyone's favourite. She'd sung it herself as she walked along.

'I think they are having lunch at the school because it is the last Saturday,' she says. As she says this it becomes true.

'But they would have told us. You'd think they would have told us that, wouldn't you?'

'They probably forgot. I think we were supposed to tell you yesterday but we forgot.'

'Oh?' Banatee is not convinced. She frowns, worried, and hands Orla her plate of roast beef, which tastes as if it has been boiled for several hours, and soft boiled carrots. Orla eats them, wondering why Banatee does not ask what she is doing at home. But somehow Banatee does not think of this, because she has so much on her mind.

Orla savours the experience of being alone in the house. The space opens around her, the rooms, the corridor and the hall, and she feels more well-disposed towards them than at any other time. She changes her clothes since that is what the girls do, automatically, whenever they come home from anywhere, and walks around in the coolish interior, seeing it in a new light.

She decides not to go back to the schoolhouse this afternoon. The teachers think Orla is off with Aisling and her parents. If she returns to the school now, they will wonder what she has been doing all morning. Of course she could invent some excuse. She could say she got carsick, or that Aisling and her parents wanted to be alone for a while. She could say almost anything. Thinking about it fascinates her: an infinity of lies, of stories, opens in her mind. Anything she can imagine, she should be able to say. But she knows she wouldn't. The kind of lies Orla is adept at are not stories, but silences. Evasion is her forte, not prevarication. Storytelling requires some quality that she is lacking – some courage, some acting talent, some bravura she will never possess. She leaves the house and saunters down to the burn.

The water level in the burn is lower than before, since the weather has been dry. It is easier than ever to hop across the stones, and inside the tunnel rocks that before were not visible at all are suddenly apparent. Orla tries to walk down the burn without getting her feet wet at all, and for the first couple of hundred yards this is actually possible. The ceiling is as green and close, the air as dim and mysterious, as before. The weather can't change that, since weather does not penetrate this cavern except by way of the water.

She goes down past the place where the raspberries were, past the waterfall and the pool she has never jumped into. She feels no desire to jump into it now, either. Indeed she laughs with relief that there is no pressure on her to do so.

'I'm alone!' she says aloud, in a low voice. Then she says it louder: 'I'm alone!' She hears her voice in the cavern, its loud tone and then a small green echo: 'alone alone'.

'I can do what I want to!' she says.

'want to want to.'

' I can do anything I want to!'

'want to want to.'

'Whatever the hell I want to.'

'want to want to.'

'Whatever the fuck I want to.'

'want to want to.'

'Fuck fuck fuck fuck.'

'uch uch uch.'

She has never said fuck before. She did not know before that she could say it, or harboured any wish to do so.

'Fucking hell fucking hell fucking hell,' she says, walking down the burn. The echo answers. 'Bleddy murderers bleddy murderers.' She tries out all the taboo words she knows. 'Fuck and bleddy and bloody and bastard.' She does not know very many, as a matter of fact, since people didn't at that time. There was a greater variety of curses and imprecations. Good heavens and Oh dear and drat at one end of the spectrum. Elizabeth said things like You have my heart scalded. And Mary Mother of God. And For two pins I'd give you such a hidin. And You little pup you. The very worst words, concerning the devil and sex, were left for the exclusive use of extremely angry or extremely uncivilised men. Still, there is a surprising store of words in Orla's head that have never before emerged into the light of day, into the sound of day. Her own ears. She has hardly ever heard her own voice, listened to her own voice, and it gets louder and louder, clearer and clearer, as she gets used to it.

'You little pup you!' she shouts. 'You have me heart scalded!' Scalded scalded. 'For two pins I'd redden your arse!' Orla has never before said any of these things, but she has heard them often enough. What she says is Oh dear and Oh golly and Gosh. Oh glory. Good grief. She doesn't bother shouting these now.

> 'They say that in the Gaeltacht
> The food is quite all right,
> You ask for bars of chocolate
> They give you bars of shite'

Shite!
  Shite!
  Fuck fuck fuck fuck.
  She begins to feel tired, and the damp greenness of the burn seems to be seeping into her stomach, pressing upon it. The shouting has exhausted her. It is as if something is dragging her whole body down to the water, as if all her blood were going to her feet instead of rushing around her arteries. She is in the middle of the burn, standing on a substantial moss-enslimed rock, but she begins to make her way to the bank. That tangle of briar and hazel and weed looks precarious, soft, insidious. Anything could lurk there but she knows that at some stage under all the mess she will find solid earth and just at this moment that is what she needs.
  'This darksome burn, horseback brown!' she says as she moves towards the bank. But her voice is not loud any more. All the energy has been drained out of it and she feels sad at heart as well.

> 'His rollrock highroad roaring down,
> In coop and in comb the fleece of his foam
> Flutes and low to the lake falls home.'

She is on the bank, her foot sinking into wet greenery and finding under it, soggy clay. She perseveres and takes a few steps in the mushy ground. It drags too, but she is relieved momentarily to escape from the water.

On the third step her foot strikes something very hard. It does not feel like rock, however. It is harder and smoother than that.

She shuffles her foot around and then moves on a step. On the next step her foot feels the same shiny hard thing under it. She begins to scrape with her feet, pushing away the grass and weeds. A white stone begins to emerge. White, smooth as a pearl.

She knows what it is. In fact she knew, really, when her feet felt the shine and the smoothness the first time. Horror does not overcome her at all, but curiosity, and she brings her hands to the job, pulling and scraping.

Skulls. Half a dozen, a dozen, small round white skulls. Tiny skeletons, with bones as delicate as the pieces of Airfix model airplanes.

Blood

A spot of blood marks her grey pants like a bright poppy.

She knows what it is. Elizabeth has had the sense to give her some advance warning. In response to a query from Orla when Orla was ten, sparked off by her curiosity about the visit of the Blessed Virgin to Saint Elizabeth and the babe in Saint Elizabeth's womb leaping for joy, Elizabeth had supplied a chequered and not strictly accurate account of some of the facts of life. For instance, she reiterated a few times that the very worst thing that could happen to any family was that their unmarried daughter would get a baby, but she did not explain how exactly this phenomenon could occur. Orla didn't know. 'But I thought you had to be married to get children?' she had asked, to which the answer was 'Well...' followed by a conclusive shrug. Elizabeth had also mentioned that every month the womb is cleaned out and then you bleed for a few days. More biological details were not offered, not because Elizabeth wanted to withhold information but more likely because she didn't have any and, oddly enough, didn't seem to feel any lack on that account. Elizabeth belongs to the class or generation that doesn't ask questions, and Orla to another category of humankind, the category that does.

But there was a lot she didn't query with regard to this matter of periods. At the time it had seemed like a remote, theoretical issue. Orla had assumed that she would never be visited by such a bizarre and outlandish experience. Practical advice was not sought, or offered. So now she has only the vaguest notion about how to deal with the substantive problem: that bright red spot.

Orla has nothing. No equipment, no money. If she had money she wouldn't anyway be able to get sanitary towels. There are none for sale in Tubber. Actually there are none for sale between Tubber and the nearest chemist's shop, which is twelve miles away. Whatever women in Tubber do, it probably does not involve sanitary towels.

She tears a T-shirt in half and uses that. It bundles up awkwardly and precariously but it is better than nothing. She could ask Aisling for advice. She knows Aisling has already got *them*, because Sandra told her: Aisling had told Sandra about it, confidentially, and Sandra told Orla, and half their class, more or less straightaway, a whispered secret, mildly scandalous, it had seemed to Orla at the time. Scandalous and embarrassing. But also triumphant. It was embarrassing to get them, but more embarrassing not to. The girls in the class, one by one, had let their secret leak out. She's got them! She's had them for ages! She got them when she was eleven! Shame and success inextricably mixed together, shrouded in a delicious mysteriousness. Open secrets, gleaming red, half-hidden.

There were many reasons for avoiding discussing them with Aisling. But Orla has noticed, occasionally, that Aisling gets quiet and preoccupied and smells slightly strongly of eau-de-Cologne, and of something else, warm and earthy.

Orla has no cologne and she doesn't think she smells of anything. Yet. But she has got them. It's an occasion for panic, but her delight is irrepressible. All last year she pretended not to hear the whispers in the classroom, which indicated to her that she was being left behind. Half the girls had them, including two or three who are younger than Orla. Orla the freak. Orla who might never get them, be mysteriously overlooked by nature, forgotten about.

But it has happened. Nature has not abandoned her. She is not going to be left out of the circle of real girls and women. Like all the rest of them she has been given her badge. Unlikely as it seemed, she is going to be a normal woman.

Orla walks down to the *céilí*, a little late, with half a T-shirt rolled up between her legs. She is alone: Pauline and Aisling couldn't wait for her. Orla had not told them what was wrong, but had managed to annoy them by acting oddly, hogging the bathroom for most of the evening.

As soon as Orla enters the classroom she catches sight of Bean Uí Luing standing near the record-player, talking to Killer Jack. Tonight Bean Uí Luing is wearing a white flowered dress, an embroidered shawl; her lipstick is bright crimson, and she is laughing heartily at some joke he has made. She looks, just now, kind and pretty and sensible. It crosses Orla's mind that Bean Uí Luing would know about periods. She probably has them herself. Maybe she would be able to help Orla? Maybe she should go up to her and ask?

'Fallaí Luimnigh!' yells Killer Jack.

The boys scuttle across the room to the girls, She sees Gerry passing Pauline and asking another girl to dance. Pauline stares at him as if she had never seen him before in her life. Are they having some sort of quarrel?

There isn't time to investigate. Alasdair bears down on Orla. Within minutes the ranks are formed, the record-player creaks into action, the feet are thumping the floorboards. Bean Uí Luing herself is out, dancing in the slow heavy style of older people, hand in hand with Headmaster Joe. Orla and Alasdair meet them when they are halfway through the steps. She dances towards the teacher, she dances back. Bean Uí Luing is walking the steps now, her feet in white patent shoes shuffling instead of hopping. Her eyelids are powdered with dark green eye shadow and she is wearing thick mascara, which makes her look unfriendly. Orla smiles at her as she and Alasdair pass on to the next couple. The smile is not returned. Maybe Bean Uí Luing didn't notice Orla's timid grin? Or maybe she dislikes Orla? Can't stand her?

The T-shirt is starting to edge its way out. Orla can feel little tendrils of cotton scratching her thighs. When the dance is over, she slips out of the schoolhouse and goes round the back to where the horrible toilets with their candy-coloured doors are. Normally she avoids using them but now she has no choice. In the putrid gloom of one of the cold cubicles, she readjusts her accoutrements. As far as she can she, in the semi-darkness, there has been very little activity going on. Maybe her period is going to be snatched away before it even started properly, because she doesn't deserve it, being obviously so incompetent? Will it be bestowed on some more worthy girl, less awkward, with a large supply of every feminine accessory?

When she comes out of the shed, someone is standing by the wall of the schoolhouse, smoking. Sandra. The little red light at the tip of the cigarette glows like a headlamp on her face. Sandra moves to hide it but seeing that the intruder is Orla replaces the cigarette in her mouth and emits a generous puff of smoke.

'Hi!' Orla smiles. She does not even have to think what to do next. Here is the answer to her problems, leaning against the wall, smoking a cigarette. 'I didn't know you smoked.'

'You learn something every day!'

Orla sidles up to her. 'Sandra,' she says.

'Yeah?' Sandra looks at her scornfully. It doesn't deter Orla in the slightest.

'I've got a problem.'

'What's new?' Sandra blows smoke into Orla's face, then throws the cigarette on the ground and stamps on it. She coughs.

'I got my periods.'

'Wonders will never cease,' says Sandra.

'I mean it's the first time.'

'Better late than never, I suppose.' Sandra's new friends talk like this all the time. She has learned their idiom of glibness much better than she has learned Irish. She even talks in the same drawl that Monica and Noeleen have.

'The thing is I have no you know things. And I don't know where to get them. And I haven't any money either.'

Sandra looks at Orla, standing in the yard in the twilight. She looks beyond her to the row of coloured doors, to the dark blue bay and the purple mountains behind it. Faint music slips through the window. Strauss. They're doing the old-time waltz. After a long time Sandra says, 'I'll give you some things tomorrow. I've got loads of them in my case.'

'Oh Sandra!' says Orla. 'You're an absolute angel. I'll pay you back as soon as I get a letter from my mother!'

'Going back to face the music?' Sandra jerks her head at the windows.

When they come back into the schoolroom, Headmaster Joe is striding down the centre of the room to the table where the record-player stands in its place of honour. You can see from the purposeful way in which he walks and from his face, which is redder and puffier than usual, that he is about to do something of exceptional importance.

'Ciúnas!' he screams at the top of his terrifying voice. This is always his cry for attention. It usually attracts it and now, since it is uttered a few decibels higher than usual, you could hear a pin drop.

'What I have to say is so important that I am going to speak English.'

The horror that shudders along the line of children sitting in a ring right around the walls of the schoolhouse is palpable. Some of them gasp, and most eyes widen in shock. Apart from the very first evening, an age ago, nobody in that hall has heard a single word of English pass the lips of Headmaster Joe. They know that for him this is the language of last resort, and that he must have something really horrible to impart.

'Today there has been a terrible, a tragic accident.'

Somebody has died, Orla thinks. Then she thinks, he knows I have been down the burn. He knows about the skulls. He knows I am connected to the skulls, although I don't know how, myself.

He pauses for half a minute, and gazes around the room. Not for effect. Checking. Checking to see who is there and who not there.

'Four girls have been drowned at Ballybane beach.'

He pauses and stares at the windows at the back of the room. The children wait for more information, such as, what the hell is Ballybane beach and who were these girls?

'They were four students at Coláiste Rosron, the nearest college to this one, four girls from Dublin.'

Some of the Dubliners exchange glances with one another, and the people from Derry and Belfast look at them with a certain amount of respect.

'They went out too far!' he roars. His face turns very red indeed and beads of sweat decorate his forehead. 'The teachers tried to save them but they couldn't.'

He sits down and mops his brow. Everybody remains silent, but a tiny ripple of sound, not apparently created by any individual in particular, begins to shiver around the line, as it always does in gatherings of this kind.

'Ciúnas!' Killer Jack jumps up and glares with narrow eyes at everybody. Then he glances down at Headmaster Joe questioningly, not knowing what the next move is. Headmaster Joe does not shirk. He tosses his head, in so far as someone with little hair can, and stands up once again.

'From now on' – he reverts to Irish, much to everyone's relief: it's clear that the danger is over – 'we will be more careful than ever. Nobody is allowed to swim unless there is a teacher in the water. When you are told to get out, get out. Anyone who disobeys will be sent home immediately. Do you understand?'

'We understand,' they chant, relaxed once more. Tragedy has passed close to them, death and danger. But it has passed on, not touching them, as the bombs in Belfast pass them by on the television screen and in the newspapers, disastrous but unreal. Headmaster Joe has been close to the edge but he has not fallen over. They are speaking Irish again, the language of the classroom, of holidays and leisure, not of real life or danger. They have caught a glimpse of the storm raging at sea, the huge waves sucking down the bodies of children. But they remain where they know they belong, safe in the childhood harbour where nothing ever actually happens.

'I have heard ...' Headmaster Joe continues in his low, threatening, furious voice, his schoolmaster pose that will never fool anyone again. He peers around, his eyes alighting on one child, now on another. 'I have heard, only this morning, that some students in this college have been playing in the river.'

San abhainn: he booms on its gentle syllables and half the people in the college jump. At least half of those present spend most of their free time playing in the river.

'That river is dangerous,' he goes on. 'It is full of deep treacherous pools, and strong currents. You can drown in that river more easily than you can drown in the sea at Ballybane. Much more easily than in the sea here.'

Headmaster Joe is a rhetorician, and it is this skill as well as the sheer brute force of his character that makes the college of Tubber such a great place to be.

'It is strictly forbidden to go near that river!' he booms, his black eyes flashing. 'If anyone is found near it, they will be expelled immediately. And that includes you, Orla Crilly.'

Two hundred eyes turn on Orla.

'Your banatee told me that you have been washing clothes in the river behind the house.'

Orla nods, stunned. That is all he knows?

'You are not allowed to wash clothes there again. Not to wash clothes, or wash your feet, or your face.'

Now he is playing for laughs, which of course he gets. Orla doesn't care. Obviously he knows nothing, not a single thing.

'There is a place to wash your face, even in Teach Uí Dhochartaigh, and it is not the river.'

By now the hall is in uproar. It is easy to get a frightened audience to laugh.

'Next dance The Siege of Ennis,' he sighs. Nobody bothers to tell him they have already done it.

The workhouse

Can you dream what you do not know? Usually the stories that unfold in Orla's head while she sleeps are mixed-up images that she recognises from the life she lives during the day, from stories she has read or heard or seen. She sees words, printed or written, people, places, moving through narratives that her sleeping self invents. But the people, the places, the words, come from where she has been when awake. Can it only be like that?

NUALA CRILLY. The words. Headlines in an old newspaper. Without reading, Orla knows the text of the article. Nuala Crilly was arrested by the Royal Irish Constabulary at her home in Tubber last week on a charge of wilfully murdering a baby two weeks ago. Bridget Gallagher, of Derryadda, Tubber, said that she had visited the Crillys' house on Friday two weeks ago. Nuala Crilly was not in when she came to the house and her mother Mary Nuala told her she had gone out for a walk. When Bridget was passing the barn which adjoins the house she heard a sound. 'What sort of sound?' 'It sounded like a baby crying.' 'What did you do then?' 'I went into the barn and I saw Nuala Crilly lying on straw and a baby with her.' 'Was this baby her own baby?' 'Yes, I think so.' 'Why?' 'It was known in Tubber that Nuala Crilly was in the family way.' 'What did you do then?' 'I said, Can I do something for you, Nuala? She said, No. Go away please.'

The next day the baby was missing from the Crilly household. When questioned, Nuala Crilly and her mother denied that she had had a child.

Nuala Crilly was tried at Milford Courthouse and convicted of manslaughter. She is condemned to be moved to Letterkenny Jail and there to be executed by hanging by the neck.

Nuala looks like Aisling. She is lying in the corner of Aunt Annie's barn, on a heap of bright yellow straw. The baby is in her arms, dressed in a white robe. The baby is bald and has shining white skin and red lips. It is a boy.

Nuala wears a red dress and her hair is long and fair. She is walking down the *buachalán* field to the burn. With the white baby in her arms she steps across the stones, lightly stepping. A boy that looks like Micheál is standing on the side of the burn, not fishing, just staring sadly at her as she walks. She enters the tunnel of foliage and walks down to the waterfall. There she takes off the baby's clothes and drops him like a stone over the waterfall. He smiles at her as he falls like a stone into the black skin of water.

They don't grow on trees

Sandra is as good as her word. Next day she brings a brown paper bag containing six sanitary towels to school, and passes them discreetly to Orla. 'Try and make them last as long as you can,' she says. 'They don't grow on trees.' Orla has no idea how long any of this will last, but she doesn't reveal her ignorance to Sandra. Her confusion is apparent, though, and Sandra mistakes it for dismay. 'Don't worry. If you run out, let me know. Auntie Sandra to the rescue!'

'Oh gosh thanks Sandra.' Orla sighs, full of guilt and gratitude. 'And sorry ... you know, sorry it didn't work out about being in the same house.'

'That's life.' Sandra shrugs and tosses her head: she has tied her hair up in two ponytails, a dotty-looking style that the girls in her house have recently adopted just to annoy everyone else. 'No bones broken. So how are you feeling?'

'Oh fine,' says Orla. 'I feel fine.'

'Some girls get pains. I do,' Sandra tells her. 'Awful cramps.'

'I haven't got any,' Orla says. Now she has something new to worry about: the absence of pain.

'You're lucky then.' But it seems to Orla that Sandra may think otherwise. Clearly, having a pain is a desirable part of the whole procedure. Maybe she'll get one later? Or the next time?

247

If they ever come back again. She'd like to have the pain, the cramp. She wants to get exactly what all the other girls get.

Chocolate orange

After supper Pauline goes upstairs, makes a racket in her room for five minutes, and switches out the light. Then she opens her window and squeezes herself out onto the ledge. A branch of the big sycamore stretches along the front of the window. Onto that she clambers like a cat and down the trunk with her.

The moon floats in windy cardings of cloud, on a sky of darkest lightest Prussian blue. The yard all gloom and shadow, yellow puddles of moonlight. Bran the sheepdog barks twice, annoyed by Pauline's soft loud thunk to the ground. Then stops. All the livestock, cows and pigs, sheep and fowl, are silent in their dreams of summer, nightmares of Reynard.

Pauline halts for a mere second to savour the comfortable dark and the almost silence and the friendly moon, the soft cool night air like new linen on her skin. She breathes deeply, smiling with pleasure and a sense of great achievement. It's not her first time. It's not her last time. They'll never catch her now.

Lighting a fag, she runs out of the yard and sprints along the lane.

At the end of the lane Gerry is waiting, in a rusty Anglia. The passenger door is open – actually it can't be locked – and she hops in. The noisy engine runs. Gerry looks at her and says nothing. He releases the handbrake and on he drives down into the valley.

'Cigarette?' she asks.

He nods.

She lights one and places it in his mouth. The car fills with smoke.

Past the familiar buildings, the post office and the schoolhouse and the church, all strange and magic in the depth of night, all clothed in the robes of their own otherness.

The beach gleams like phosphorus in the moonlight; the water is black satin with a path of silver running from the horizon almost to the shore. Waves plash softly against the sand. Splush splush splush. Plop! Splush splush splush splush. PLOP!

Underfoot, small creatures shift in the sand, barely perceptible, like leaves rustling.

Four other students are already gathered in the boathouse. A fire has been lit near the door. The flames cast long shadows on the stone walls. The students sit round the fire, drinking from one large flagon. Coke.

'Caidé mar?' one of them shouts when Gerry and Pauline arrive.

'Caidé mar a drink?' Pauline takes the flagon and slurps down some of the warmish Coke. She passes the bottle to Gerry who drinks too, before putting another flagon on the floor.

'Where did ye get aholt athat?' It's a boy named Jimmy.

'Tubber.'

'He drove there.'

'Got a lift?'

'Got a lenda the car.'

'Ye wha?'

Gerry receives due credit for his achievement in borrowing his faratee's car.

'De ye not think ye'll get found out like?'

'No. If I did I wouldn't have taken it.'

'Goodonye boy!'

One of the girls, Maureen, has a guitar. She picks it up and begins to strum. Another girl – it is Monica – starts to sing and soon they all join in. We all live in a yellow submarine, they sing. Yesterday. She loves ya yeah yeah yeah.

Pauline sings along, swaying to the rhythms of the songs. Heat from the flames licks her face. Happily she gazes through the arch of the boathouse door at the satin water and the black mountain at the other side of the lough. Streetlights twinkle all night long in the town across there, chains of lamps against the browny blackness of the mountain. The sky is never black, but navy-blue and light blue with streaks of peach. Chocolate orange, thinks Pauline, remembering the strange taste.

'Chocolate orange!' she sings, to the strum of the guitar. 'Don't ya love to eat chocolate orange in the middle of the night when the stars just aren't!'

When all the Coke is drunk the couples lie in each other's arms on the floor, and kiss until four a.m., when the sun rises over the hill behind them and the water in front becomes the colour of mangoes.

At the cottage

Orla meets Micheál again, this time in the farmyard of Dohertys'. He is herding the cattle from the field into the byre, for milking. It's just before teatime: Aisling and Pauline are in the house, fighting over the bathroom. Pauline has become a daily hairwasher all of a sudden, she who in the past seldom seemed to wash anything at all. The sun is still high in the sky, burnishing the sea below, and burnishing Micheál's reddish skin and hair. The air is rich with the smell of woodbine from the garden, the smell of cows, the smell of summer heat departing.

Micheál is wearing not his green ravelling sweater but his white shirt. Its sleeves are rolled up, revealing arms, reddish brownish frecklish. Orla fixes her eyes on them.

'Hello!' he says. It's quite a lot, coming from him.

'Hi–i,' drawls Orla. Nerves tickle her inside, but not unpleasantly.

'Ye were down with your Aunt Annie the other day?'

She looks at him in the eye, angrily. So this is what it's about? Putting her in her place. 'Yes.' She can't keep the chill from her voice, nor does she want to. 'She wasn't in.'

'Was she not?'

'I knocked and knocked.' Orla is on the defensive.

'A nice woman your Aunt Annie.' He doesn't seem to be lying, but you never know with country people.

'I'd a present to give her from my mother.'

'Ye'll still have that so?'

'Naw. I left it on her windowsill.'

'She'll like to get that.'

Orla sees in her mind's eye the brown packet on the red windowsill. She sees Aunt Annie lying in a heap on the floor of the red barn.

'Yeah,' she sighs. 'It's elastic stockings!'

He laughs. 'They'll come in wild handy for her, so they will!'

'Yeah, she's bad legs, you know.'

'Terrible things, the bad legs. Och aye!'

He smiles at her again. She looks at his eyes. They are green, large pools of dark mossy green, fringed with dark red eyelashes. The skin on his face has grown dusky with the sunshine, and his hair too seems to have got darker, not redder. When Orla looks at his face, something happens to her whole body, something that has never happened before. It's as if she were going under ether, as in the dentist's chair, but the ether is not smelly or frightening. Not at all. It's as if she were going underwater, under glaucous, clear water. Under water, but breathing deeply and calmly of the freshest air.

She cannot take her eyes away. And neither can he.

They stare at one another for what seems like a long time.

'Micheál!' It's his father, Charlie. He pokes his head around the side of the byre. 'What's keepin ye?' He sees then, Charlie does, and he withdraws, redder than usual in the face.

'I saw her the other day. Your Auntie Annie.'

'Did you?'

'Aye. She was in a bad way. She'd fell on the floor of the barn so she had and she couldn't get up.'

'That's terrible.'

'Them bad legs of hers.' He looks at her closely, but not unkindly.

253

'Is she all right?' Orla asks.

'Aye. I helped her up and back into the kitchen. She'll be fine.'

'Good.' Orla feels relieved that she was not dead. Relieved and disappointed at the same time.

'Ye could go down to see her,' he says. 'So ye could.'

'Yeah. I will.'

He turns to go, but before he disappears in a flash of smoke mumbles: 'Um, are ye going to the *céilí mór* tomorrow?'

'Yes,' says Orla quickly. She hasn't any choice has she? The *céilí mór* or any other *céilí* is obligatory. She dances with Alasdair at *céilís* though. Not *muintir na háite*, the people of the place.

'Yes.' she looks into his eyes again. 'Yes. Are you?'

'Aye, maybe,' he says. 'Maybe I'll be down at the burn later on ye know, fishin. I'd see ye there. Down near your auntie's,' he says, as he turns on his heel and follows his patient cattle home.

Auntie Annie has a crowd in

After tea Orla washes her hair and rubs it furiously with the towel. She puts on her green cords and asks Aisling if she may borrow her blue and white T-shirt.

'OK.' Aisling gives Orla a puzzled look. She has never made such a request before. 'Why?'

'I've nothing to wear,' says Orla, who spoiled two of her T-shirts before she got the things from Sandra. 'I'm in a mess. I've got my visitor, out of the blue.'

As if she'd been getting them all her life.

'Oh glory!' Aisling sighs. 'Well if you need any, you know, I've mountains of them. Mummy gave me about ten packets.'

'Thanks but I've loads too,' says Orla. 'I mean you never know when you'll need them, do you?'

Aisling looks at her oddly but doesn't pursue the matter.

Orla continues, 'Actually, I've to go and visit my aunt, you know, the aunt who lives down by the shore, before the *céilí*.'

'Oh yeah.' Aisling only vaguely remembers the aunt. Orla and her funny relations.

'You know, your mother gave me something for her, from my mother.'

'Right. Can I come as well?'

'Well ...'

'My parents brought you to the café . . .'

What can Orla say?

'All right,' she capitulates wearily. Aisling hands over the T-shirt. It's tight on Orla, but in it, in Aisling's T-shirt, she feels very well. The cotton is thicker, the colours purer, than any she has ever had herself.

'Suits you.' Aisling eyes her thoughtfully. 'You should get one of them yourself when you go home.'

They walk together along the road to the shore, dawdling in the evening light. They pull fuchsia from bushes and suck the honey from the tiny pistils, and pink dog roses to put in their hair.

At the shop Aisling stops to buy a choc ice. Orla waits outside, sitting on the wooden windowledge, looking at the mixture of houses opposite: a thatched cottage side by side with a small bungalow roofed with red Spanish tiles. She likes the bungalow better. That's where she'd love to live, in a little bungalow like that, with a cheerful red roof and big picture windows. It surprises her that the cottage has not been knocked down. Most of the old houses have been, and just as well too, in her opinion. 'Sure people had no comfort,' Elizabeth says, in her wise-old-owl voice. 'No comfort. It's all very well . . .' It's all very well, oh yes, it's all very well, it's all very well.

Aisling buys two choc ices, one for Orla.

'Gosh!' Orla is flabbergasted. 'Gosh, thanks.'

'Seeing as you've no cash . . .'

'No. And I won't have now either.'

'Ah well, only a day to go, can you believe it?'

No.

Micheál is at the bridge around the bend at Auntie Annie's.

'Oh glory!' says Aisling. She's been saying that for a few days, oh glory. 'What on earth is he doing here?'

Orla betrays nothing, she believes, although Aisling notices that a change of mood has occurred. Micheál is standing at the bridge, staring into the water as if at some spectacular sight, a drowning man perhaps. He is dressed in his white shirt, or a white shirt, again, and has also put on a waistcoat, not too fancy, and his cowboy boots.

'Cool Hand Luke!' whispers Aisling. It is at that point, as she says these words, that she realises.

'Hello.' Orla decides to be reckless and utter this brave speech.

'Hi.' Micheál takes his eyes off the burn and looks at her. She forces her eyes to meet his, although now she knows what effect this has on her. The burn babbles along under the bridge; it has a babyish sound here, a happy baby gurgle.

'I'm calling around to em em Annie's.'

'Och aye yer Auntie Annie.'

'So ... eh ...'

'Och I'll drop in meself. Say hello.'

Orla feels something break inside her head, like the shell of an egg. Her big secret is disintegrating. Micheál, Aisling and Orla troop across the yard and into the house.

It's dark inside, as in all the old, small-windowed houses. And, despite the lack of sunshine, it's hot in the kitchen, where the range is burning brightly. Auntie Annie is seated to one side of it, and on the other are Killer Jack and Bean Uí Luing.

Orla and Aisling exchange surprised glances, and Aisling mouths 'Oh glory!', her eyes and lips stretching into a suitable O of amazement.

'Caidé mar atá sibh?' asks Killer Jack, sounding like a normal person, not a teacher.

'Táimid go brea,' mutters Orla.

'Isn't this the lovely cosy house?' Bean Uí Luing, in one of her brilliant red cardigans, has her feet stretched out to catch the heat from the flaming turf fire. 'It's the nicest house in the whole valley, I always think!'

'Yes,' says Aisling. 'It's a real country house, isn't it?'

Orla looks at the ticking sunray clock, the uneven rocky floor, the painted dresser stocked with blue plates and an odd assortment of ornaments: a yellow and white shaggy dog, a brilliant blue woodpecker, a little girl in a Dutch bonnet sitting by a nut-coloured wooded stile. She looks at the bare bulb dangling from a twisted wire in the middle of the ceiling. Can Aisling and Bean Uí Luing be serious? Who could find a single thing to praise in this gloomy, old-fashioned, ridiculous house? A house that Orla has often wished would burn to the ground and be forgotten for all time.

Aunt Annie jumps up from her chair and gives Orla a hug. Orla's first impulse is to pull away – this is certainly what she would do if she were alone with Auntie Annie. But all eyes are upon her. She must submit politely to the tortuous embrace. Auntie Annie's funny face brushes her skin; her warm, work-hard hands caress her shoulders. For a second Orla shudders with revulsion. Then something inside her head relents. The warmth of her aunt sinks into her shoulders, the touch of her skin feels familiar and desirable. Orla closes her eyes and sees Elizabeth. Feels Elizabeth's arms around her, feels her hands washing her face, brushing out her hair. Soon she will be home with her mother. She will sit in the kitchen with Elizabeth and tell her everything, everything good and everything bad that has happened during this holiday in the Gaeltacht. They will talk English and drink tea and have a laugh together.

When she opens her eyes Micheál and Aisling are staring at her. Killer Jack is fiddling with a tape recorder on the kitchen table. Bean Uí Luing is drinking tea.

Auntie Annie thanks Orla for the elastic stockings, and then starts to get more cups and plates for the new visitors. She clatters around the room, banging the cups and saucers down on the table, looking every minute as if she is about to drop something. Usually this clumsiness and lack of co-ordination nettle Orla so that she has to leave the room. But nobody else seems to notice.

'So she is your aunt?' Killer Jack leaves his tape recorder and, lighting a cigarette, looks at Orla as if she were a curious plant.

'Yes.'

'I didn't know that. I've never seen you here before.'

'No.' Orla isn't sheepish. She just tells him the truth. 'I didn't have time to visit her before now.'

'I see,' he says, nodding sagely and puffing clouds of smoke across the table, where Auntie Annie is buttering brack. The smoke makes Orla want to cough but she does her best to prevent this happening. Allowing anything as noisy as a cough to emerge from her mouth when teachers are present would be anathema to her, even now when she feels more comfortable with them than she ever has before.

Micheál and Aisling are sitting at the back of the kitchen, one on each side of the wooden chest Annie uses for layers' mash, with a gap of red wood between them. They gaze happily at the kitchen, of which they have a good view, but maintain absolute silence.

'How is yer mammy?' Auntie Annie asks, in her now low, now high voice. Bang-crash goes a cup and saucer.

'She's well,' answers Orla.

'What's that?' Aunt Annie is deaf. That is another one of her defects. Even when you find something to say to her, she can't hear it.

'She's well,' Orla shouts.

'And yer daddy?'

'He's well too.' Orla shouts on. Micheál and Aisling allow themselves a tiny smile, which Orla does not see.

'And how's Roddy?'

'He's well too.'

'Is he at school?'

'He's on holidays.'

'What?'

'He's on holidays.' Orla yells. 'He's at home in Dublin.'

'Why didn't he come to the Irish college?' Auntie Annie pours boiling water from a battered kettle into a teapot. Her hand shakes and the water splashes the buttered brack. But nothing more disastrous occurs.

259

'Oh gosh!' Orla looks desperately at Aisling, who grins encouragingly. 'He just didn't. I think he didn't want to.'

She is tired of the conversation now, but so is Auntie Annie. No more seems to be required.

Aunt Annie pours out tea for everyone, Aisling jumps up and helps pass round the cups, and the buttered brack.

'Yum!' says Bean Uí Luing. 'This is the nicest brack I ever tasted.'

Orla goes to sit between Aisling and Micheál on the red chest. They eat and drink, chatting softly. The warmth of the room increases and the clock ticks loudly on the mantelpiece. Orla finds her sense of well-being burgeoning. The room encloses her like a cradle, warm and old and dark and comfortable. Peace seeps into her soul from the mellow walls, the rocky bed of the floor. Flames flicker in the range, spoons clink against plates, voices rise and fall in meaningless chatter: it is a tune that has been played in this kitchen often before. For hundreds of years. Right here in this room.

Killer Jack changes the tune. 'Time to do some work!' he says, depositing his cup on the table and plugging the tape recorder into the socket high in the wall over the range.

'All right!' Auntie Annie plonks herself in a chair at the table and smiles at him happily.

'What are you doing?' asks Orla, spontaneous for once.

'Annie is going to tell me some stories.'

Orla can't believe her ears. 'Oh?' is all she can say.

'And it's fine with me if you stay and listen, isn't it Annie?'

'Wha?' asks Annie.

'You do not mind if they stay and listen?'

'Wha?' asks Annie. Orla rolls her eyes to the ceiling. This deafness!

'They would like to listen to the stories. Do you mind?' he shouts at the top of his voice.

'Och no sure I don't mind.' She sounds like Orla's father. That's exactly what he would say.

'Well, there's the *céilí*,' Orla murmurs. Nobody hears her. Nobody ever hears her. She waits for somebody else to say the same thing. Aisling.

'Well I'm afraid we'd better be getting back to the *céilí*. It's late,' Aisling announces. Bean Uí Luing looks at her watch.

'I didn't notice the time passing!' she says. 'I'll give you a lift, girls, if you like? I've got the loan of Headmaster Joe's car.'

'Oh yes!' says Aisling, before Orla can stop her.

Micheál refuses the lift, somewhat to Orla's disappointment. He stays sitting in the kitchen while the women say goodbye and tumble out under the low portal to the yard.

'Bye-bye!' yells Orla to Auntie Annie, who sees them to the door.

'When will you call again?' Aunt Annie asks, wringing her hands nervously

'I'm going home soon,' Orla says. 'But maybe . . . I don't know. Maybe sometime soon.'

Aunt Annie nods, confused. Orla gets into the car. Bean Uí Luing reverses out of the yard, and Aunt Annie waves at them until the car turns the corner and drives away.

'You're lucky, to have an aunt who lives in a house like that,' says Bean Uí Luing.

'Oh yes!' Aisling smiles at Orla. 'It's really lovely.'

The car is moving quickly along the narrow road, between the dangling hedges of rose and fuchsia. Orla looks at the dark lilac hills, low and regular as hills drawn by a child's hand. She looks at the little cottages sinking into the fields that spread from the foot of the hills like blankets. She wonders if Aisling and Bean Uí Luing are lying.

People tell so many lies to other people in order to protect them.

But she does not know if they are lying or not. And she realises, not for the first time, that it doesn't matter one way or the other.

Aunt Annie's house, her father's house, has many flaws. It has a cobbled-together, home-made feel to it, as if it had been built haphazardly from whatever bits and pieces of stone and wood had been found lying around the valley. It is old and awkward, poor, simple and eccentric, like Aunt Annie herself. You could be ashamed of all that, or pleased with it.

This evening the house had felt warm and comfortable. Aunt Annie had stumbled and twitched, shouted and whispered, as always, in that strange, jerky, unpredictable way of hers, that frightened Orla and made her cringe. But her arms had been warm when she had held Orla in her embrace. Killer Jack was interested in what Aunt Annie had to say, and Aisling hadn't, as yet at least, passed any critical remarks about her. Bean Uí Luing had praised her baking.

For once all the flaws of her aunt and her aunt's house seem insignificant. Orla is content.

The field

The field is unkempt. Like most fields in Tubber, it has lain un-cultivated, unspoiled by human hands, for twenty or thirty years. It teems with flowers and grasses, seeds, feral fertility. Golden fat-eared rye grass, fuzzy fennel grass. Button buttercups on coltish stems, foxgloves of deep shellfish purple, open to the sun. Prickly hedgehog clumps of clover, white and mauve, frothing meadowsweet, banks of the yolk-yellow flowers known to children as scrambled egg. Into this field Micheál leads Orla.

'Let's sit down,' he says, indicating a patch of field. She sits down. The grass seems to grow around her, high, curtaining.

He sits beside her.

She listens to the air moving in the grass, to the grasshoppers singing. The air is full of the smell of seeds, of meadowsweet, of foxgloves. In the next field, flax sways, blue as waves.

Micheál puts his arm around her shoulder.

Her heart pounds. Her head, her body, her blood are filled with a sweetness like the raspberries on the bank of the burn, like the salt water caressing her skin, like the sun in the high blue sky, the stars, the drooping dog roses, unimaginably pink, blossomy. Music from golden fiddles.

She puts her arm around his waist.

They say nothing.

They sit arm in arm, side to side, in the long grass. The grasshoppers sing their endless creaking summer song. The blackbirds call. The burn babbles on at the end of the field.

Orla hears none of this, sees none of it. And hears all of it, sees all of it.

The hedge circles around the field, hemming them in, a perfect O of hawthorn and bramble. For half an hour, for eternity, they sit at the centre of the world.

Teenage fun

'Tonight!' Pauline whispers in a moment of grandiloquent generosity, recklessness.

'Humph?' Orla is cocooned in soft, sweet thoughts. Micheál. The burn. The field full of buttercups. The water lapping against her skin. So locked in is Orla that she hardly hears people talking to her sometimes, most of the time. Knock knock wakey wakey, they say. 'Um?' she says, opening her eyes wide, shocked, unwilling to leave the happy hotbed of her daydreaming.

'Tonight after supper.' Pauline is regretting already. Too late. 'In the yard, OK? Bring Alasdair?'

'Alasdair?'

'Oh never mind!' With luck it won't happen.

But it does. Even down to Alasdair, in his maroon jumper with his bat ears shining in the moonlight, a bottle of Coke and a packet of fags clutched carefully to his bosom, at the gatepost of his banatee's.

Then the midnight ride through the silent valley and the boathouse rising like a ghost of itself from the beach.

Dreamy it is for Orla, who has never been on the shore at night, never dreamt such a thing possible. Such disobedience, such risks, such craziness. In the boathouse, the fire flickering, bottles everywhere, accumulating night by night; it's a wonder nobody notices them by day but they don't apparently.

She sits with Alasdair near the fire. The big girls and boys are smoking, the Coke bottles and the cider bottle are opened, waiting to be drunk. The girl called Maureen is playing the guitar now. Hey Mr Tambourine man play a song for me. Let me take you by the hand and lead you through the streets of London I will show you something that'll make you change your mind. Parsley sage rosemary and thyme. Tell her to weave me a camb-er-ic shirt parsley sage rosemary and thyme without no seams or needlework then she'll be a true love of mine.

The couples sing along, dissolve along, melt into the emotion, sentimentality, sleepy dreaminess of it all. Scarborough Fair. Out across the lough twinkle the lamps of the big town against the summer night sky, in the heavens flash the blue stars, glow eyes around the fire, intertwine arms . . . beat hearts.

Alasdair puts his short fat arm around Orla.

She lets her head loll on his comfortable maroon shoulder.

Cold water cold water canyon, sings Maureen, shaking wildly, getting wilder by the minute. I know I never would know you. Cold water deep in the canyon. I just wanted to show ow ow ye.

Alasdair tries to kiss her. It's what everyone else is doing, except Maureen, bent over her guitar, hair falling blonde and wild onto its strings, in love with the instrument perhaps, in love with the music, in love with the night, with the fire, with the Coca-Cola. Mad as a hatter mad as singers have to be. Cold water cold water canyon . . .

Orla pulls away.

He makes no protest. In fact he looks deeply relieved. From his pocket he pulls a packet of fags and lights one for her. Orla drags. Her first cigarette.

Splutter splutter goes Orla.

Splush splush splush go the waves against the sandy shore.

Caught

The tide is low, leaving a wide swathe of hard sand between the stones and the edge of the waves. Rain falls on it, the first rain they have had in more than two weeks. It is falling very softly but persistently, peppering the papery surface of the sand with thousands of dark spots. There are no stars tonight. The sky is a murky cup of black clouds over the dark muddy world of beach, rock, sea.

'Stay in here!' Gerry calls Pauline to the boathouse. They've been coming to the beach every night since last week, sometimes with companions, sometimes on their own. Tonight they're alone. Who but Pauline would venture out in such terrible weather?

'No!' says Pauline. 'It's the last night we can come here. I don't want to spend it in that hellhole.'

'Hellhole hellhole,' echoes back from the cliff.

'You'll get all wet.' he continues. 'Please.'

'I'm all wet anyway,' Pauline shouts back. Wet anyway wet anyway. 'I'm going for a swim.' She's out of her clothes and in the water before he can stop her, splashing around in the blacky grey waves, the rain pinging down on top of her.

'Come on in,' she yells to him. Gerry surveys the scene. Pauline's white arms thrashing up and down in the water. The rain getting heavier all the time. The nothingness around them – he can see no hills, no rocks, no cliffs. Everything is subsumed in the cold miserable mist. He shivers, tired and weary of it all suddenly. But he pulls off his clothes and jumps from the slip without enthusiasm. The water is as cold and unpleasant as it looks. So much for the Gulf Stream.

He swims towards Pauline, who is giddy now, racing ahead of him, out to sea.

'Come back!' he yells. 'You can't go out there.'

'Scaredy cat!' She turns and looks at him. 'Cowardy cowardy custard stick your head in mustard.'

It feels like mustard the water, as nasty as mustard. The rain gets heavier and heavier, it curtains her – he can hardly see her although she continues to shout from time to time.

'Come back, Pauline.' His voice is weak, he can hardly be bothered shouting any more. 'Come back come back.'

That's when he hears the engine, its chugging muffled in the rain. It is approaching the shore. Pauline hears it too, and swims towards the slip.

They are clambering up to the boathouse when the torch is turned on.

'Caidé mar atá sibh?' Killer Jack says, in his most sarcastic tones. 'Bhfuil sibh go maith?'

The céilí mór

It is the cause of my sorrow that I cannot visit you in the lonely
valley where my love is, there is honey on the rushes there and
butter on the cream there and the trees are in flower until the
autumn begins. And I am the boy from Lough Erne who would
not betray the nice young girl I don't need a dowry from her I
have riches enough of my own. I own County Cork and the
Glens and half of Tyrone and if I don't change my ways I'm
the heir to the County Mayo. Dada da da da da da da dadada-
dadd. There was a big buck from down beside Bandon and a
ship had he little song síodraimín sizzorseen so.

Orla prepares, wishing she could have a bath; her period is very
light but it makes her feel messy and smelly, inside and out. She
washes her whole body with a facecloth, rubbing her skin all
over with soap and rinsing in tepid water. Aisling has lent her a
little cologne. She dabs it behind her ears, on her wrists, on her
tummy. After that she feels cleaner.

She has a new dress for this occasion, a dress she made herself
on Elizabeth's old Singer sewing machine. It's a plain dark blue,
with a white collar. She wears it with her sandals and no socks at
all, since she has none that are not grey.

She and Aisling walk the mile to the village together, aware that it is almost the last time they will do this. The valley is laid out before them, looking calm now, its colours dark lilac, dark August green. The bay is shadowy, black and purple, the sky lowering. The last time the last time.

When they come into the schoolhouse, their sadness lifts: the big room has been transformed. Who would have suspected that Headmaster Joe had such creative talents? (Bean Uí Luing in fact is responsible for the decorations, but the girls give her credit for nothing.) Balloons and streamers dangle from the ceiling. There are candles lit on the high windowsills, and Chinese paper lanterns cover the bare bulbs. A table stacked with delicious little bottles of Football Specials and plates of crisps is placed in one corner.

Headmaster Joe has a new suit; it's not black but green, a greenish tweed suit. Bean Uí Luing is wearing her mother-of-the-bride outfit, minus the hat. Every girl and boy has made some sort of effort to look better than usual. Those who have not kept back a dress or shirt have washed their hair. A few boys wear ties. One or two have polished their shoes, encouraged to do so by the banatees. Everyone looks fresh, excited. They have left their everyday personalities behind them, and risen to a new occasion.

Pauline and Gerry are in attendance, looking a bit weary but otherwise not worse for wear. Last night, Killer Jack drove them home to their houses. But first thing this morning he collected them – arrested them – and carried them off to Headmaster Joe. Expel them, he said, Expel them.

Headmaster Joe had decided against it. There is only one day left, he reasoned.

'What won't they do in a day?' screamed Killer Jack. 'It's the principle of the thing.'

'Leave us,' ordered Headmaster Joe, his eyes flashing.

Having dismissed Killer Jack, he launched into a lecture that lasted for over an hour and left him considerably more exhausted than its recipients. His voice rose and fell and so did his blood pressure, expressing its vagaries in his face, now red, now white, now ashen, now fiery.

'I trusted you and you failed me!' he screamed at Gerry. He had little to say to Pauline whom he had always considered a hopeless case. 'You put this girl's life in danger. I don't know what else you did and I don't like to think. You could end up in jail for this you know, if I reported you to the guards.'

Gerry felt his self-esteem diminish, inch by inch, until at the end of the hour there was nothing left of him but a miserable little speck of self-loathing and fear.

But at least he was not to be expelled.

Killer Jack was furious. He wanted to punish Gerry in particular in some appropriately terrible way. 'What do you want me to do? Hang him?' asked Headmaster Joe. 'Hanging's too good for him,' snarled Killer Jack. 'What he needs is a good kick in the arse.' Headmaster Joe raised his beetle brows. 'I hope you didn't take it upon yourself...?' Killer shook his head, sadly. The restrictions life placed on teachers in Irish colleges were very hard to bear. 'Well,' said Headmaster Joe. 'I've a clean record, so far. And they go home tomorrow anyway.' 'What if she's...?' 'What can I do about that now, *a thaisce*?' He shrugged his shoulders. 'If she is, good luck to her. But all you found them at was swimming.' 'Skinny dipping,' corrected Killer. 'And they've been up to more than that. I've had them under observation for a week.' 'So why didn't you do something about it until she nearly went and got drowned on us?' Headmaster Joe's face reddened, and his eyes began to spark. He clutched his heart. 'I've a clean record,' he said. 'And I'm never going to do this again. It's more than my life is worth.'

'Please yourself, and pay the consequences,' said Killer Jack.

So Pauline and Gerry are at the *céilí mór*, just like everyone else. Gerry has a cold in the head but Pauline is as right as rain. They both avoid Killer Jack, who makes no effort to return the gesture. Much of the night he spends in an orgy of winking

271

meanly at Pauline and scowling ferociously at Gerry, trying to kill him with looks. Gerry's career as a star is, of course, ruined. But he feels he has got off lightly.

Headmaster Joe takes his place by the record-player from force of habit. But tonight there will be no records: there is a band in a corner, a small *céilí* band, invited in from a neighbouring parish. Its members sit and wait, accordions and fiddles on their knees, while he opens the proceedings.

With thanks, with regrets, with congratulations, with hopes that they enjoy themselves. He keeps his speech as short as he can – twenty minutes.

Then it's The Walls of Limerick.

The music breaks out, the room is filled with ripe, mellow sounds. The boys move *en masse* to the girls: Alasdair, still in the wine sweater but with his hair slicked back, asks Orla, and Seamas asks Aisling. The couples, trained now like the Kirov Ballet, take up their positions. The fiddler lifts his bow and the room is filled with ripe, merry music.

In and out the dancers move, in and out and round about. The hands clasp, the feet bounce, the lips smile. Over to the right side, over to the left side. Take your partner and on you go. The barrier of arms drops, the stream of dancers passes through. Along the schoolhouse they flow sedately to the music. The Siege of Ennis. The Little Cape of Clonard. The Fairy Reel. The Couple's Jig. The night moves on: Alasdair and Maurice, Paul and Alasdair. The patterns form and unravel, the bodies swing.

'And now, *Baint an Fhéir!*'

It's everyone's favourite, the best of all the dances, the fastest footwork, the wildest swings. Alasdair and fifty boys move across the floor to the waiting girls.

Micheál walks into the schoolhouse.

Orla sees him, everyone sees him. He is dressed in his white shirt and blue jeans. His hair springs from his head in a dark red crest. He walks straight over to Orla.

'An ndéanfaidh tú an damhsa seo liom?'

'Déanfaidh agus fáilte.'

Alasdair asks the next girl, Aisling. Seamas asks the next girl, Monica, her mousy hair bouncing in a ponytail, a big red bow surmounting her lively head.

The partners line up, five opposite five. Micheál smiles across at Orla and she smiles back. The music strikes up. The dance begins.

In and out and in and out. Over and back and swing your partner. Swing swing swing.

The couples swing. Whirlpools, storms, propellers spinning. The schoolhouse is hot with human electricity. The feet thump, the ponytails fly, the blood races. The music accelerates, faster and faster fiddles the fiddler, faster and faster pleats the melodeon. Feet are tapping and ears are reddening and hearts are thumping.

Headmaster Joe surveys the scene from his perch by the creaky record-player. The Irish college dances before his eyes, every step in time to the music, every movement perfect. It's Carrickmacross lace, it's the river running, it's the salmon leaping, it's the ploughman ploughing, it's the spinner spinning, the boatman sailing, the fellow fishing, the fire flaming. It's the dancers dancing.

It's the *céilí mór*. He wipes his forehead with a white handkerchief. From his slim black briefcase he removes a cigar. He lights it and the blue wisps of smoke snake across the schoolhouse, over the heads of the dancing scholars.

Tomorrow they all go home.

Home again home again
jiggedy jig

In Oldchurch Crescent, all the mothers are waiting. Their eyes shine, their hearts beat, their tongues wag.

'They'd a great time!' Elizabeth says. 'Orla had me killed with letters, I didn't have time to read the half of them. I don't know where she got the time. Or the stamps.'

'They're late,' says Sandra's mother, twisting her hands together and looking anxious. Many things make her anxious – especially other mothers in the school, and especially Elizabeth.

'Ah how could they be in time? How could they know exactly when they'd come?'

How would Sandra's mother understand the complexities of a long journey, a bus, traffic? She hasn't a clue. Some haven't a clue.

'It'll be along in a minute.' Nuala smiles kindly at Sandra's mother, whom she likes and for whom she feels sorry. 'Don't be getting worried now. They'll be home before you know it and soon we'll be wishing they were back again.'

'Oh indeed.' Elizabeth nods as if a great profundity had been uttered and was now being confirmed. 'True for ye.'

Aisling's mother tells them, not for the first time, that their daughters looked brown as berries when she saw them at the weekend, and that she didn't think they'd want to come home at all at all.

'Here they come!' someone cries.

Eighty eyes swivel towards the corner of Oldchurch Crescent.

Forty mouths smile in delight.

Forty youthful voices waft from the windows of the bus. 'Singing ay ay yaddie ay ay yaddie singing ay ay yaddie yaddie ay!'

The bus stops and its door slides open. Sean O'Brien, in green tweed suit, tweed tie, his glasses like two television sets on the bridge of a nose, steps out.

Forty mothers rush to the door. He stands aside. He lets them on, knowing there is no stopping the tide of maternal love when it is in full spate.

'Did yez get a good tan, let me have a look at yez? Did yez have a great time? Did yez learn a lot of Irish? Sure yezell talk nothing but Irish now!'

'Wus all right,' say forty voices, give or take.

Now

There is a heritage centre, vast as a cathedral, in the middle of the valley where I spend my holidays. Outside it stands a statue, touchingly rough-hewn, of the most famous of the local writers. Videos, photographs, wall hangings, snatches of music, commemorate the others within. Every day, visitors in their hundreds pour through the marble halls of the centre, learning a little about the community, admiring its resilience and genius: this is an area where Irish has survived and where it sometimes seems to prosper. There is a radio station, and people have started to agitate for an Irish television channel. You can hear Irish spoken in the schoolyard, in the pub, even in some of the shops. You can hear it on the crowded beaches. It's the Gaeltacht triumphant – not a bit like Tubber.

I am sitting on the beach as usual, in the heat of the afternoon. The islands loom black and mysterious on the horizon, and the sea is a clear calm jade. The beach is busy, but not as packed as it is at the weekends. It's the middle of August. The holiday season peaked a week ago, and already is ebbing away. Although the beach is more comfortable than it was, the comfort and space come accompanied by a faint, familiar feeling of dread. The summer, the holidays, are drawing to an end.

I have been in for a swim and am now lying on a towel,

reading. Every so often I glance over my shoulder and examine the bathers in the water, checking that my children have not drowned.

I see Micheál.

He is standing about knee-deep in the waves, holding a small girl by the hand. She has on a blue bathing suit. Her hair is long and curly and red.

Micheál's hair.

My heart pounds and all the stiff components of my body lose their starch, flop limp inside me. I return to the page of my novel in an effort to collect myself, although of course there is no question of reading. When I feel a bit calmer I steal a look at the water's edge again. Maybe it is not him? It is easy to make a mistake in these matters.

But not with Micheál, whose looks are distinctive. And anyway every curl on his head and every line on his body are as well-known to me as my own, as my children's. I have not looked at him for years. But he is in my head, he is in my dreams, he is in my body, forever, along with Elizabeth, who died three years ago, and my father, who is in a home in Dalkey. Micheál is more active in my dreams than either of them, or than anyone else, perhaps because he featured in my reality for such a short time.

What is he doing here?

The summer after the Irish college I went to Tubber, with Tom and Elizabeth, to visit Auntie Annie. That second summer I was fourteen, taller, thinner. I'd had my periods for one year. Micheál was sixteen and still fishing in the burn when he could. But when we met it was not in the burn, but in the Fairyland Ballroom. We fell in love. Rather, we acknowledged that we were in love and had been since last summer. For the whole summer, it seemed – it was three weeks, actually – we loved each other idyllically. At night we plunged headlong into the traditions of the place: dancing in the Fairyland, the Carrowdonnell, the Railtown Inn, the

277

Strand Hotel. I felt superior to everyone I encountered in these places. I was slumming it. But I loved the beat of the country-and-western drum. I loved the hot sticky halls full of pulsing bodies. I was one with the crazy venality of it all, the loud throbbing fertility dances.

The days were quiet, like lake water lapping. During the day, when we could escape, he from his work, me from the house, we lay on the sand, or on the hillside, or in the long grass on the burn bank. We kissed. We kissed. We kissed.

When I left I was steeped in love for him, love like warm water or warm wine or warm butter, flowing through me and over me. I did not see how I could survive without him. I sat in my convent classroom drowning in this love.

There were dances, in the convent, organised by the nuns at special calendar festivals – Halloween, Christmas, St Patrick's Day – to keep the girls away from real dances. At the first of these decorous occasions I danced with Aisling's brother, Sean. He wore glasses, and claimed to have read a book by Jean-Paul Sartre. Besides, he was good-humoured and handsome in a squeaky-clean, well-groomed way, and besides, I felt I knew him inside out, long before I met him, thanks to Aisling's stories.

It was a passionate, tempestuous, disastrous relationship, lasting six or seven years. Long after I recovered from it, I married my husband, my husband who is back at the house, reading or studying, while I roast on the sand.

A woman joins Micheál and the little girl. She is young, I think, much younger than me, with long fair hair. She's fattish. What have I heard about him in Tubber? Not much – people are not fools, they know sensitive areas and do not tread on them. But I heard, nevertheless, that he went to England and managed a pub. That was fifteen years ago – he never got anywhere academically, didn't even do his Leaving.

Of course it was out of the question.

Marriage.

Maybe he still lives in England. I see him in a holiday village, on the Isle of Wight where Elizabeth came from. Why not? If she could come from there to Tubber, he could go there. That is the way of the world, coming, going. Staying. He manages a quaint little inn with a deep golden thatch, serves cider and ale over a knotty pine counter. And around the door grow roses, roses, and his little girl shakes her auburn curls in the southern sun. The bedroom is, there's a white lace quilt on the bed, the window looks to France.

Or north, perhaps.

For the rest of the week, the last week of the holidays, I frequent the beach, hoping to see him again. If I see him one more time I will speak to him and find out everything. Learn his story.

But he does not return, and I do not spot him in the heritage centre, or any of the pubs, or the supermarket, either – which is surprising. He must have been passing through. He must have been doing a tour, stopping a night here, a night there.

Since then, I have not seen him.

BOOK ENDS
opinions
interviews
and more

About
Éilís Ní Dhuibhne

Born
Dublin, 1954

Educated
Scoil Bhríde, Ranelagh, Dublin;
Scoil Chaitríona, Eccles Street,
Dublin; University College
Dublin; University of
Copenhagen

Lives
Dublin

Fiction
The Inland Ice and Other Stories
(1987); *Blood and Water* (1988);
The Bray House (1989); *Eating
Women is Not Recommended*
(1991); *Singles* (1992); *The Pale Gold of Alaska and Other Stories* (2001);
Dúnmharú sa Daingean (2001); *Midwife to the Fairies* (2002); *Cailíní
Beaga Ghleann na mBláth* (2003); *Fox, Swallow, Scarecrow* (2007)

Books for young people
The Uncommon Cormorant (1990); *Hugo and the Sunshine Girl* (1991);
The Hiring Fair (1993); *Blaeberry Sunday* (1994); *Penny Farthing Sally*
(1996); *The Sparkling Rain* (2002); *Hurlamaboc* (2006)

Plays
Dún na mBan trí Thine (1994); *Milseog an tSamhraidh* (1997); *The Nettle
Spinner* (1998)

Non fiction
Voices on the Wind: Women Poets of the Celtic Twilight (as editor, 1995); *W.B. Yeats, Works and Days: Treasures from the Yeats Collection* (as editor, 2006)

Awards and prizes
Stewart Parker Award for Drama, three Bisto Book Awards for children's literature, Butler Award for Prose and several Oireachtas awards for novels and plays in Irish. *The Dancers Dancing* was short-listed for the Orange Prize for Fiction in 2000.

Éilís Ní Dhuibhne began writing in her teens. Her first short story was published in 'New Irish Writing' in the *Irish Press* when she was an undergraduate student at University College Dublin, and a succession of stories followed. After graduation, she worked in a variety of jobs and began a PhD in Irish Folklore at UCD. In 1978 she was awarded a research scholarship and spent a year at the University of Copenhagen, working on her doctorate and learning Danish. She married Bo Almqvist, a Swede living in Ireland, in 1982. They have two sons.

Following her marriage and the completion of her PhD, Éilís began writing seriously. Since then she has published more than twenty books, in both English and Irish. She has also written plays, television scripts and many lectures, articles and reviews. In addition, she has taught creative writing at the Irish Writers' Centre, Trinity College Dublin and UCD. She has worked as an assistant keeper in the National Library of Ireland since 1982. She recently co-curated the world-renowned Yeats Exhibition at the National Library, and co-edited *W.B. Yeats, Works and Days: Treasures from the Yeats Collection*, a book accompanying the exhibition. A member of Aosdána, Éilís has won many literary awards and is a frequent speaker at literary events around the world.

A collection of essays on Éilís Ní Dhuibhne's writing, *Éilís Ní Dhuibhne, Perspectives*, edited by Rebecca Pelan, will be published by Arlen House in November 2007.

Éilís Ní Dhuibhne on writing
The Dancers Dancing

In 1986 or so, I wrote 'Blood and Water', a partly autobiographical story drawing on childhood experiences of visiting my father's home-place, a glen in the Gaeltacht on the shores of Lough Swilly in County Donegal. The story dealt with my own ambivalent feelings about this place, and about my relatives there, who were not, frankly, the relatives I would have chosen for myself. A working-class child of country origins, I would have very much liked to have been the daughter of a duke, or at least of a family that contained a single person who had a university or a secondary school education. Most children I knew seemed to belong to families of the latter kind, although the children of dukes were naturally enough in short supply.

Anyway, I wrote the story, describing a holiday in my father's valley, analysing my feelings about it, and using as the central image, a metaphor for intellectual density and misunderstanding, a pat of butter. In Donegal it had been the custom to smear a bit of butter on the wall of the dairy or kitchen after every churning, for luck. I had seen these ancient dabs of butter attached to the wall of my father's family home in Donegal, but had never known why they were there. Nobody explained. Perhaps

> I would have very much liked to have been the daughter of a duke, or at least of a family that contained a single person who had a university or a secondary school education.

283

they had forgotten what it was, or didn't notice it, or, most likely, felt such a custom was too silly to be worth explaining. My aunt, who owned the old family house, still churned, at least until I was eight or nine, and the butter she produced was one of the many Irish country things I was enjoined to admire and appreciate, and – this was much harder – actually eat. The taste of it made me sick. I hated it. It represented the negative side of Donegal for me. Some aspects of Donegal I loved passionately, even when I was eight: the nature, the beauty, the donkeys, my innumerable third cousins, who were wonderful playmates. But the dark past, the strange rituals, I mistrusted deeply. I had ambivalent feelings about the languages of the place: it had two, Ulster Irish and Ulster Scots, both of which were foreign to me, a speaker of Dublin Irish and Dublin English. I didn't like the toilet facilities much either.

That was long ago, in the 1960s. But by the 1980s, when I wrote 'Blood and Water', my tastes had changed. Everything about Irish country life fascinated me: its customs, traditions and beliefs, its languages (although not, I must admit, its butter). I had studied Irish folklore for many years at university and had come to an appreciation of my own past. By then I realised what the pat of ancient butter meant, that it was smeared on the wall to appease the forces that can cause churning to fail. (Like all industry related to cattle and milk, churning was a delicate task, subject to conditions over which the churner, the woman of the house, had little control.) Smearing the butter on the wall was a form of magic and was still in practice up until the 1960s in parts of Ireland. Understanding this ritual worked like alchemy for me – it transformed my view of my past, my childhood, my ancestors, from one of diffident boredom and scepticism, at best, to one of enchantment. Knowledge is magic.

'Blood and Water' was what Alice Munro calls a 'breakthrough short story' for me. It was the first piece of fiction in which I drew on my own childhood experiences, and my first visit to the territory of childhood as a writer, a visit I was to repeat again and again, as a novelist, short-story writer, and writer of fiction for children. Indeed, although I have never intended to write only about children or teenagers, and have, and hopefully will, write about other kinds of people, I continue to find this age group intriguing and fascinating. I tend to the belief that childhood and adolescence are the most interesting parts of human life, as well as the richest and the most rewarding for exploration in literature.

Retrospectively, I see that this awakening occurred around the time I became a mother, an experience which is deeply interesting in itself for a writer (as for anyone else). And it also coincided with a time when I began to revisit Donegal, a place with which I had been deeply in love as a child but had forgotten about for over fifteen years. Place matters to me, and affects my writing, always.

'Blood and Water' was, like many of my earlier short stories, published by David Marcus in *New Irish Writing*. Later it appeared in my first collection of stories, my first book, to which it gave its title, *Blood and Water*, and in the first *Blackstaff Anthology of Short Stories*, both of which appeared in 1988. By then I was a member of that phenomenon of the 1980s, a women's writing group. Someone in that group whose opinion I valued, Dolores Walsh, a playwright with a passion for social justice who wrote a number of plays about apartheid, suggested that I write a novel based on that short story. Something about this opinion impressed me – possibly the

> Place matters to me, and affects my writing, always.

respect I had for Dolores and the strength of all her convictions, and possibly my own sense that in 'Blood and Water' I had struck a vein that merited more prospecting. I paid little attention to the advice at the time, but it lodged in my memory, as good advice does.

Almost ten years later, after I had written three other novels (one unpublished) and a few collections of short stories, I began to work on the novel which is now *The Dancers Dancing*. The inspiration for it came in the summer of 1997 when the IRA initiated its first significant ceasefire, which eventually led to the Good Friday Agreement and the cessation of the Northern Ireland conflict. I began to think of the summers I had spent in the Irish college in Donegal, in 1965 and 1966, when I was eleven and twelve, the summers to which I refer rather cursorily in the short story 'Blood and Water'. An interesting feature of the Donegal Gaeltacht experience for me as a Dublin child was that there I met, for the first time, many young people from the North of Ireland, from Derry and Belfast. In fact it was these cities that supplied the Donegal Gaeltacht colleges with their students for the most part – my friends and I from Scoil Bhríde in Ranelagh were anomalies. Dublin schoolchildren tended to go to Connemara or Kerry or Cork, to learn Irish in the summers. Even in the 1960s, most Dubliners would have died rather than go to Donegal, since the journey entailed driving through County Tyrone, in Northern Ireland, a place that most Dubliners believed would be blown to pieces the minute they set foot in it. Many people in the South still regard Donegal as an Ultima Thule, even though it is not all that far away.

These thoughts occurred to me, that summer of 1997, listening to the news about the ceasefire. I was in another Gaeltacht at the time, Dún Chaoin in County Kerry. The contrast between the vibrancy, self-confidence and energy of the Gaeltacht there on the Dingle Peninsula, and the little marginalised quiet Gaeltacht where I had gone during the summers of 1966 and 1967, also struck me.

It was these two points that 'triggered' *The Dancers Dancing*. Drawing on 'Blood and Water', which deals exclusively with the relationship of its first person narrator to her Gaeltacht background and ancestors, I began to write a new novel, which would deal, according to my initial plan, with the relationships between the girls from Dublin and the girls from the North.

> The diffident attitude which I, and many people in the South, had to the Northern situation was one I was concerned to explore.

Although my own Gaeltacht experiences, in the mid-1960s, pre-dated the Troubles, I decided to set the novel in 1972. The diffident attitude which I, and many people in the South, had to the Northern situation was one I was concerned to explore. Another more immediate reason for choosing 1972 was that an IRA ceasefire had been called in that year, obviously a ceasefire which was very shortlived. I began to write *The Dancers Dancing* as another ceasefire was announced, a ceasefire which was to endure (although not without terrible lapses).

What I remembered best from my childhood summers in Donegal was, however, not the girls from Derry and Belfast, or the *bean-an-tís* or the *céilís*, or any of that, but the river. I always loved playing in water, and especially in rivers, little narrow mountain streams. On Saturdays when I was very young my parents used to bring us on a drive to somewhere not too far from Ranelagh, in Dublin, where we lived – Dollymount for swims in summer, Brittas for walks, and the river in spring and autumn. In Brittas there was a stream

The river was full of mysteries, it seemed to me. You never knew what would come out from under a stone.

where my brother and sister and I messed about for hours, with toy boats or bits of twigs. During summers in Donegal I continued the practice. On my first summer there without my parents, when I was eight, and staying with a large lively family of cousins, I spent most of the two weeks in the river which flowed under a stone bridge beside their house, fishing for tiny fish called pinkeens. The river was full of mysteries, it seemed to me. You never knew what would come out from under a stone. The weeds and plants which grew in it and on its banks were many and strange. Its capacity to surprise was infinite, as it rushed along, babbling over rocks and stones, hellbent on reaching its destination. I didn't know where it came from, although I knew where it was going – down to Lough Swilly, where it spread out, a wide dark brown slow water, before it mixed with the sea in a place we were forbidden to swim, presumably because of the currents.

The river in Donegal was called the burn – like a lot of short rivers in Irish country places, it seemed to have no proper name, just as the river in Dún Chaoin where I spent my holidays and where I wrote *The Dancers Dancing* is called *An Abhainn* (the river) or even *Abhainn Baile na hAbha* (the River of the Townland of the River!). I spent the summer when I was eight in the burn. A boy from Glasgow, also on holiday with his family, was my water mate, although we never exchanged a word as we paddled and fished in the cold, companionable stream.

When I went to the Irish college, like Orla in the novel, I found the burn again – in new locations, which I had not discovered in my earlier childhood. The other girls with whom I lived took to it with greater or lesser enthusiasm.

Some were not enthralled. They did not like getting their clothes wet. Or they just didn't get the point of spending hours wading in cold running water. Others shared my love for the river and outstripped me in daring. They ventured further downstream and upstream than I would have, left to my own devices (I was curious but timid). They found deep pools, they dove into them. It was wonderful, magical, and slightly mad. These were girls on the cusp of childhood and adolescence. They were not sexually awakened, although they might dress up a bit for céilís and pretend to prefer one dancing partner over another. They were wild. Wild about the river.

In 1978–9 I had spent a year at the University of Copenhagen, as a graduate student, and there I attended a seminar on the fairytale given by Professor Bengt Holbck, a great Danish folklorist who was writing his mammoth and brilliant study *The Interpretation of Fairytales*. I remember him telling us that lakes and wells, swans and ducks often occur as symbols in fairytales. Water almost always has a sexual meaning. Men, he said, male storytellers, often didn't seem to understand this, but women storytellers were invariably aware of it, and made this clear in the way they use the symbol in their tales.

It occurred to me, looking back on this obsession with water, that somehow there was a connection. In the novel I intended to suggest some link of that kind, but the river in *The Dancers Dancing* means much more than that. It is a symbol of life and a metaphor for eternity: 'Men may come and men may go, but I go on forever.' The river is also a place of beauty and mystery: to me it seemed that anything could be hiding in there, in that little country river. It represented the great potential of the world to yield astonishing treasures.

Although I was unfamiliar with W.B. Yeats's poem 'The Stolen Child' at the time of writing *The Dancers Dancing*, its expression of a child's longing to live in 'the water and the wild', informs the novel, in part. Originally I called the novel *The Burn*, but Anne Tannahill, at Blackstaff Press, suggested I change the title. *The Dancers Dancing* was her idea – a phrase from the novel that also links the book to Yeats, whose line, 'How can we know the dancer from the dance?' from his poem 'Among School Children', inspired mine. Although I was reluctant to abandon the title *The Burn* at the time, I am glad I did. The motif of dancing runs through the novel; it represents unease and clumsiness, to begin with, and finally – when the students learn to dance – becomes a symbol of harmony, the quintessential symbol, as used by Yeats. For Orla, the heroine of *The Dancers Dancing*, the well-danced dance serves, like the symbol of the magic butter in 'Blood and Water', as a metaphor for understanding and self-acceptance.

A novel is a complex thing. Sometimes I think of it as a building, a house – much of my thinking is in terms of houses – a house of many rooms, a symphony of many voices, and the challenge is to design, construct and decorate it as well as one can. But, however apt the metaphor, when it comes to the crunch the writer knows that even if there is a flaw in the design, even if something goes badly wrong, no one is going to die. Some readers might be bored, or the artist disappointed. But that is it. Writing a novel that fails is not a hanging offence. The world will get over it.

> Writing a novel that fails is not a hanging offence. The world will get over it.

This gives the novel writer a wonderful freedom.

Although art is demanding and the artist needs to take pains, ultimately it is a sense of irresponsibility that is the writer's greatest gift. The childlike gift of creative irresponsibility which the girls in *The Dancers Dancing* have, and which encourages them to break rules, to explore forbidden territory, is also an asset for the writer, an innate gift which needs to be nurtured rather than abandoned.

Mostly I wrote *The Dancers Dancing* in my house in Dublin, sitting at my big old computer in my cluttered bedroom. But I began to compose *The Dancers Dancing* in Kerry, in our little summer house in Dún Chaoin. And it was there that I worked on my descriptions of the burn, examining *Abhainn Baile na hAbha*, the river that runs through Dún Chaoin. The house is a good place in which to write. It is quiet and there are few distractions. I sleep soundly and long enough to have vivid dreams. Sometimes I dream stories – coloured images, fully-fledged narratives, usually of a bizarre and interesting nature, at least to me – and I sense that I am tapping into whatever source it is that helps me write.

When I get up I go down to the big empty room which constitutes the whole of the house downstairs, and listen to music as I drink my coffee. Outside there is a field full of long grass, weeds, wildflowers in summer. I can stare at that as I breakfast. Sometimes an animal emerges. Most often a hare. Or a swallow. Sometimes a fox. Sheep, the domestic animal which is closest to being wild, occasionally wander past and stare inquisitively at me as I drink my coffee, before moving on, at a sedate and dignified pace. Not in the least bit sheepish.

The grass, like the river, seems to me a metaphor for the imagination. So much comes out of it. Those wild animals – they are there, hiding in it, sometimes emerging, like pinkeens from under rocks in the burn. The flowers, which come in their dozens from spring right through to autumn, starting with the primroses and violets, going on to the early purple orchids, then the profusion of June and July, the buttercups, the dandelions, the eyebright, the selfheal, the scabious, and many more, until the bright orange montbretia come in August and September.

The grass, like the river, seems to me a metaphor for the imagination.

In this place writing is not work – in Dublin, it can begin to be that, to be a chore. In the country, even if there is a deadline, and there often is, it is easy, it is play, it blends into the daily pattern, it is an essential component of that tapestry of walking, listening to music, swimming, cooking dinner. It is a part of life, and fun, as it should be. I often start my novels in this place, in the field of long grass, where ideas flow into my head without any effort on my part.

Declan Kiberd on reading
The Dancers Dancing

'There's no there there any more' Gertrude Stein
sadly said of Oakland, California; but the same observation
might have been made of the Donegal Gaeltacht in 1972.
Supposedly a repository of traditional Gaelic culture and
values, to which four Dublin girls are sent for a summer
sojourn to improve their Irish, it turns out to be a
surprisingly modern place. Its teenagers are more sexually
precocious than the visitors from the capital;
they sport 'fast' platform shoes; and they use
the same mass-produced furniture in their
bedrooms.

Éilís Ní Dhuibhne in *The Dancers Dancing*
has produced one of the most compelling and
understated exercises in the female
Bildungsroman. Her Dublin girls cannot learn
the Donegal dialect from their hosts – a skill
which, if mastered, would anyway make them
ridiculous in a capital city whose elites speak a 'civil service'
Irish, stiff with correct grammar and syntax. But they can
learn other lessons – about the hidden injuries of social class;
about the cultural gap which separates Northerners and
Southerners at the height of the Troubles; and about the
hybrid nature of a national identity which has already been
sufficiently expanded to include English mothers as well as
Irish fathers, Protestant fathers as well as Catholic mothers.

Ní Dhuibhne's book was first published in 1999, a year

> ... one of
> the most
> compelling and
> understated
> exercises in
> the female
> *Bildungsroman*

after the Good Friday Agreement announced that a county such as Derry might be British or Irish or both at the same time; but its narrative shows that such a redefined Irishness had to be learned in youth before it could be proclaimed in middle age. Her chapter headings can make play with this double layering of time: 'The truce is over (but not to worry it's 1972)'.

If the form of Irish taught in Dublin has little use-value in the Gaeltacht, this is true of many other aspects of education and upbringing too. Orla, the central character of the four, comes from a family intent on bourgeois proprieties: her bricklayer father must now be styled a building contractor. She herself seems at times less interested in reviving Irish than in stamping out such Hiberno-English expressions as 'youse' (second person plural of 'you'). Yet the crowded house of her *bean-an-tí* in Donegal reminds her all too pointedly of the fact that, when her father was on strike, her own mother had to take in lodgers so that she might receive a good education at secondary school.

That education, though strong on theory, fell short on practice: and Orla's mother, for all her carefulness, did not think to alert her daughter to the likely onset of her menstruation. More generally, the Dublin girls know next to nothing about the war being enacted in Derry, not far from their Donegal setting, during the prosecution of Operation Motorman by the British Army. In that summer of 1972, the journalist Mary Holland interviewed an IRA volunteer who insisted that he was dying not for Mother Ireland but simply to protect the neighbours in his street.

The girls from Derry whom Orla meets are thin, fast and derisive of Southern attitudes: and their background in nationalist enclaves of dire unemployment suggests a possible equation with Gaeltacht dwellers, who suffered from the same condition. The Northern girls are undernourished but modern. They are already aware of their bodies, but not so good at Irish. They talk with utter freedom only when together, yet they know how to manipulate adults. When one of them goes on hunger strike, it isn't hard to feel the force of the implied equation between Gaeltacht and ghetto. In the end, the differences between the Southerners and Northerners come down less to matters of nationalism than to questions of social class. And the Southern girls, like honest young people everywhere, try hard to understand.

Orla, being the complex child of an Irish-English marriage, longs to build a bridge between worlds, between the labouring poor and respectable middle class, between Galltacht and Gaeltacht. But the Gaelic values into which she is inducted often seem hopelessly abstract: Irish dancing, in those pre-Riverdance days, is less a sensuous challenge than a sort of Euclid Theorem performed with nervous legs. Worse still, the headmaster of the Gaeltacht college believes so little in his own mission that he reverts to English whenever he has a crucial message for his charges, 'so youse will all understand'. The novel is haunted by that very Hiberno-English which the respectable are intent on abandoning: yet whole sentences and paragraphs written in it suggest that, at its best, such a dialect is filled with expressive potentials, and, moreover, that those who still use it are often much more quick-witted than the politer sorts. If respectable people still think in English while using halting Irish words, then others who still think in Irish are capable of using beautiful English phrases. No wonder that poets from W.B. Yeats to Tom Paulin have argued that Hiberno-English posed the 'real' language question for modern Irish people, too ashamed to recognise the beauties of a hybrid language which had evolved out of the desperate bargain struck between English and Irish in the nineteenth century. Yeats believed that all prestigious activities, from the writing of editorials to delivery of church sermons, should be done in Hiberno-English, but that the Irish were too colonised in their minds to do this.

Orla herself is often ashamed of her eccentric Aunt Annie, about whom she feels (as many do about Irish) that 'something' should be done (presumably by other people). She avoids Annie, much as Southerners avoid issues raised by the Northern conflict – but, inevitably, a confrontation of sorts with both deferred national questions must occur.

Deeper still, however, is Orla's confrontation with her own emergent womanhood, against the natural backdrop and secret potentials of that hidden place called the burn. It is here, in the presence of the female divinity of the river, that much is resolved, so that the Euclid Theorems may be cast aside to make way for real dancers really dancing. Near the end, by a subtle shift of voice, Ní Dhuibhne adds further depth to this narrative of growth and demonstrates how a woman can take power by the simple but audacious expedient of writing her self. This second look at experience can transform a person from one imprisoned by it to one freed of it.

> Ní Dhuibhne ... demonstrates how a woman can take power by the simple but audacious expedient of writing her self.

The subtlety of this marvellous *Bildungsroman* lies in its refusal of any sense of a grand narrative. There is no major catastrophe, because everything happens elsewhere, further up the coast, in Derry, or back in the past. This is, after all, an account of a relatively happy childhood, and a happy Irish childhood at that, delivered with tenderness of touch and an utter exactitude of language. Perhaps, in an age of angst-ridden exposés of parental tyranny and youthful trauma, there can be no more subversive or more honest a story than that.

ALSO BY ÉILÍS NÍ DHUIBHNE

FOX, SWALLOW, SCARECROW

Anna Kelly Sweeney is a writer of popular fiction intent on worldly success.

Leo is an idealist who lives in rural County Kerry, and devotes himself to poetry, culture, and innumerable worthy causes.

When Anna falls in love with the handsome and enigmatic journalist Vincy, and Leo with troubled publicist Kate, the consequences of their glimpsed happiness reverberate beyond their own insulated worlds.

Panoramic, strikingly original, and compulsively readable, this new novel by acclaimed writer Éilís Ní Dhuibhne is an intelligent, witty, and always fiercely humane insight into modern Ireland.

ISBN 978-0-85640-807-6

£8.99

www.blackstaffpress.com